THE MONKEY ISLAND MURDER

ALSO BY ROSALIND BARDEN

The Cold Kid Case

The Cannibal Caper

The South Seas Shenanigans (Forthcoming)

THE MONKEY ISLAND MURDER

A Sparky of Bunker Hill Mystery

ROSALIND BARDEN

To my mother Marie and my uncle Jake,
both book lovers who would have enjoyed the
Carla and Reginald books when they were young.

CONTENTS

THE
MONKEY ISLAND
MURDER

PROLOGUE

I think this was the worst day of my life.

I know I'm only eleven, but still.

Can I tell you about it?

It seemed like a dream that I saw in flashes.

Okay, there were actual flashes of light, with the cop spotlight swinging over the drizzling September sky, searching, searching for Bookie clinging to the roof of the Monkey Island building in the flatlands of downtown Los Angeles, 1932. Most of the roof was glass, so when the spotlight hit the glass panes, it was like it hit mirrors, lighting them up extra bright and flashing in my eyes, blinding me for a second even though I squinted.

There, I spotted Bookie's foot. Then his hand. His fedora rolled along the steep glass roof and tumbled down to where Mug, the overgrown cop, stood shouting up at Bookie.

I worried Bookie would slide off. Why did it have to rain now? It was only a light drizzle, but it was enough to make the slanted glass panes Bookie clung to as slick as grease.

Like I said, this was the worst day of my life. But even worse for Bookie.

Then the spotlight found Bookie and fixed a round, glowing circle over him. His fingers were digging into the metal strips that held the glass roof together. His shoes were digging, carefully, against the wet glass, trying to push himself up. His thick black hair stuck up in all directions. His nice suit he'd only just stolen was a rumpled mess. Was he crying? Bookie crying? That never happened.

The drizzle got heavier. I saw water running off the glass roof. Please, Bookie, please hold on.

Mug was shouting things at him. There was so much noise and commotion with dozens of cop cars, a hundred cops, reporters, lookie-loos, snoopers, laughing idiots—it was hard to hear anything. Lots in the crowd were pointing up at Bookie and yelling things like, "There's the murderer! Don't let him get away!"

Bookie wasn't the murderer. I should know—I was there. Okay, I didn't actually see everything, but I was sure it wasn't Bookie. It couldn't be.

I listened hard. It sounded like Mug was calling Bookie "Sue." What? I must have been hearing that wrong.

"Aw, come on, relax! Hey, Sue, I got your favorite cell all warmed up and ready for you! The one with the window that you like! Got a hot drink and a sandwich and a nice cozy blankie all for you!"

"I'm scared!" That was Bookie. My Bookie, who'd rather jump into a pit of lava than say anything like he was scared. Now, in the glare of the spotlight, I saw: Bookie for sure was crying.

"I know, I know. Hey, Sue, I'll be here! Don't worry!"

"I don' wanna go back! I don' wanna!"

It was like my Bookie turned into a little kid. Did Mug lock Bookie up a few times in the good ol' days, when Bookie was a little criminal? Like me.

But not like me, because I'd never been caught, never been locked in the big house like Bookie. I came pretty close this summer after being framed for killing about a million people. But I slipped through Mug's big fingers. One thing I knew: Bookie vowed never to be locked up again.

As Mug shouted cheerful words about the nice, warm cell waiting for Bookie and called him Sue, of all things, and Bookie sobbed back at him, I spotted a tall, skinny character I never liked to spot: Whisper-Whisper, the City Hall fixer who pulled the puppet strings behind City Hall's closed doors.

Let's just say, Sparky wasn't his favorite kid. I'd caused him plenty of grief this summer by messing with his schemes.

With him were his two kid cops who were firmly in his pocket and did whatever he said.

To hide, I slid under a parked cop car. It was like a stinky lake under there. The huge puddle soaked through my white sailor dress. At least I could still see them. I hoped they couldn't see me.

Wait. Something was wrong. A danger alert went off in my head. The kid cop who'd blasted the pistol-toting floozie this summer with a rifle, after a nod from Whisper-Whisper, was holding his rifle again.

With rain dripping down the brim of his cop hat, the rifle kid cop looked up at Whisper-Whisper, who was taller than the kid cops. Whisper-Whisper's long neck with his bobbing Adam's apple, was craned back, looking up at Bookie. Rain ran along the brim of his Panama fedora to dribble down the back of his neck. Angrily, he pulled his fedora off his blond head. He shook it but, too late, it had lost its shape from the rain.

Whisper-Whisper noticed the kid cop looking up at him. He looked down at the kid, frowned at his wet fedora. Then he made a small nod, so small you'd miss it unless you were looking straight at him. Like I was.

I recognized that nod. It was the same nod Whisper-Whisper made this summer right before the kid cop took the bull's-eye rifle shot that knocked the floozie down, permanently.

This same kid cop was now pointing his rifle up at Bookie sobbing in the glare of the spotlight. Bookie was an easy target. Oh, no. No, no, no.

Bookie always said to be careful about acting too crazy, especially when people were looking, because that was the difference between going to the loony bin or the jail pen, and as bad as both were, the bin was worse than the pen.

Sorry, Bookie, crazy was called for now.

I jumped out from under the cop car, jumped on the kid cop, and bit his hand. As hard as I could.

The rifle shot exploded as the kid cop fell back.

I took my teeth off his hand so I could turn around to see if he hit Bookie. My ears rang from the rifle shot, but I could still hear screams and running feet. Then I saw Bookie. He was holding on. No, wait, he was sliding, sliding.

He kept sliding until he slid off the roof directly toward Mug, who looked terrified but held out his arms, like he was trying to catch Bookie.

Bookie slammed onto Mug, knocking the giant cop to the ground.

"Sparky!" Whisper-Whisper snarled. "Get her!"

The rifle cop was still under me, moaning, "That crazy girl bit me! Get her off!"

The other kid cop leapt at me, but I was faster. Whisper-Whisper joined the chase, but being small has its advantages. I zipped and dodged in and out of the sea of big people legs packing the wet sidewalks and street. I started sliding on the slick street, so I kicked off my school shoes. I wasn't used to shoes. They slowed me down.

I kept dodging through legs. I had to find out if Bookie was okay.

Finally, I was able to squeeze close to Bookie. He was sprawled on top of Mug's chest. He was still sobbing. Now other cops were pulling him off Mug, who was groaning. There was something wrong with Mug's arms, bent kind of funny. "I'm sorry, Muggie!" Bookie bawled.

Bookie seemed alive and well, so time for me to vanish.

I heard Whisper-Whisper shouting, but further away in the crowd now. I heard "Hey, watch it, mister!" from annoyed people he was probably shoving over.

I kept dodging through the legs until I reached a handy alley that I knew led to a shortcut I could slip through—a dark door to a speakeasy that had another dark door in the back, opening outside to the next block. "Hey, who let that raggedy kid in here!" the swells shrieked. Others laughed and toasted me with their drinks, which were illegal, being it was 1932, with Prohibition and all. I was out to the other side before the bouncers grabbed me.

I could have hopped the Angels Flight tram to ride up steep Bunker Hill from the downtown Los Angeles flatlands. That was the easy way, and the easiest way for me to get caught.

Whisper-Whisper no doubt had more cops searching for me now. Besides, Angels Flight was too close to the ratty Monkey Island tourist trap to be safe.

And to think, only hours before, I was so excited about Bookie taking me to Monkey Island with its glass roof and for-real monkeys. Now I felt like a chump.

I took the hard way, scrambling up the steep hillside, clawing in the wet dirt, keeping hidden in the bushes. It was tough climbing in this stupid dress. School didn't allow the sailor suits with pants that I had been wearing. Even better for climbing would have been the tough old overalls I used to steal when I used to be a street punk. That's before I started living in Creepy House this summer with Tootsie LaFemme, the former silent-screen vamp, and her assistant Gilbert Grossman, who looked like a goblin with his bald head and scar over his eye. Creepy House was where I headed. It was home now. That's an idea I was still getting used to: home.

I was a mess by the time I got to the top of Bunker Hill. Being a mess was how I usually was.

I found an out-of-the-way spot to hide, behind a slop bin, in the shadows away from streetlights. I'd pause here until I was sure no cops had followed me. The fading rain tapped my curly rat's nest of dishwater-blonde hair and dribbled down my freckled face that kids at school made jokes about. The day started out hot, but now, with the sun long gone from the cloudy night sky, I shivered in my soaking dress.

I probably should backtrack and tell you how this, the worst day of my life started.

School. That's right. It started with my first day back at school.

Monday

Today could have been a day like any other. The sun came up, right? From there, it went downhill. Fast.

Tootsie was so excited by my first day back at school, she actually roused herself from her huge carved peacock bed, with painted wooden feathers at one end and a giant peacock head at the other.

"Sparky, you will be the star today at school! Think of it as your movie." She held my freckled face in her hands and smiled at me. Tootsie wore a flowing, dark-red wrap with a pattern of red-eyed, pouncing black leopards. About a foot of black fringe swung as she waggled my freckled face back and forth with glee. "I'm so happy for you."

"You will do so well, my little Sparky!" That was Gilbert the goblin, beaming so hard, his scar running over one eye turned bright red. When he got worked up, his strange accent from somewhere across the ocean got even heavier. It got extra heavy today.

At least someone was happy. It sure wasn't me.

We were in Gilbert's sparkling white-tile-and-chrome kitchen. It was the most modern part of the house. Gilbert matched his kitchen. He wore a long white apron over his white shirt sleeves. He always kept his dark tie neatly tucked between buttons on his shirt. His bald head was shiny, like the chrome in his kitchen.

I was shocked to see the kitchen when I first snuck into Creepy House. I expected to see bloody kiddie parts dangling from the ceiling and boiling in pots because neighborhood kids said a vampire lady lived here. That's why they called it Creepy House.

Gilbert sure wasn't serving up boiled kids today. He set a colorful plate with a green-and-pink leaf pattern in front of me on the white-and-chrome kitchen table, then a matching napkin, a knife, a fork, and a glass. Sometimes it took forever to get something to eat from the goblin.

Carefully, he poured orange juice he'd freshly squeezed into the glass. Then, grinning extra big, he brought over a tray covered with a cloth that matched the green-and-pink plate. He pulled the cloth off with a flourish.

What was on the tray was something I'd never seen in this kitchen before, never seen anywhere before. They were pastries that looked like fat twists wrapped around brown, sweet-smelling, nutty filling that was so thick, it struggled to ooze out from between the twists and turns. I felt like crying.

With a fancy silver serving spoon (he had lots more where that came from), he scooped one up and laid it on the green-and-pink plate. The smell wafted up my nose and down to my stomach. I knew I was supposed to use the fork, but I wasn't exactly from polite society. I grabbed it in both hands and jammed it into my mouth. Oh, my.

"Gilbert was up very early to make these goodies to celebrate your first day back at school!" Tootsie chirped while the goblin beamed.

School.

Why did they keep talking about it? Normally, I'd shove at least another pastry down my snout, but suddenly, I lost my appetite. I sat back and didn't move.

"They're so good, she doesn't know what to do!" Tootsie said to the goblin. Of course, she didn't have a plate, a glass, or a pastry, because she never ate breakfast and hardly ate at all. She had to stay slim in case an audition came her way.

"Ah, well, the rest will be waiting for you when you come home," Gilbert smiled at me.

I stared at my half-eaten pastry, then my mind wandered to the newspaper on the table. "New Mayor" read the headline, and something about "Tough on Crime!" and "Law and Order!" The close-up photo was of the roughest looking hard case I'd ever seen. I should ask Bookie if he knew this guy.

I couldn't focus on this interesting new Mayor any more than I could focus on the pastry.

School was ruining my life.

"The clock is ticking!" Gilbert announced. "Time for your bath!"

Tootsie's fringe swung as she flounced with Gilbert and me to the downstairs bathroom that was mine now. "Got to get you bright and shiny for your first day back at school!" she declared.

"Bright and shiny!" the goblin repeated.

Did I tell you I was no fan of baths?

This bath business would happen every school day from

now until forever. I might as well be locked in the big house. I didn't want to think about it.

School had rules on what kids were allowed to wear. Girls had to wear dresses, so Tootsie bought me a dozen sailor-style dresses that were mostly white with blue trim. She figured, since I was willing to wear the sailor suits with pants this summer, maybe the sailor dresses would be okay. What choice did I have? School also required shoes, which I hated.

They made you wear shoes in the big house.

When I was done putting on my prison duds, I headed back to my room to pick up the new school supplies Tootsie bought me. Normally, walking into my pretty pale-green-and-blue room made me smile. Normally, new pencils, pencil boxes, erasers, and paper would make me excited. Not today. The pencils and papers in my room were part of my trip to the lockup.

I patted Clara Bell, a stuffed leopard, and her boyfriend, who was flattened into a rug. When they were still alive, they used to be Tootsie's pets in Paris when she was still a silent movie star. My friend Bobby corrected me that they were not leopards, but another spotted cat called a cheeseball or something. So what if he was a smart bookworm? Maybe he didn't know everything.

"Wish me luck," I told the leopards. They never said anything, but I knew they understood my pain.

School supplies tucked in my new school bag from Tootsie, I headed to the mansion's sunroom, which was the only room in the house with clear glass panes on its French doors. The sunroom French doors were also the only ones with cut glass transoms above them that scattered rainbows around the room when the sun touched them. Those doors led to her overgrown, hidden jungle of a backyard. The rest of the windows in the house had colored glass panes with smaller clear glass transoms above. The windows stayed shut, and only the transoms were cracked open a little, even when it was hot weather, like now. The huge cooler machine in the basement conked out more often than not, so wasn't much help.

The colored glass was how Tootsie liked it. Hidden from the outside world, she felt safe. Can't say I blamed her. The world was nuts. Especially today, with school looming.

I nearly fell over when I stepped into the sunroom and spotted the goblin standing by the French doors. He was out of his apron and done up in his beige chauffeur gear with the tall boots that made him look like a jungle explorer in the movies.

"I shall drive you to your first day of school!" he declared.

Oh, no. That meant driving me in Tootsie's mile-long, gold-colored movie star sedan. When the other school kids got a gander at that, they'd give me grief for the whole school year.

Tootsie danced into the sunroom with her vitamin doctor on her arm. "You'll arrive in style!"

Doctor knew my number. He read my face and made that smirk of his on his thin, pale face. He wore one of his usual expensive summer suits that were identical but for color. Today it was a dark gray suit. Good for a funeral.

"You know, I think I want to walk to stretch my legs some. Clear my head. Get ready for the big day and all that," I told them.

Tootsie seemed surprised. She and Gilbert exchanged uncertain looks.

Doctor came to my rescue, as he sometimes did. "Exercise is good for the children. Perhaps she should walk," he said in his cool, quiet voice while eyeing me with his smirk.

"Well, I suppose," Tootsie said, still unsure. Gilbert looked disappointed after dressing up in his chauffer gear. "Yes, perhaps," Gilbert sighed. Whatever Doctor said held a lot of weight in Creepy House.

I noticed a tin in the goblin's hands. "But you must remember your lunch. I have made a special treat for you today." He smiled as he carefully slid the tin into my school bag. That was one thing to look forward to.

"You will search for room 3A," the goblin said cheerfully. "That is your homeroom at school."

Before anyone changed their minds, I darted through the French doors, across the jungle yard, and toward the back gate. I heard Tootsie call after me, "Remember, ignore what the bad kids say! Hold your head high!"

Easier said than done.

My feet hurt.

I had no problem scrambling around Bunker Hill and the downtown flatlands below—in my bare feet. Me and shoes weren't meant for each other.

The closer I got to school, the slower I walked. That wasn't only from my hurting feet. I knew what waited for me.

Sure enough, when I reached school, the packs of kids milling outside went quiet. They stared at me. I heard a girl say to her group of friends, "Wasn't she in jail this summer?"

I should have listened to Tootsie and kept my mouth shut. Before I could stop myself, I shouted at her, "No, I wasn't!"

Okay, I was almost locked up for murder this summer before I cleared my name. The point was, I didn't go to jail.

Kids started snickering. I spotted the boy who promised he'd "get me" when Tootsie and Doctor took me here to sign up for school. He noticed me noticing him. He laughed and said, "You shouldn't have come back."

I felt my fists go tight, ready to punch. I would have, but then the school bell rang. All at once, the kids herded inside. Some of the mean older boys, who always gave me a hard time on Bunker Hill, made a point to shove me. Nice.

Goblin told me to look for room 3A, my homeroom.

It was hard for me to find the right door in the crowd of kids. The brown tile on the floor that ran halfway up the walls made the sounds of the noisy kids even louder.

Up ahead, I spotted Bobby, neat as a pin and his blond hair combed just so, as usual. He saw me, waved, and mouthed "lunch." Right. I was supposed to find him in the lunchroom. It was all part of the plan to keep me on the straight and narrow at school.

He disappeared into a classroom. He wouldn't be in the same room as me because he was twelve, a year older.

My other friend, Marigold, was my age, eleven. I wouldn't see him at this school either. He went to a different school, far away, run by his mom's church. Every morning, his crazy great-uncle Old Bob, who trained stunt horses for the movies and dressed like a cowboy, drove Marigold to school. Rumor had it Marigold was named after one of Old Bob's movie star horses. Marigold fancied himself something of a movie star too, so much so that I nearly punched him in the nose a few times. But I never did. His face was too pretty.

The other kids who followed Bobby into his classroom were the known smarties and bookworms. Yeah, Bobby would be in the brainy kids' class.

Wait, was that the weird kid from the weird pet shop on Bunker Hill? Inside that musty basement shop lived spiders, peculiar fish, a puppy-sized lizard tugging on a leash, a bald monkey in a sailor suit, and a rooster and guinea pig with a hankering for math. The shop also sold lots of books with strange symbols on the covers.

The kid was hard to miss. Head to toe in black, he wasn't dressed like the other kids. He kept his black hair longer than other boys, and it hung in his dark eyes. He spotted me staring. He stared back and made a small, sly smile before he went inside the smart classroom.

How about that? The weird pet shop kid was also a brainy kid.

One thing I did know, Bobby didn't like him much and got buggy at the thought of me talking to him.

Come to think of it, Bobby sometimes was suspicious about me talking to Marigold, even though they were buddies.

Bobby, Marigold, the pet shop kid: they all stood on my last nerve.

Finally, I saw "3A" painted on one of the doors. The halls were nearly empty now. I was about to go in, when I nearly jumped from loud oinking sounds coming from close behind me. I whirled around and saw it was the same boy who told me I shouldn't be here.

"You're a dummy in the dummy class full of dummies," he laughed, and started oinking in my face.

Wouldn't you know, but about when I was winding up to slam my knuckles into his face, a teacher popped out of the classroom.

Oinking boy did a quick vanishing act, leaving me standing there with my arm in the air.

"Time to come inside, young lady," she said.

I followed her inside. The only empty seat left was right in front, right in the middle. Could this day get any more perfect? And I meant that as a joke.

I noticed the kids in this dummy class were of different ages. The mean older boys were grouped together in back. "Hey, Sparky!" one called to me and threw a balled-up paper. He missed. The paper bounced off the head of a smaller boy, maybe nine or ten. "Ow!" the boy howled and started crying.

Wack! The teacher slammed her ruler on her desk. "Everyone, quiet! Young lady," and she pointed her ruler at me, "take your seat. Now."

The room quieted down, but I still heard snickering as I sat at my desk that was smack-dab in front of the teacher.

Dummy class. I couldn't believe it. But I could. Come on, I'd been out of school for over a year. I should have expected this. Being a street kid, I didn't see the point of school. Even before my cousins left town without telling me, leaving me to fend for myself on Bunker Hill, I'd stopped going to school. The kids made fun of me for the one threadbare dress I wore every day and my too-small shoes that were falling apart. They were the only clothes the cousins gave me to wear.

No one seemed to care if I went to school or not. Well, except for Bobby, but he wasn't a grown-up. When I started staying with Tootsie and Gilbert in Creepy House this summer, everything changed. They actually cared about what I did. So it was back to school for ol' Sparky.

But dummy class? It was so embarrassing.

After glowering at the kids, the teacher launched into stern instructions about coming on time, good behavior, paying attention, the usual school stuff. She wrote her name on the chalkboard: Miss Clark.

Then attendance. Each kid said "Here" and raised their hand when the teacher called their name. She got stuck on one name and kept repeating it over and over. That kid must have skipped school on the first day. At least I wasn't that bad.

Suddenly, Miss Clark was rapping my desk with her ruler.

"Ambrosia Brown, when I call your name, you answer 'Here' and you raise your hand. You do not daydream. Didn't I just explain about paying attention in class?"

What?

Oh, right. That was my real name. The one I never used. Only school used that name. I'd forgotten.

I said "Here" and raised my hand to snickers from the older boys in back. I did what I was told, but too late. I hadn't been paying attention in class.

That meant Miss Clark marched me with my nice new school bag stuffed with nice new pencils and Gilbert's lunch to the Principal's office.

Could I do nothing right?

Behind the door that had "Principal's Office" painted on its frosted glass panel, were two rooms. The back room, behind another frosted glass door, was where Principal lived during school hours. The smaller front room was guarded by his secretary, Miss S, who was built like a locomotive and took no nonsense.

"Getting started already, are we, Sparky?" she said, eyeing

me, after Miss Clark dropped me off. "You know the drill. Get in the chair."

I did. This was a place I spent more time in than any classroom. I sat on the hard metal chair to the side of her desk.

Principal cracked his door open. I saw his pudgy, bald head peek out to see who the bad kid was. His bespectacled eyes widened when he spotted me. "It's only half past eight, and you are here already?" He gasped and shut his door.

Miss S gave me her hard look. "Keep quiet. Don't move. You'll be here for a while so you might as well make yourself comfortable."

She knew full well it was impossible to get comfortable in the punishment chair. What could I do? I was at Miss S's mercy. I sat, said nothing, and tried not to twitch.

Sure enough, Miss S kept me there a long time. The hours crawled by. There were no windows to open in her little domain, which made it hotter and stuffier than anywhere else in school. The heat made me sleepy. Every time I felt myself drifting, starting to tip over, I heard a sharp, "Sparky, wake up."

Finally, the bell rang that meant lunch.

She didn't let me go right away. She shuffled papers for a bit before saying, "All right. Lunch for you. But don't get too excited. No recess. Eat, then park yourself back here."

Oh, no. But what could I do? I was her prisoner. I was in the big house.

The lunchroom was packed. The kids mostly ignored me this time. I wasn't sure where to sit until I saw Bobby waving at me.

"You're late," he pointed out when I sat in the chair he saved for me.

"Ah, yeah, I was held up by. . .stuff."

Bobby wasn't buying it. "Sparky, it's too soon to get in trouble at school." His blue-eyed angel face looked at me in a serious way. His face would have been perfect except for the dent in his nose. That was my dent I put there after he stole a kiss. Bobby had crazy notions in his noggin that we'd get married one day. I think not!

I put up with Bobby. Not sure why, but I did.

To be fair, I wasn't sure why he put up with me, either.

"Remember, we'll spend recess in the library to help with your studying," he said.

Didn't sound fun, but more fun than being stuck in the playground with the oinking boy. Definitely more fun than Miss S's punishment chair.

"The thing is, I can't come today. I have to. . . ." I trailed off.

Bobby finished for me: "Stay with Miss S all during recess?" He frowned. "Just try to keep out of trouble tomorrow so we can go to the library together."

Bobby had a sandwich, an apple, and a cookie. They were probably packed by Helen, his family's housekeeper.

I pulled Gilbert's tin open. A sandwich. Not too exciting, though Gilbert's sandwiches were steps above your typical sandwich. Then, what's this? Something was wrapped in brown paper spotted with greasy stains. I pulled at the paper, which took some doing because it was stuck to whatever it was hiding.

When I finally unwrapped the treasure, my mouth hung open. It was two sticky bars drizzled with chocolate and thick with layers of jam and more chocolate. Gilbert, you have outdone yourself.

I noticed Bobby's eyes staring. He liked the goblin's cooking too.

"We'll share." I pulled one sticky bar from the brown paper and gave it to Bobby.

"Thanks!" He gave me his cookie and his apple.

I had to admit I was hungry after hardly eating anything this morning. I polished off my sandwich, Gilbert's treat, and Bobby's cookie. I stashed the apple in my school bag for later.

Along with his lunch, Bobby had a stack of books. "There's a book here that I think will help with your spelling." Yep, spelling sure wasn't my strong point.

While Bobby busily looked through his books, my eyes wandered the lunchroom, and stopped at the pet shop kid. He sat by himself in the far corner. He must have felt me looking at him. He turned. Through his fringe of black hair, I saw one eye. It winked. He added a sly smile. I quickly looked away. Good thing Bobby was still messing with his books and didn't notice.

After lunch came more dull times with Miss S. She did spice things up by giving me a bowl of paper clips to sort by bent ones and not-bent ones. At least that made the time go by. I still felt sleepy in the hot room.

Eventually, I think she got sick of me. "Back to class," she ordered.

When I opened the door to my homeroom, the older boys snickered. Some kid—I couldn't make out which—started chanting, "Sparky's a murderer! Sparky's a murderer!" The others laughed until Miss Clark got stern and told them to be silent "unless you all want to make a trip to Miss S."

On my desk were school books that must have been passed out when I was trapped with Miss S. Under them was a bad drawing of me with so many freckles, my face was a blob. Behind me, I heard more snickers.

That was about how the rest of the school day went.

After the school bell rang, I got more oinking and a couple of shoves from the mean older boys. Outside, I ducked around the corner to avoid Bobby.

I dodged Bobby, but instead, I slammed into the pet shop kid so hard, I knocked myself down. He made a little laugh, helped me stand, and picked up my school bag from where I'd dropped it. He didn't give it back. Staring at me through his fringe of hair, he whispered, "I'm done with school too. But I'm not worried. Why? Because I'm planning to stow away on a ship bound for the other side of the world." He gave me a particularly intense look. "You can come too." Finally, he handed me my school bag. Then he walked away.

What was he talking about? That kid was as crazy as his pet shop.

Can I tell you I was more than done with school? I was done with everything.

I should have headed back to Creepy House with Bobby so he could help me with my spelling. Gilbert probably had more of those chocolate jam bars. This morning's pastries would also be waiting for me. No doubt the goblin would be whipping up new yummy eats.

I liked Creepy House, my new home—my first real home, if you thought about it. I had my own room, another first for Sparky. I loved the pictures of Tootsie from her silent movie days that covered the walls of Creepy House, the layers of mismatched carpets, and the mess of vases, doodads, sofas, and poufy stools. Best of all I loved Gilbert's kitchen and Tootsie's maze of closets upstairs that were filled with costumes and props from her old movies.

But I couldn't deal with Bobby, Tootsie, and Gilbert today. Because today had been an awful day. I needed to stop by the five-and-dime, head to Bookie's office in the back. I needed to take a break from my new life with a home, a clean kitchen, school, and homework by stepping back to my other life with Bookie, crooks, and no questions asked.

Here's a tip: if plugging's on the menu, some kid standing by will hardly make a difference.

I wasn't thinking about that when I strolled into the Bunker Hill five-and-dime store that never had customers, only Bookie's overgrown gorillas and the other shady characters working for him. The usual crew sat at tables playing cards by shelves of dusty sewing thread and hair pins no one bought. I'd just gotten steamed at all these characters, especially Bookie. But I couldn't stay mad. Much as I hated to admit it, I was used to these idiots and missed them.

"Hey, Sparky," from Gorilla #1. "How's it going?" from Gorilla #2.

"We got our scholar coming down to see us. How's school?" That was from Spots, the pudgy character with a bum foot who liked sporting spotted ties.

I came here to get away from school talk. This wasn't fair! I mumbled something and headed as fast as I could down the short hall to Bookie's rooms in the back.

"Yeah, well, I didn't like school either. Same as the Army, and look what they did to my foot," I heard Spots say to the gorillas.

I had to check in with Bookie on the regular anyhow to see if he needed me to run any of his mysterious packages down the Hill to his boss Chum-Chum, who had no problem operating out of his storefront in the wide-open across from City Hall. Like Chum-Chum told the cops, he had dirt on everybody. Dirt was like currency in City Hall.

Kids made the best runners for an operation like Bookie's. With me being eleven, I could dodge grown-ups and slip through shortcuts that big cops like Mug couldn't.

I didn't live on the streets anymore, but I still had to work for Bookie because I traded a lifetime of free work for a tip that helped to clear me of murder last summer and save me from the hangman's noose. Bookie kept me busy. It was the life I was used to. Like Bookie said, sometimes the cookie didn't crumble how you wanted.

So that he knew I was coming, I stepped hard on the squeaker Bookie hid under the rug outside his office. He hid the squeaker there so he had a second's warning if any crooks charged in with shooters meaning to fill him with lead. Bookie was prepared.

Today Bookie seemed distracted. He didn't look up at me when I stepped on the squeaker. He usually did. Maybe he figured it was me. But still.

I had to admit, being forced back to school put me in a mood. Bookie not saying anything, even to yell at me, added to my mood. My mood made me start kicking his file cabinet. My shoe on the metal made a nice loud clanking, banging sound. The more I kicked, the more it made the sound. The harder I kicked, the louder it got. Yeah!

"Stop that!" Finally, he noticed me. "You gone mental or something? I'm in the nuthouse here."

I smiled at him. But his notice of me faded just as fast. He sunk down in his chair and rubbed his temples like he had a headache. His big brown eyes seemed lost.

Bookie fancied himself a sharp dresser. He took a lot of care—too much, if you asked me—ironing his own shirts and making sure all his gear for the day matched. Bookie told me the Chicago bosses always dressed sharp. I supposed that meant he wanted to be just as sharp as them or have them like him or something.

Today he wore one of his new, high-end outfits that showed up in his office at night in canvas sacks. In other words, he didn't buy them. His outfit was a pale-yellow suit with an even paler-yellow shirt with contrasting dark-green cuffs and collar. His tie was gold with random darker-gold, dark-red, and dark-green dots and cross-hatching. His pocket hankie matched the tie. He wore the gold cuff links and gold watch and chain that his boss Chum-Chum gave him not long ago. The last mayor used to wear that watch, chain, and cuff links, but no more. What can I say? Politics was a tough business. Bookie's fedora sat on his desk. It was the same pale yellow as his suit and sported a dark-green band with random dark-gold, dark-red, and pale-yellow dots and cross-hatching.

All very sharp. Though today, the sharp was a bit rumpled. His tie wasn't so straight. His pocket hankie wasn't folded just so. The ironing job on his shirt was so-so. It looked like he'd been running his hands through his slicked-back hair, because it stuck up in a funny way. I knew better than to laugh.

He didn't say anything, didn't look at me.

What else could I do but start up again? Hey, it was fun. This time, I decided to run backwards into his file cabinet, hitting it good and hard with my butt. That made an even better sound. I think I dented the metal.

He moved his hands over his tan face, then through his black hair, messing it up even more. He still didn't say anything, so I made another run.

Just before my butt crashed into his file cabinet, he finally said, "Hey, hey, Sparky," but soft, not like my usual Bookie.

I stopped, waited.

"How about I take you for a little ride."

Ride? Like to fit me with a pair of cement boots for the bottom of Echo Park Lake because I was ramming his file cabinet? Or more likely, to drive me somewhere and have me run out to pick up an envelope or drop off an envelope. The usual, not too interesting routine.

"You wanna see Monkey Island?" he asked.

What?

Monkey Island?

The Monkey Island?

Did I ever want to see Monkey Island! Never in my wildest dreams did I think I'd see that tourist trap full of monkeys being crazy on their own island. Or have Bookie, of all people, actually pay to take me inside.

"Look at you, jumping up and down. I guess that's a 'yes.'"

Before I had a chance to be embarrassed about acting like a little kid, before I had a chance to ask myself why, all of a sudden, out of the blue, Bookie would take me someplace fun I'd want to see, something he'd never ever, ever done, Bookie did a quick rubdown of his hair, popped his fedora on his head, and was up and heading out to his sedan, with me hopping behind (yeah, I know, but you'd do the same for Monkey Island). I left my school bag in his office. I didn't want any school junk ruining my Monkey Island fun.

When we reached one of his sedans, he mumbled, "Maybe I can get you an ice cream or something." He paused. "I won't put that on your tab."

I think I screamed. Bookie put everything on my "tab" that I had to work off. He'd never given me a freebie, ever.

I bounced on the car seat all the way down Bunker Hill to the Los Angeles flatlands below. I kept thinking Bookie would snap out of his funky mood, tell me to quit being a clown, change his mind, and U-turn back up the Hill. But he didn't. His mind seemed miles away as he looked straight ahead like I wasn't there. Even after I started making the loud blowing-squashy noise with my tongue that always made him mad and bark at me for being low-class, I got nothing.

It was so strange, so unlike Bookie, I stopped bouncing and making low-class noises. Inside, I was still bouncing as high as the moon. Monkey Island!

Monkey Island was in an old building from the last century near the Grand Central Market downtown. I'd been by it a million times. I heard about it from other kids, how packed it was with for-real, wild, crazy monkeys doing monkey things. You had to pay to get in. That was the rub. Now, unbelievable as it seemed, Bookie was paying.

What I didn't expect was the smell.

After Bookie paid the ticket man outside, and the man pulled the door open for us, I was pushed back by the power of that stink.

I'd had to do my share of hiding in slop bins to dodge cops, but this smell? Oh, howdy, it was way more powerful.

I desperately wanted to see the monkeys. So I bucked up, held my breath, and ran inside.

It was an old building, like I said. Inside, I could see the bare brick walls because they weren't covered with paint or plaster. There were two ancient elevators, like mechanical monsters with giant turning wheels that pulled the elevator cabs up and down. I saw stairs made of fancy ironwork that traveled up and up to a second, third, and even fourth level. Each level had walkways that went around the building and had railings made of the same fancy ironwork. Off the walkways, I noticed doors, all closed. I'd bet they were closed because of that smell. Did people live behind them? Were businesses behind them? Couldn't tell. The fancy iron stairs traveled up one more level to a catwalk below the steeply pitched glass roof. A grid of iron held up the entire glass roof. The stairs, the elevators, were off to the sides of the building, leaving the space in the middle wide open all the way from the ground floor to the roof. The afternoon sun poured down from the glass roof, lighting the open space inside. I'd never seen anything like it.

I could've stared at that roof all day, but the monkeys were what I came for. In the middle of the open space, below the glass roof, was a fake mountain rising to the height of the building's second level. Circling the mountain was a moat of water, ringed with a railing of the same fancy ironwork. Kids, parents, all sorts, hung over the railing. They hooted, hollered, and threw things at the monkeys.

Were there ever monkeys. Every inch of that fake mountain was covered with monkeys hooting and hollering back at the people. They scrambled to catch what the people threw. Some of it was food, but some of it wasn't, from how the monkeys spat it out and screamed at the laughing people.

Some of the kids held ice cream cones. I stared hard at them licking the cold goodness with huge smiles on their faces. I tugged Bookie's sleeve and pointed at the kids.

"Yeah, right, ice cream," Bookie mumbled, but like he was only half paying attention.

"Ice cream! This is the first time ever you got me ice cream!" I admit I started jumping up and down.

"Crazy things happen. Haven't you figured that out by now?" he said. But he wasn't looking at me. He was scanning the open space, like he was searching for someone.

I spotted the ice cream stall against one side of the brick wall. I grabbed Bookie's sleeve again and tugged him toward it. "Yeah, yeah," he muttered, still glancing around for someone or something.

There were so many ice cream flavors in tubs behind a frosty glass case. The colors! Orange, pink, gold, chocolate brown swirling with bits of—could it be?—cherries! I felt as frozen as the ice cream—what should I pick? Behind the counter, the man with a white cap, snow-white apron, and face the same color as the chocolate ice cream, helpfully suggested, "Maybe Miss needs two scoops. Works every time if you can't decide."

This talk of two scoops, meaning double the money, made Bookie's head snap back to attention. I saw his teeth clench, and the growling sound he made when he wasn't happy came rumbling from behind those teeth. But that didn't last, like he couldn't focus on this two scoops problem. He pulled out his notoriously tight wallet and tossed coins on the counter.

I was so happy, I started crying. Tough ol' Sparky. That's right. Crying over ice cream. Before you crack a remark, keep in mind: two scoops. If you saw those colors behind that frosted glass, you'd cry too.

The man with the chocolate smile came to my rescue. He chuckled. "Well, now, Miss, how about I help you a little?"

I snuffled and nodded up and down like a crazy person.

He chuckled more. "Start by telling me which color strikes your fancy best."

With shaking hand, I pointed to the tub brimming with dark brown and swirling bits of what I dared not dream were cherries.

"Ah, chocolate cherry swirl!"

I was right!

"Good choice. That's my favorite."

I gasped, more tears sprouting. Did the Ice Cream King see me as an equal, or at least having really swell ice cream taste? This was more than I could bear.

"Know what goes really well with chocolate cherry swirl?"

I shook my head no, back and forth like the crazy person in reverse. I was ready to put myself completely in the Ice Cream King's hands.

He pointed to a tub overflowing with pink wonder. "Strawberry."

Oh, my. Oh, my, my, my. I jumped up and down and couldn't speak.

The Ice Cream King smiled as he scooped my ice cream into a huge, toasted waffle cone. Gently, he placed it in my shaking hands. "Be careful now. And start eating it right away because it's already starting to melt."

I couldn't. I had to show my prize to Bookie. I turned, but he was gone.

I ran toward the island and looked for him in the crowd hanging over the rails.

I spotted Bookie, but not at the rails. He was off to the side, near a shadowy passage with a low ceiling that led away from the sunny glass roof. He was talking with a man wearing a light summer suit and a straw boater hat with a dark band. Must be the character Bookie was looking for.

This character wore a smirking grin I didn't like. Bookie looked nervous. I saw Bookie's hand twitching. Straw boater? Cool as cucumbers. His thin, wiry self looked like he was lounging even while he was standing. Bookie said something, and Straw Boater raised his hat to rub his hair like he was thinking about this proposition. That hair was so blond, it looked nearly white. His face was red and sore like he just got baked with a brand-new sunburn. He popped his hat back on and pulled his grin wider. He said something back I couldn't hear, but I got the feeling he was treating Bookie like a joke.

I wasn't the only one eyeing Straw Boater. Standing to the side, not too close, but close enough to get a load of any action, was a moll. No two ways to put it, she was a for-real gangster's moll. Toughest-looking processed blonde I'd ever laid eyes on: cap with black veil brushing half her face that looked like it had an inch of pancake stuck tight like concrete, orange paint over gum-chewing lips above a fox neck wrap, the kind where the dead fox heads are biting their own tails forever. The dead paws dangled over her shoulders.

That struck me as a hot thing to wrap around her neck on this boiling September day. The mustard-colored fabric on her dress that hugged her like it was glued on, seemed kind of heavy, like wool. That was too thick for this weather. She must be from out of town, maybe came off a train this morning from a locale where September wasn't so hot. Same for Straw Boater, but in an opposite way. Popping that straw hat on his head was almost going overboard, like, look at me—I'm used to hot Septembers.

Yeah, the two were a pair, but acting like they weren't. I wondered where they came from. I wondered what they were playing at with my Bookie. Whatever was going on, I wanted to find out. I also had to show Bookie the ice cream wonder his coins bought.

I ran to Bookie's side, holding the ice cream cone high to keep it safe. "Bookie! Look at my two scoops!"

Straw Boater looked at me, his eyes like hard blue diamonds. With his smirk, he said, "Cute kid," in a way that said I was anything but.

Bookie looked down at me. His tan face was wet with sweat. "Get lost," he said, low. Then added, "But stay close, okay?"

Straw Boater heard this. He leaned his head back and har-har'd. "That kid your muscle or something?"

I wanted to sock that character, but Bookie moved his chin, though not too much, telling me to take a hike, but a close hike.

This was strange. I eased back toward the monkeys. Truth be told, their monkey howls were calling my name. I decided to study them while I enjoyed my two beautiful scoops. At the same time, I'd dart my eyes toward Bookie and try to figure out what was going on.

Funny thing was, the longer I stayed inside Monkey Island, the more I got used to the smell. It was still there, but somehow, not as bad. Hiding in slop bins was also like that. At first I'd want to heave. Then, after a while, the stink was tolerable.

As I sidled up to the railings surrounding the monkey moat, the smell did get stronger. I decided to hold off on licking my ice cream until I got used to it. I still had fun watching as the scoops dripped down my hand, the pink and the chocolate mixing together. It was so pretty. My very first ice cream cone ever.

The monkeys noticed my ice cream too. They hopped up and down screaming. They were a rough-looking lot, dirty and skinny. Whoever owned them must not have fed them much and relied on the sightseers tossing them candy and old pieces of toast.

I leaned forward to get a better look. Then—horror! Those two beautiful scoops tipped off the cone and fell into the moat. I shrieked. I was so surprised, my hand opened and out tumbled the waffle cone. I hadn't had a bite or a lick of any of it.

The other kids, and some of the big people, laughed at me. I would have taught them all a lesson with my knuckles to their kissers, but I couldn't move my eyes from my beautiful lost ice cream. The two scoops pulled apart and floated in the water that was a dirty green color with brown swirls. The water was so thick and dark, I couldn't see through to the bottom.

The water seemed to move and be pulling the scoops, along with my waffle cone, cigarette butts, a doll's head, and shoelaces straight toward the monkeys. The monkeys knew the score on how the water worked and were waiting for my prize. They jumped up and down and screamed so loud, they sounded like they were tearing their throats out. The closer the ice cream and cone drifted toward them, the more they fought. They bit and pounded one another with their fists. A man nearby laughed and said to no one in particular, "Just like people, huh?"

When the scoops hit the island shore, a monkey bigger than the others shoved them aside and grabbed both scoops in his hands. He stuffed my ice cream in his huge mouth before the others could claw the scoops away. He lifted one clawing monkey and heaved it into the water. Then the big monkey reached down to grab my bobbing waffle cone. He crammed it into his mouth. Still chewing the cone, the big monkey pushed through the monkey crowd as he climbed and fought to the top of the mountain. Once there, he finished chewing the cone fast while beating aside smaller grabbing monkeys. He swallowed the cone, then made a huge scream, like he was the ice cream king now.

The monkey in the water gasped and struggled. The other monkeys didn't care. They moved their eyes back to the human crowd, hoping for more handouts. Soon enough, the water's current carried the struggling monkey back to the island. It had a hard time climbing up because the other monkeys kept shoving it back in the water. "Just like people, huh?" the man said again.

I had to agree with him. Monkey Island wasn't what I thought it'd be. I wanted to go back up Bunker Hill. The monkeys, the screaming, my lost ice cream didn't make my mood better. I felt worse.

Suddenly, I realized I'd been so busy watching the monkeys, I hadn't been checking on Bookie. I hoped he didn't see me drop that ice cream into the monkey moat. He'd get mad and never, ever buy me ice cream again. He'd be even more steamed that I wasn't keeping an eye on him like I was supposed to.

I used my sailor dress to wipe the melted ice cream off my hands. Normally, I would have licked off every drop, but now I felt too sad. I moved my head to look around. Where was Bookie? Not by the ice cream stand (of course). Not by the monkeys. Not by the entrance doors.

I walked away from the island to search for Bookie. I discovered a large cage against the wall opposite the ice cream stand. A sign above the cage read, "Big Otto." The cage was empty. Maybe Big Otto escaped. Good for him. Whatever happened to Big Otto, Bookie wasn't near the cage or in it. He was nowhere.

I heard something. Was that Straw Boater laughing in a sneering way? I followed the sound. It led me toward the shadowy passage. I heard Bookie. He was somewhere in the passage. His voice sounded nervous, panicked even. What was he saying? "Wait! What? Come on!" Was Straw Boater about to plug him full of holes?

I ran, then stopped hard. Straw Boater staggered from the shadows, into the open area, and fell. Bookie stepped from the passage. He stopped and stared down at Straw Boater, who wasn't moving. His straw hat rolled away, wobbled, and dropped down to the floor.

As if feeling my eyes, Bookie looked up, saw me, and shouted, "Run for the car!" He started running toward me.

Just as I unfroze and turned to run, I saw the moll. She was standing near me. She raised her hand, pointed at Bookie, threw back her head, and screamed, "Murderer!"

All at once, everyone in Monkey Island turned to see Bookie running away from motionless Straw Boater. Screams echoed around the brick walls. The man who said the monkeys were just like people pointed at Bookie and shouted, "There's the killer!" People jostled me aside as they ran toward Bookie.

The sight of this mob stopped Bookie in his tracks. His escape was blocked. Through gaps in the crowd, I saw his panicked face. He knew he was trapped. Then he realized he was near the iron stairs. He ran, leapt over the fancy iron railing, landed on the steps, and ran up, up. A group of shouting men and kids ran after him. Everyone was pointing.

Others decided to ride up the elevators to follow Bookie. So many jammed inside, the doors wouldn't close. The elevators' giant mechanical wheels twitched, made grinding sounds, then stopped. The elevators went nowhere. The people inside tumbled out and joined the mob running up the stairs.

I pushed through the crowd of people pointing up at Bookie until I could see him. Ice Cream King was also watching Bookie run up and up. He tipped his head so far back to see, his white cap slid off. He didn't notice.

Bookie reached the fourth level. He ran along the walkway, then stopped to look down at the hooting, hollering people stampeding up the steps toward him. Even from down where I stood, I could see he was breathing hard. His face was damp and chalky.

He ran back the way he came so he could rush up the next set of stairs leading to the catwalk. He climbed onto the catwalk, but then seemed lost. Under the glass roof, he scrambled one way, then another, trapped. The fast-approaching mob saw this and laughed. They knew they had him.

Suddenly, I saw Bookie's hands reach above. It was a hatch! He pushed and pushed until I saw it pop open. He jumped, then wiggled onto the steeply pitched roof. Through the roof's glass panes, I saw him scrabbling on the other side, trying to get a grip on the glass.

The mob booed. They poured onto the narrow catwalk. It started jiggling. Too many people! The crowd below watched and screamed louder. All at once, everyone tried getting off the catwalk. A few jumped to the fourth level. The mob pushed, shoved, and trampled, knocking more to the fourth level. Now the catwalk was swaying wildly. With a crunching sound, part of it broke loose from the wall. Everyone who was still clinging, jumped off to the fourth level.

One man, the guy who said the monkeys were like people, overshot and fell, screaming, straight down, down through the central open space. He landed in the monkey moat with a massive splash, soaking everyone nearby with the stinky green-and-brown water. He popped to the surface, gasping. He realized with horror that the current was carrying him toward the monkeys. Oh, yes, and they knew it too. The biggest snack of them all was heading straight their way. They jumped and screamed with joy as the man struggled to swim away.

He wasn't having much luck. I overheard a woman wondering out loud, "Maybe someone should help him."

I didn't have time to wait and see.

I ran outside. Maybe I could spot Bookie, do something, anything to help him.

Already, the cop car sirens were screaming as they sped toward Monkey Island.

And you know the rest.

The worst day of my life.

After Bookie slid off the Monkey Island roof and I escaped Whisper-Whisper and his two kid cops, I took my time going back to Creepy House. For sure, I was going to get questions, lectures.

I went in by my usual way, through the back gate next to the garage where Tootsie's shinning gold movie star car lived, through her overgrown jungle of a backyard, and through the sunroom's French doors.

As I pushed the doors open, I heard a commotion. Tootsie burst from the hallway into the sunroom. She wore a pink wrap printed with orange dancing bears. Her face was smeared with orange goo that matched the bears. From under her pink turban, blue goo oozed. Green goo oozed from under orange mitts on her hands.

She pounced on me and grabbed me in a hug. I felt the multicolored goo sliming me.

"Sparky! We received a wonderful call today! I have an audition, the best audition in the world! I know this will be the one! I can feel it! I am so happy!"

Gilbert followed Tootsie into the sunroom. The scar on his face was bright red and his eyes were also red. He dabbed them with a hankie. "I am so happy you are here for the good news, Sparky!" he told me. "Your Bobby heard our news, but he had to go home. No matter. Later, we will celebrate. But not now. We must prepare for this audition. We must work extra hard!"

I knew what that meant: Tootsie's parade of wacko people she thought she needed to make her look young and perfect for her auditions.

Sure enough, out of the hallway emerged the two face broads, stern looks on their faces. "The youth treatment must harden. That kid is smearing it."

"Hey! I'm just standing here!"

"Don't mind them," Tootsie smiled. Then she drifted to the face broads, but not before both the avocado hair lady and hair lady #2 joined the pile to comment on all her youth treatments. The face broads and the hair ladies got into a tense discussion with a spat boiling just below the surface, like usual. The hand lady arrived to worriedly insist more goo must be shoved under Tootsie's orange mittens—it was an emergency. Mr. Exercise in his tights came by and pulled Tootsie's arm one way. "Stretch, Mademoiselle!" Then pulled her other arm the other way. "Stretch!" It got even more crowded when her voice coach, Mr. Beele, put in his two cents: "Mademoiselle, you must say 'Ahhhhh!'" Tootsie, with arms pulled, hands oozing goo, repeated, "Ahhhhh!"

Seeing Beele was never good news for me. He was suspicious from the moment he'd laid eyes on me in Tootsie's mansion this summer. Beele was of the opinion that a sound beating would be perfect for me.

When Tootsie's dance teacher showed up and started trading dark looks with Mr. Exercise, my good ol' goblin came to the rescue. He took my hand and led me through another of Creepy House's many hallways to his bright kitchen.

"I am so sorry, my Sparky, but I cannot do cooking while she prepares for her audition. Doctor says the cooking smells will interfere with her slimming efforts."

Yep, this happened before.

On the white kitchen table, I saw a sandwich resting on a purple-and-gold spotted plate. Gilbert's sandwiches were first-rate, made with thick, thick slices of bread. But "What about the pastries from this morning and those jam-and-chocolate bars you made for my lunch?"

Gilbert beamed. "Ah, I made those before the audition call, before Doctor's orders. They are safe. I have many left. And," he winked, "when those run out, I shall order from the bakery you like."

Goblin was my hero.

To prove his point, he placed a pastry twist and a chocolate jam bar on a matching purple-and-gold plate and laid it on the table. I dug in.

Was this heaven? I crawled back to Creepy House late, with my new shoes gone, my new dress a muddy mess, and I was sure my hair was worse. No one noticed because they were so busy being thrilled about this latest audition. Instead of questions, I got a chocolate jam bar and a yummy, crunchy pastry twist. Can't get much better than that.

Just as I was thinking this most terrible day in my life was turning around, Doctor, like the shadow of doom, appeared in the kitchen doorway. He looked me up and down, from my dirty bare feet to my ratty hair. He frowned. He knew I'd been up to no good. Can't fool Doctor.

Luck struck again when Doctor was surrounded by raw-food lady, slimming man, and their questions about the "quickest advisable conquest of belly fat." They pulled him in the direction of the chaos surrounding Tootsie. I noticed they were trailed by spiritual man, who was humming in his white robe and turban, like usual.

I'd seen all of Tootsie's usual wacky crew, except the dress lady, her assistant, and the jewelry man. I didn't need to wonder long, because Gilbert dreamily murmured that the three of them were upstairs, "Assembling the perfect wardrobe. This audition requires the look from her silent films that she is famous for."

"Yea! Her vamp look is better than her new 'I'm-at-the-beach' look."

"Yes, but the vamp must be modernized. New and classic at the same time."

Sounded awful, but what did I know?

As long as everyone was busy with Tootsie's audition, they wouldn't notice what I was up to. That was the main thing.

Bookie was in the pen, and I had to do whatever it took to get him out.

TUESDAY

The morning papers weren't looking good for Bookie.

I sorted through the newspapers on the kitchen table while the goblin bustled about packing my school lunch and getting me more orange juice and pastries from yesterday. He muttered about the pastries not being fresh anymore, and how he must call the bakery to remedy that problem immediately.

Normally, talk of the bakery would be music to my ears, but this morning I had more important business to pay attention to. I had to find out what was happening with Bookie.

All the papers had a photo of the "Monkey Island Victim," Claude Cavalerie, an actor. Sounded like a fake actor name. His photo looked like one of Tootsie's actor pictures, with the lighting just so and his mouth slightly open like he was about to say something. I wasn't the best reader by a long shot, but from what I could figure out, the guy was a washed-up silent picture actor who left Florida for Hollywood a dozen years back. There was another interesting tidbit about this actor: he looked nothing like Straw Boater. Claude had dark hair and a dark mustache on a pudgy face. Straw Boater had white blond hair, no mustache, and his sunburnt face had a wiry, lean wise guy look. Funny, huh?

Bookie's mug shot didn't do him any favors. His hair stuck up in all directions and he looked like he was growling. The newspapers pegged him as a "crook," "con," and "flat-out criminal." Okay, true. The name under his mug shot was strange. It must be wrong. I only knew him as Bookie. Others called him Books or Hothead. I decided I'd ask Bobby about the weird name in the rags.

The papers reported witnesses saw Bookie running from Straw Boater, aka Claude Cavalerie, sprawled flat on the floor in Monkey Island, which I saw. Then the stories branched off in all directions. One paper said that witnesses saw Bookie raising a knife. I didn't see anything in Bookie's hands. Another paper said Bookie had a machete in one hand and a sword in the other. I for sure would have noticed that. A third said Bookie mowed Straw Boater/Claude Cavalerie down with not one, but two tommy guns, one in each paw. Oh, come on. For those who weren't the best readers, like me, the rags also had drawings of Bookie's different rampages that made him look like a lunatic. The papers couldn't keep their stories straight!

The topper was the guy who fell into the monkey moat. He said Bookie pushed him into the moat, and he was nearly eaten alive by monkeys before cops pulled him out. Bookie was outside on the roof by the time that character fell into the moat.

This smelled like a frame-up.

Why?

My thinking was cut short when the goblin cheerfully reminded me of my bath. Right. That.

On my way to my bathroom, I passed the room with a shiny wood floor and walls of mirrors that Gilbert called the gymnasium. Tootsie was inside, up early in her tights. Mr. Exercise pulled her here and there: "Stretch!" While being pulled, her dance teacher instructed her to do dance steps that were too complicated for me to follow. Mr. Beele had music churning on the Victrola. "Repeat after me," he ordered. "Ah, oo, eee!" Tootsie repeated: "Ah, oo," then, "Ouch!" when Mr. Exercise yanked her too hard.

Mr. Beele, a small man with almost no hair and a little stick he liked waving around in time to music, suddenly noticed me standing at the doorway. He eyed me suspiciously through his round spectacles. "It. Again," he said unhappily.

"Don't pay attention to Mysteeree. He's doing my errands this morning." Tootsie told him.

"Seems like a layabout."

I made fast tracks to the bathroom before he said anything else. When I was wanted for murder this summer, Tootsie told him I was her houseboy named Mysteeree so he wouldn't realize I was the same kid on the wanted posters. He still pegged me as no good from the get-go.

I realized I still had bits of Tootsie's multicolored goo dried on my face and hair from when she slimed me yesterday. After scrubbing mostly clean, I changed into the fresh sailor dress Gilbert had ready for me in the bathroom. The one I wore yesterday might be too dirty and torn for even Gilbert to repair. Plus, it was also slimed with Tootsie's multicolored goo. He also left a new pair of the same shoes. Before school started, Tootsie got a whole bunch of the same sailor dresses and Mary Jane shoes for me. Tootsie and Gilbert knew I went through clothes like nobody's business.

On the way to my room to pick up my school bag and pencil box, I remembered I'd left them in Bookie's office before he drove with me to Monkey Island. Whoops. If I hurried, I could make it to the five-and-dime, fetch my bag, and get to school on time.

Running, I dashed to the kitchen to pick up my lunch tin from the goblin. I rushed out. "Such an eager student!" I heard Gilbert declare happily.

Not exactly.

Even with my feet hurting from yet another new pair of shoes, I still made quick time to the five-and-dime. I planned to ask Spots, the gorillas, any of the usual characters, what news they had heard about Bookie.

When I stepped inside, I didn't recognize the two toughs sitting at one of the card tables. Otherwise, the store was empty. Strange. They stared at me, and not in a friendly way.

Before they could stop me, I ran to Bookie's office, stepping on his squeaker rug on my way in. A kid, about my age, stood next to Bookie's desk. No one else was there. The kid looked up from a book he was holding.

"Hey, that's my book. Give it!"

The kid cocked his head. Without looking down at the book and keeping his eyes on me, he crunched a handful of pages in his fist and then tore them off. "Book? No, it's my toilet paper," he smirked. He threw my book over his shoulder. Then, from Bookie's desk, he grabbed the apple that Bobby had given me yesterday. "Your apple?" He took a huge bite from it and chewed with his mouth wide open, which even I knew you weren't supposed to do. He laughed, making part of the apple slide out of his mouth.

I was about to charge him until I realized the two hard-looking toughs in the five-and-dime were now standing behind me. They had carefully not stepped on Bookie's squeaker so they could sneak up on me.

I was done here.

I darted between the two characters. They lunged at me, but only managed to grab my dress sleeve. It tore off as I pulled away. I heard them running after me as I flew through the five-and-dime's front door. I kept running until I couldn't hear them behind me.

Out of breath, I sat down hard on the curb near the Angels Flight tram stop at the top of Bunker Hill.

Who were those idiots?

Something was familiar about the way they dressed. Yeah, they reminded me of how the moll at Monkey Island dressed. They wore wool clothes that were too hot and heavy for September in Los Angeles. The kid talked funny too. Come to think of it, Straw Boater had the same accent.

One thing was clear, this kid and those two toughs took over Bookie's office. He wouldn't like that much. But he was locked up and couldn't do squat about it.

I couldn't go to school without my books, my pencils. By now, I'd be late.

In for a penny, in for a pound. I might as well skip school today. That made it a perfect day to visit Bookie in the pen.

Gilbert left me pocket change in my school bag, and you know what happened to that. Because I had no coins, I offered a choice from my lunch tin to the man collecting fares for the Angels Flight tram. I peeled the brown paper away from the chocolate and jam bars so he could appreciate their wonders. The goblin also stuffed in one of the pastry twists. "I don't like no sweets," the man said as he grabbed the sandwich. He gave me a round-trip ticket in trade.

I always enjoyed the impossibly steep ride down Bunker Hill on the little Angels Flight train cars, especially when the car going up passed the car going down so close, it looked like they were going to crash.

Once at the bottom of Bunker Hill, it was a short walk to the old jail. It was best to step carefully when going to the old jail because it was behind the old downtown central police station. There were still plenty of cops working in the station, though they'd been moving a bit at a time to City Hall, which was only built a few years ago. The previous City Hall had since been flattened into a parking lot.

Bookie sent me to the old jail a few times to drop off packages to locked-up crooks, so I knew the routine. The jail bulls inspected whatever I brought in. It was a real art hiding or disguising whatever wasn't allowed from the sharp eyes of the jail bulls.

I didn't have any contraband in Gilbert's lunch tin today, but the jail bull jabbed the pastry and the chocolate and jam bars with a rusty knife. He pulled one bar from the sticky brown paper. "I have to test this," he said as he slid the bar into his mouth. He chewed. "Mmm." He smiled. He jabbed what was left a few more times with his knife. "Okay."

I put my hands on the tin to take it back, but the bull held tight. "When you come here, you ask for people's official names. You don't come and say, 'I wanna see Bookie.' I know who you mean, but next time, maybe I'll decide I don't. We have procedures here, kid."

Fine, but I didn't know Bookie's official name, like Bookie didn't know I was really Ambrosia Brown. Crooks just went by crook names. That meant my crook name was Sparky.

I didn't say anything smart. I knew the jail bulls were touchy. He let go of the tin and said, "You'll have to wait. He's already got a visitor."

As I walked into the visiting room, I nearly fell over when I saw Bookie chatting with Chum-Chum. I ducked behind the benches for waiting visitors so Chum-Chum wouldn't spot me and wonder what I was up to. Bookie always warned me to be careful of Chum-Chum. When I had a package or envelope to drop off, I was to leave it on Chum-Chum's desk, take any package or envelope he had going back to Bookie, and get out. "Don't hang around Chum-Chum," Bookie warned me. "Don't mess with him. Do not ever, never make him mad."

I watched Chum-Chum from the safety of my hiding place. He held his goldfish Rosie in her round bowl. He adored that fish with her long orange tail. She swished around in her bowl to look at Chum-Chum, then turned away to stare at Bookie.

Chum-Chum wore his usual outfit, a long silk robe over a

white silk pajama set with a white silk tie, white silk pj shirt, and razor creases and cuffs on his white silk pj legs. Today his robe was dark red with a pattern of dancing devils playing different musical instruments. His red slippers with black tassels matched the devil robe. He had multiple rings on each finger. Even though plenty of real rocks passed through Chum-Chum's pudgy hands in a back-door-midnight sort of way, all the gems on his rings were paste.

Chum-Chum smiled at Bookie. Bookie smiled back and chatted in a happy way I'd never seen before. Bookie was always so nervous at the thought of Chum-Chum, but he sure didn't look nervous now.

I couldn't hear everything, but I think Bookie was saying there was a mouse in his cell, and he was thinking of making a pet out of it. A pet? That didn't sound like the Bookie I knew. Bookie was going overboard to lay on the chatty charm, or something. Chum-Chum smiled and said in his strange little girl's voice, "Oh, that's so cute. I love it."

Soon Chum-Chum hefted up his short, round self to leave. Bookie stood too. "Please come back anytime!"

Chum-Chum waggled his fingers at Bookie. "Toodle-oo." He waddled away. The jail bull opened the door for him and Rosie. "Have a good day, sir!" The bull smiled. Chum-Chum grunted in reply.

With Chum-Chum gone, the happy Bookie melted away. He slowly sat back down and slumped in his chair. He looked suddenly small in his baggy blue prison denim. His face became blank.

I bounded out from behind the benches. "Bookie!"

He sharply sat up, like I'd scared him.

"What are you doing here?" He frowned at me.

"I got something for you." I slid the tin toward him. Bookie never ate sweets or pastries, but they'd be good for trading on the inside. He pulled the tin close, but didn't lift the lid.

"You shouldn't be here."

"Bookie, there's some real fishy business going on. The papers say the dead guy is some washed-up actor who doesn't even look a little bit like that guy wearing the straw boater hat. They're saying you had swords and machetes. You're being framed!"

Bookie looked away and didn't say anything.

"But Chum-Chum came here. He's going to get you out."

Bookie's lip curled. "No, he's not."

I blinked, confused. "But he was happy, he was smiling. He brought Rosie with him."

"He drags that fish everywhere." He looked back at me. "You don't know Chum-Chum. He's not doing squat." His eyes drifted away. "There's lots of ways to lose, Sparky," Bookie said. "Lose at cards, lose at dice, lose at life. Lots of ways to lose, Sparky. Get lost. I'm a dead man."

I didn't plan it. It just happened. I started to cry—right out in the wide open like a little girl.

Bookie jerked to attention. He looked embarrassed. His eyes darted here and there to the other cons with visitors. I could tell they were watching me on the sly, but not in an obvious way. Cons were careful about letting on what they saw. But they saw.

Even so, I couldn't stop.

"Hey, hey," Bookie said in a hushed kind of way. "Relax, come on. Quit being such a little girl."

I kept crying. I didn't know what was wrong with me.

"Why do you care what happens to me? Huh?" His eyes suddenly blazed.

I blinked at him. Tears running down my face, I sputtered, "But you're there. You're always there." This was true. When the cousins abandoned me, Bookie showed up in my life. Even if everyone in my life disappeared, I knew Bookie would always be there. Sure, Bookie was Bookie, a complete crook who was always mad about something. But he was there. No matter how messy I was, how bad a speller, Bookie was there.

"You're stupid," he growled.

"I know," I sobbed. "I'm in the dummy class in school!"

"Dummy class" made the other cons' eyes do a double take. I'd bet they'd done time in dummy class before graduating to the big house.

Bookie's eyes darted around. My scene was making him nervous. He smoothed away his angry face. "Forget what I said. Yeah, you know what, I think something'll turn up. Chum-Chum has his ways. Don't pay attention to me. I'm just in a mood. I'll be out before you know it."

I knew he was lying.

He bent forward and hissed at me. "Knock it off or do I have to jump over there and tan your ass?"

That got me back to my senses. Bookie wouldn't want the other cons to know Chum-Chum wasn't helping him, that Bookie wasn't under his protection. My sobbing could be a giveaway. Bookie was right. I was stupid. Quickly, I snuffled away the tears. "Sorry," I mumbled.

"Yeah, you better be." His eyes quickly scanned the other cons, who moved their slyly peeking eyeballs back to themselves. "Things'll work out."

I knew they wouldn't. I had to take matters into my own hands.

Bookie would not want me to do this. He'd yell in my ear if he were here.

But he wasn't. He was in the pen, charged with murder. I had to help him.

I paused at the glass storefront window and glass door of Chum-Chum's office. I could see City Hall across the street reflected in the glass. Chum-Chum always kept the venetian blinds on his door and window cracked open. Through them I saw Chum-Chum at his messy desk making kissy lips to Rosie as she swirled around her bowl. The rest of his shadowy office was crammed with teetering boxes, broken dolls' heads, old food, bottles of hooch. The mess mix changed every time I went there.

I never set foot in Chum-Chum's office unless Bookie sent me on a run with an envelope to drop off and pick up. I never showed up on my own. Ever.

I took a deep breath and pushed the glass door that he kept cracked open with a doll's head as a doorstop when it was hot. As I stepped over the doll's head, I felt his fan blow the roasting air from inside his office against my hair and face. Chum-Chum's slippers were off, and his bare toes massaged his usual pan of ice. He had his ways of keeping cool.

At the squeak of his door opening wider, his fish-kissy face vanished and his head jerked up to see who was there. When he saw it was me, the hardest expression I'd ever seen took over his face. He stared and said nothing. His toes stopped massaging the ice. Rosie turned in her bowl to watch me.

I was sweating, and that wasn't from his hot office.

He kept saying nothing. I saw anger growing on his face. His empty eyes, cold as the ice in his foot pan, bored into me.

Since he wasn't saying anything, I'd better get to it. "Bookie needs help. Please help him. Please?" I was shaking now. My voice was small, pitiful. I planned to be a bit more forceful, maybe try to spell out how useful and what a great crook Bookie was, how deserving of Chum-Chum's help he was. But I could barely speak.

I saw now why Bookie was so afraid of Chum-Chum. His face darkened and become cold fury.

Here I was, this nothing two-bit kid—a kid in the dummy class, no less—daring to ask Chum-Chum a favor, something Bookie told me never to do. "You'll regret it for the rest of your life."

Without even thinking, I managed to gasp, "I'll trade you. I'll trade you something for Bookie."

Chum-Chum cocked his head and gave me a strange smile. "It'll have to be something else, won't it, Sparkles." He laughed with his weird half-baby, half-horse laugh. He knew my name was Sparky. He called me Sparkles to let me know what a little nothing I was whose name wasn't important. "This something-something'll have to be an especially nice something, won't it, Sparkles?"

Was I crazy? What was I thinking? Why did I say that?

Panicked, I turned and ran from his office, flinging open his door so hard, his blinds clattered against the glass. I half-tripped on the doll's head doorstop, cracking it. I heard Chum-Chum laughing behind me.

I ran for blocks in the downtown flatlands. I didn't pay attention to where I ran.

When I had no more breath left, when I was too overheated to keep running, I had to sit down on the curb. I put my head in my hands.

I'd never be able to find something valuable enough to trade for Bookie. I hadn't done second-story work for Bookie for the longest time, so I didn't know the hottest spots for jewelry snatching anymore.

A cold feeling filled my chest despite how hot I was. Tootsie's jewels. She had some sparklers you wouldn't believe. They beat by a mile almost everything I'd ever taken for Bookie. I was sure it would be a cinch to pinch them. I was already in the house. I didn't have to sneak in.

No, no, no. Tootsie and Gilbert had been too good to me. I couldn't, not to them. They weren't just any ol' rich strangers. They were my friends. My new family.

What was I going to do? I told Chum-Chum I'd get him something. He'd take it as a promise. If I didn't deliver a valuable to his satisfaction, he'd send his goons to collect. If I didn't have a valuable, they'd collect an arm, a leg, my head, instead.

Bobby might have an idea what to do. But I couldn't ask him. He didn't approve of my hanging out with Bookie. He'd be upset if he found out I'd gone to a jail—a *jail*—to visit

Bookie. Bobby didn't know about Chum-Chum. He was a criminal on a whole worse level.

I slapped my forehead with my hands. Think, think.

Maybe, just maybe, if I could solve the crime, find out who really killed Straw Boater and why, that would be enough to force the city to let Bookie out of jail. If Bookie was out, then I wouldn't need to trade something with Chum-Chum for his help, right?

Because I'd brought it up, Chum-Chum would expect me to pay, whether Bookie was in or out. I couldn't think about that now. I had to figure out what happened at Monkey Island. I had to get Bookie out of the slammer.

Once he was free, I'd worry about Chum-Chum.

"Hey, Spark!"

I looked up toward the familiar voice. It was Spots, shuffling with his bandaged foot. He was carrying a bulging canvas sack.

I knew that sack. Bookie gave it to Spots or one of the other five-and-dime characters to make the rounds. With Bookie in the pen, I wondered who gave it to Spots. I was about to ask if he got it direct from Chum-Chum, when Spots answered my question.

"Chicago putting me to work." Breathing hard, he stopped by where I sat on the curb. "They know I can only move around so much, but it's like, faster, faster, quicker, quicker. They're trying to get rid of me, wear me to the bone so I fall over. Why? 'Cause I'm old! 'Cause I'm a war vet, with an injury!" He held up his foot that was always wrapped like a movie mummy with strips and strips of cotton bandages. "Horse stepped on my foot. Officer's horse."

Chicago, huh?

I thought about the wool clothes worn by the moll, the kid who bit my apple, and the two toughs in the five-and-dime. I thought about the strange accent the kid and Straw Boater had. When the moll shouted "Murderer!" at Monkey Island, she also sounded funny. Chicago made sense. Did the Chicago bosses send them to town? Why?

I decided to quiz Spots more. I'd have to quiz carefully. Spots could get cagey fast if he thought he was being questioned.

"I got bit by a horse," I told him. I was thinking of Dodger, the retired movie star horse owned by Marigold's great-uncle, Old Bob. He kept Dodger in a little horse house behind his big house that he shared with Marigold, Marigold's mom, and a couple of her brothers, his nephews. The horse house opened onto an alley. Old Bob kept the top half of the door open during the day so Dodger could check out who came and went. One person Dodger didn't like coming was me.

Spots shook his head. "Horses. They use 'em to replace people, you know? Especially old, crippled war vets they wanna get rid of."

I stood up from the curb and walked with Spots as he continued shuffling. "You wanna know how old I am?" he asked.

"How old?"

"I'm so old, I remember there used to be olive trees here. That's why they call it Olive Street, Sparky. There's no olive trees no more, but I remember."

"What's an olive tree?"

"What! You're joking. Dontcha know: martinis, cocktails?"

I shrugged. That was Chum-Chum's business.

"They're like a fruit."

"An apple?"

"No!" He stopped in the middle of the sidewalk. He looked up at the sky like it'd give him answers. "Well, now that you bring it up, Sparky, maybe a green apple. Real green and if you kept it soaking in vinegar, like a pickle." He looked down at me. "Smaller too. Like a little bitty green apple."

"Don't sound like anything I wanna eat. No thanks."

"Ah, come on in. Let me give you a taste of what this is all about."

Spots motioned for me to follow him into a stop. It was a downtown saloon, or former saloon, like all were nowadays with Prohibition. There was a huge sign on the door: "No Booze Served Here!" Yeah, sure. Not up front, but behind a door in the back there was probably plenty of booze.

Spots held the door open for me. "Ladies first! See, Sparky, you can always tell a gent, right?"

"Sure. Thanks, Spots." Bookie told me he always held the door open for dames. But I'd seen him do otherwise. Charging ahead, forgetting the broad in his wake, red lipstick frowned down, powdered forehead in an angry crunch. Yeah, Bookie couldn't keep a gal too long. Maybe he should take a lesson from Spots, if he ever got out of the pen. Out of the hangman's noose.

That thought put me in a down mood again. But I couldn't be glum. I had to stay alert for the right time to quiz Spots.

I'd followed Spots into places like this before, as well as Bookie's other crew, Bookie himself, and sometimes I'd go in by myself if Bookie ordered it, to pick up an envelope or drop one off, or both. I liked these dark, smoky dens.

I'd never been in this particular ex-saloon, but it pleased me from the get-go. It was the old style, with a huge, long bar of dark wood carved up with doodads and ladies with fin tails. I felt my mood lift. Like a simple-minded little kid, I skipped to the bar.

"Hey, lookie that. The little sweetheart wants to quench some thirst," Spots laughed. I waited for him to catch up. After he flopped his canvas sack on the bar, I let him lift me up onto the stool. He always liked to do that. "You're getting too big for me, Sparky!" But he was laughing, forgetting his bum foot for just a little while.

A thin man wearing a long white apron and a mouth like a straight line wandered over and put his hand on the canvas sack. Spots snatched it away. Holding it close to his chest, he pulled out one envelope and handed it to the barman. "For you."

While Spots watched him suspiciously, the barman slid the envelope into an unseen space below the counter. When he stood back up, he held another envelope that he handed to Spots.

Spots nodded, "Okay." He grabbed the envelope. "Gimme a pen." The barman wandered to the other end of the bar, then wandered back with a pencil. "Yeah, yeah, pencil, that's what I meant." Spots made notations on the envelope, then slid it and the pencil back to the barman. "Make your mark on it."

The barman made a big X. Spots waggled his fingers at the man, then he stuffed the envelope into the sack.

"Okay, then," Spots said. Envelope business over, he changed the business to me. "Little girl here could use something to wet her whistle. Put some olives in it. She don't know what they are."

The barman stared at me with his straight-line mouth, but this time he let both eyebrows go up, then down. He stared some more. "You like bubbles, little girl?"

"Bubbles! Sure!"

"Maybe I put some cherry syrup in it."

"No!" That was Spots. "That doesn't go with olives."

"Yeah, fine. I put some tomato juice in."

As the barman tinkered with the mix, Spots called to him, "You got some 'a those cucumber slices? I was telling her that olives are like pickles. Maybe if she sees cucumbers, she'll see where the pickles come from."

"Yeah, I got some. I'll put a bunch 'a stuff together. Maybe she'll like it."

Spots grinned at me and nodded. "That's the ticket. She's going to school now, see? This is like education and learning."

"My folks wanted me to go to farm school," the barman said over his shoulder as he worked.

"Did 'cha go?"

"Nah. Stuff happened. Had to leave town."

"I know that feeling."

I didn't mind the two of them wasting time jawing. I was enjoying sitting at the bar. I could see myself in the mirror that was spotted with age. There were shelves on either side of the mirror and above it. Along with the usual rows of glasses, a couple of old-time sail ships sat on one of the shelves. Not real ships—small ones, like toys, but nicer. I wondered if this was what the pet shop kid was talking about when he said he'd stow away on a ship bound for the other side of the world. Maybe he was planning to sail the high seas on a ship like one of these. A real one.

The barman brought me back from drifting on the high seas when he slid his masterwork in front of me. It was a squat, heavy glass sloshing with red bubbles, curls of lemon peels and carrots, a wooden spear stuck with pickled tiny onions, cucumber triangles, and pickle chunks. Another spear was stuck with a bunch of green nuts.

How about that?

Sometimes a bar gave me something to drink along the lines of tomato juice or cherry syrup in seltzer water. But nothing this fancy. And not so much extra stuff. Green nuts and pickles!

I slurped and dug in. Spots laughed.

The watching barman raised his eyebrows again. "I'll get some dessert."

This was getting better and better.

Before I knew it, the barman was back with a glass of bubbling red cherry syrup complete with a spear thick with sweet, squashy cherries that only came from a jar.

They both watched as my snout went deep into this bubbling, sweet heaven. Then, of course, I had to switch back to the tomato bubbles with the green nuts and pickles.

"So I guess you like them olives, huh?" Spots chuckled.

"Guess she do," the barman added, watching me with his straight-line mouth and moving eyebrows.

"What olives?" I asked. I didn't see any little green apples.

"Those olives," Spots said. "Or, one olive." He pointed to the one green nut I hadn't eaten.

"That's a green nut, Spots."

"Green nut," the barman said, almost in a whisper, like this was too crazy for him to wrap his head around.

"Green nuts!" Spots half-shouted, half-laughed at me.

He pointed at the green nut.

"Yeah? So?" I said.

"Sparky, that's an olive."

"An olive, all right," the barman added like an echo.

I looked at it. "That's not an apple."

Spots sighed. "An olive is not exactly an apple. You have to pickle it first, like a pickle. Remember, I told you about the cucumbers?"

I stared at him.

"Did Knuckles give you the line about green nuts?"

I shrugged. Knucklehead once showed me a jar of what he told me were green nuts. He chuckled about it, so now I could see he was pulling my leg. Knuckles was Bookie's only pal. He was a big talker and kind of an idiot, but I wasn't ratting him out.

"That Knucklehead is nuts." Spots shook his head. "Green nuts! Well, as long as Bookie puts up with him, none of my business."

"How's he doing?" the barman asked, mouth a straight line.

Spots was quiet, then said with a sigh, "Not looking so good, pal." He shook his head.

This was my chance. "Bookie was framed!" I meant to say this in a normal voice, casual-like. But it came out so loud, bubbles from both the cherry syrup and the tomato juice exploded out of my nose.

Spots bent his head. The barman turned his back to bustle with his glasses and olives.

"Whenever you go to the slammer," Spots said in a serious way, "not that I want you to—but accidents happen, understand? So, in the slammer, you'll learn that everyone is framed. Every single one. Framed."

"But Bookie didn't do anything!"

"There's not a con on this earth that's ever done anything."

"But it's not fair!"

"Yeah, that's life, Sparky. Life summed up in a green nut-shell." He pulled the last green nut-olive from the spear in my glass and popped it into his mouth.

This wasn't going according to plan.

"Listen, Sparky, let's get a move on." He wiped my red-bubble face with his spotted hankie, then lifted me back onto the floor with a grunt. "Ladies don't hang out in bars. I shouldn't be taking you into places like this."

Spots snatched up his sack and waved at the barman. The barman waved his glass polishing cloth at Spots before turning his straight-line face back to his glasses.

I trailed Spots to the door. He held it open for me again. "Ladies first."

Out in the sun, I felt tears sprouting from my eyes. Like a baby kid.

"Hey, hey, Sparky," Spots said.

"Nobody's helping Bookie. Nobody." I was thinking of Chum-Chum. "Chicago framed Bookie. They took over his office."

Spots looked down the sidewalk to the right, to the left, then back at me. "Listen, there's not a lot that little people like you and me can do about much of anything, really. There's big fish with big money, big power. Sometimes the little people get squashed when the big fish play ball. Maybe that's what happened to Bookie. Or maybe not. But there's nothing that nobody can do. Especially little people. Be careful, Sparky. You don't wanna get squashed too."

He leaned his weight on his good foot for a bit, then added, "Hey, kiddo, I gotta get moving. Gotta make the rounds. Chicago isn't as flexible, time-wise, as our good ol' Books, understand?"

Spots turned and shuffled down the sidewalk as fast as he could shuffle. He didn't look back.

I stared at him. What did he mean? I wanted to run after him and yell until he fessed up what he was talking about. But I knew his lip was zipped and would stay zipped. He probably told me more than he meant to.

Bookie was getting squashed by the high-rolling fish. Maybe I'd be next.

I didn't believe there was nothing I could do because there was one thing I could do right now: tail Spots and see where Chicago sent him next.

I was careful to keep a good half block behind Spots and duck into doorways if it looked like his head might turn. I needn't have worried. He mainly looked down at his bum foot to watch where he was stepping. If the downtown crowds got between me and him, Spots wasn't hard to find because he regularly yelled, "Hey! Watch my foot! I'm a war vet, you bum!" Then I saw commotion ahead when he shoved whoever wasn't watching his foot.

His first stop was at a larger ex-saloon. I'd been in this one before with Bookie. I knew for certain there was a speakeasy behind a secret hidden door panel in back. The door led down a dark, spooky stairway to another door. That door opened to a huge space with chandeliers, brown velvet booths, live band, dance floor, and waiters dressed like old-fashioned gents in white wigs and long satin coats. It was a hangout for the swells.

After Spots shuffled inside the saloon, I crouched down outside and peeped through the front picture window. The blinds were pulled down, but there was enough of a gap at the bottom for me to see inside. Sitting in the back, in the shadows, I saw Bookie's two huge gorillas. They sat on either side of the secret panel leading to the speakeasy. Their new job must be to make sure no low-rent louts went into that classy joint. Chicago must have booted them from Chum-Chum's crew. Interesting. Was Chum-Chum okay with that? I wondered if Spots was next.

Spots gave a quick wave to the gorillas. Smiles lit up their rough faces. They waved back. Spots did the same envelope routine with the barman, but faster, like he was making up time lost from dawdling with me. Another quick wave to the gorillas, who looked sad to see him go, and he pushed open the door. I dropped down hard on the sidewalk. Luckily, he didn't see me.

Spots was moving fast, for him. After more shouting and shoving people not minding his foot, he shuffled up the steps and through the double doors of a ratty flophouse that didn't have the best reputation. I watched, waited.

I didn't have a long wait. It looked like someone pushed Spots out the paint-peeling front doors. He half stumbled down the steps to the sidewalk. "Hey! Hey! I have a war injury here!" Beyond shouting, he didn't do anything. He pulled off his rumpled beige pork pie hat that matched his rumpled beige suit and rubbed his thinning head. He shuffled away.

I didn't follow because he no longer held the canvas sack. That must mean he'd finished his stops and dropped off the final take at the flophouse. That must mean the flophouse was involved with whatever Chicago was up to.

There was only one way to find out for sure. I had to get inside.

Carefully, I crept to the flophouse's front double doors. They squeaked when I pulled them. I froze. I didn't see movement through the doors' dirty glass panes. I kept pulling.

I walked into a lobby that was more like a wide hallway. The thin rug had bald patches and holes. There were a few papers tacked to the walls describing what happened to people who didn't pay.

Then I saw a man slumped over the check-in counter. He was dead! No, wait. He snorted. I stepped closer. The phone on the counter rang and rang. He snorted, grumbled, but didn't wake up. After a few more rings, the phone gave up. The only sound was rattling from a small fan on the counter that was aimed to blow on his head.

I got closer. He stunk of booze. I looked around the counter and stood on my tiptoes to peer over. There Spots's canvas sack was, dumped on the floor like he'd dropped it there. Who pushed Spots out the doors? I didn't see anyone else.

Time to explore. I walked slowly up the stairs that were covered with the same thin, itchy-looking carpet. Off the second floor landing was a long hallway. I walked down it. The air was hot and dusty. Some of the doors were closed, some were open. I took quick peeks inside the open ones. I saw a man playing cards with himself, a woman plastering on makeup, a man smoking, two men arguing. Nothing gave me a clue about what was going on, other than this was a typical flophouse.

I moved to the third floor. Same deal. No luck on the fourth floor either. The higher I went, the hotter the building got. On the fifth floor, it was different. All the doors were closed tight except for one. I tiptoed toward it. I stopped and looked in.

Straw Boater.

He was stretched out on his side atop the room's thin, stained mattress. He faced the wall, but I knew it was him. He wore the same light summer suit. The same straw boater hat with the dark band was perched crookedly on his head. He was as motionless as a dead rock.

Chicago had moved the body, moved it and planted the story with the papers about the dead guy being some silent picture actor out of Florida. I started shaking and felt like shouting, but I checked myself. I had to stay cool.

I backed away from the room.

"Where's your room key?"

I spun around. Behind me was a thin, short girl with lifeless mouse-brown hair that hung in stringy mats around her face. Her mouse-brown eyes were just as lifeless. Her thin dress with unraveling hem reminded me of what the cousins gave me to wear when I lived with them. She wore old shoes, but they didn't match. One looked much larger than the other. Her socks were different colors, and both had holes. She listed a little to one side, like she was about to fall over. Hard to tell if she was my age or older or younger.

"If you didn't pay for a room key, you gotta scram." She spoke quietly. She didn't take her eyes off me.

"Sure, sure." I took off running to the staircase. Before I headed down, I turned to look back. She was still watching me. I ran the rest of the way down to the ground floor.

I had to tell someone, but who? Spots might already know, so he was out. Chum-Chum only cared about the valuable something I was supposed to give him. If I told Bobby, he'd be shocked I was running around a flophouse in the first place.

The only thing I could do was the thing I really didn't want to do. The thing Bookie, Spots, the gorillas, everybody would tell me was a bad idea. Chum-Chum would hate it most of all.

I had to do something. I was out of options.

The man was still slumped over the front counter, still stunk of booze. I picked up the phone next to him.

"Operator, get me the cops. I found a dead man."

I heard the roar of police sirens. I ran outside. I saw sedans swerve and pedestrians jump out of the way as the cop cars pulled in front of the flophouse. Cops poured out of the cars and up the steps. Mug struggled out of one of the cop cars. Both his arms were in casts. Even so, he elbowed the other cops out of the way until he got to me.

"The dead man from Monkey Island is here! Upstairs!" I shouted to Mug while pointing to the stairs.

For a quick moment, Mug stared at me like, *What in the world is Sparky up to now?* But a possible dead body took up all of Mug's thinking space. He jerked his chin toward the stairs and the other cops charged forward. They followed me up the steps to the fifth floor.

I pointed to the room's open door. "He's in there!"

Running up five flights of steps was a lot to ask for a big cop like Mug. He had to pause for a minute, face red, breathing hard. The other cops waited until he recovered. Then Mug elbowed me aside with his casts. "This is a police matter. Stay back!" Mug charged in and the other cops swarmed outside the room.

As I watched, the skinny girl appeared behind me like a ghost. I didn't notice her until she hissed, "You rat." I turned around and before I knew what was happening, she hauled off and socked me so hard in the jaw, I fell back.

Just as quick, she vanished, running down a side hallway. I heard the tapping of feet going down what must be another stairway.

I couldn't believe it. How could something so small and beat-down be able to knock me, tough Sparky, to the flophouse's threadbare floor?

Before I could think more deeply about this, Mug was stomping out of Straw Boater's room. He didn't look happy. He growled: "You! There is no body!"

What? The girl must have been a lookout. When she heard the sirens, she must have figured out I'd called the cops about Straw Boater. Then she alerted other Chicago characters in the flophouse. They quickly hauled Straw Boater away, possibly using that back staircase she'd just fled down.

I tried explaining this to Mug, but I only ended up babbling and making his Mug face an angry red: "It was that girl! She must have done something. She's a lookout! You gotta catch her, not me!"

Mug's head shook back and forth. "You talking about Shrimpy? That skinny girl? You want me to believe she's dragging grown men's bodies around, up and down stairs?"

"No, I meant, there's gotta be other Chicago people. There's fishy stuff in this flophouse! You gotta do something to help Bookie!"

That didn't quite come out right.

Some of the other cops looked amused. They knew my goose was cooked.

All at once, I knew it too. I scrambled away from Mug. I ran, but I ran into the hallway's dead-end. There was a window on the dead-end wall. I tried pulling it open, but it was stuck fast with years of paint. Even if I could open it, jumping five stories down to the hard concrete alley below would break me apart. I wasn't thinking straight, scrambling around like the trapped rat that I was.

"Give it up, Sparky," Mug ordered as he loomed over me cowering in the corner below the window.

Then an arm pushed Mug aside. "This one's mine," the voice belonging to the arm declared.

As Mug moved away, I saw the lady cop, the one with the lava eyes I'd seen before, glaring at Chum-Chum. She was tall for a gal and built like a battering ram. She wore a dark-blue dress down past her knees, decorated with a police badge the way other broads wore a corsage. Her stockings were dark and her shoes were no-messing-around schoolmarm thick. Her hair was pulled into an angry bun topped by a police cap. The worst were the burning eyes boring into me. I looked away. This trapped rat was doomed.

"Take this thing back to the station, to my office," she ordered Mug, all the while not taking those fiery eyes off me.

"Yes, ma'am!" Mug said cheerfully. As she turned and left, his eyes followed her. He looked awestruck. For a moment, he forgot about me, as his admiring eyes followed her. Then he jerked his head back to the problem at hand: me.

"It's over, Sparky. You're coming in."

Sure enough, the cops hauled me down the staircase, past the man who was still slumped over the front counter, and outside to a cop car. With orders from Mug, I climbed into the back, like a prisoner. Wait, I was a prisoner. At least they didn't slap me in cuffs. Mug struggled into the front passenger seat, which was tough with his arms in casts. The casts must have been Bookie's fault, from when he slid off Monkey Island's roof and landed on Mug. Youch. Another cop climbed into the driver's seat and pulled out into traffic.

Ordinarily, I might have asked the driving cop to turn the car's sirens on and go fast. But this wasn't ordinary times. After years of escaping Mug's grabbing hands, I was riding to the big house.

Mug shook his head. "I thought you were going back to school, going on the straight and narrow." He kept shaking his head.

There was nothing I could say to that. I tried going back to school. School wasn't the life for a trapped rat like Sparky.

With Mug giving directions, the other cop hauled me into the old downtown central station, up a flight of stairs, and left me in an office that must belong to the police lady.

This station was in the same complex as the jail where Bookie rotted away. The police were in the front building, and the cons were in the back building. Wherever they locked me up, I hoped it would be close to Bookie so I could talk with him, see him. Then again, Bookie may not want me being around so much, annoying him.

"Don't try to run," Mug told me as he pushed the office door closed with his foot. "There's nowhere to run to anymore, Sparky."

I sat on one of two gray metal chairs across from a gray metal desk. The same type of basic gray metal chair sat behind the desk. There wasn't much else in this office: a gray metal file cabinet, a map of downtown LA on the wall with pins stuck in it. Except for a phone, the desktop was empty.

This lady cop was new to Bunker Hill and downtown. Even before she was involved in the downtown cannibal case this summer, I'd heard about her tough-as-nails reputation. Downtown wasn't her usual beat. She must have recently been transferred here from somewhere else in the city. That could explain why her desk was empty. Or maybe she didn't have a lot of stuff.

As I was puzzling about her empty office, the door slammed open behind me. I turned. There she was. Her eyes bored down at me. "Did I give you permission to sit?"

I jumped out of the chair. Her eyes did not leave me as she moved behind the desk and sat herself down in the matching metal chair. "Close the door," she said, low and menacing.

I was tempted to run out the door and keep running, but with all the cops packed in the huge open room outside the door, I wouldn't get far. Like Mug said, I had nowhere to run.

I closed the door. I stood facing her but was too afraid to look at her. I heard her fingers tapping a rhythm on the empty desktop.

"I used to be just like you. Trouble with a capital T." She paused. I heard the rustling of her dress uniform, like she was leaning forward over the desk. "But I know exactly what to do with you. What turned me into what I am today."

That can't be good.

"We've been doing a little looking into your. . .situation."

Oh, no.

"We understand you did go back to school. But yesterday you got into trouble. Today you committed truancy." She paused again. "We understand you're living with. . . .an aunt." She said this last bit like she wasn't sure she was completely buying it but would let it pass for now.

"We've notified the school and notified this aunt of yours that from now on, you will report directly here after school."

What would Tootsie and the goblin say? I felt myself sinking.

"And you will stay here for two hours every day after school doing exactly what we tell you to do with no complaints, no trying to run away, no trying to hide."

Could the horror get any worse? It was like school times ten.

At least I wouldn't be locked up in the jail building overnight, like poor Bookie.

Her dress rustled again, as if she was leaning back to study me. "You will find that I'm not soft and lenient like your Sergeant McNaughton."

Who? Was she talking about Mug? That must be his official name. Like mine was Ambrosia Brown.

I hardly called chasing me back and forth around Bunker Hill, trying to catch me and toss me in an orphan home as being soft. I supposed, since the cat was out of the bag about me living somewhere, Mug wouldn't try tossing me in an orphan home anymore. Unless they found out this "aunt" story cooked up by Tootsie, Doctor, and Gilbert was as phony as a two-dollar bill.

"Think of me as your worst nightmare."

What? I mean, what?

"Get out."

I didn't move. I dared peek at her eyes. They blazed. "Get out!"

My hands slipped on the brass doorknob as I fumbled to get it open as fast as I could. When I did, I nearly ran into Mug lurking outside. His face was cheerful. "Stay right there, Sparky," he said, jolly-like.

He peeked into the cop lady's office. I heard her voice bark, "Put her to work."

"Sure thing, LT," he replied, still chipper.

Mug escorted me into the huge open room full of cops outside her office. "I think you'll like working here," Mug said. "There's lots to do and learn. I think you'll end up staying with us."

You've got to be kidding. This was exactly how Mug sounded when he learned I was going back to school, like school was a wonderland kids loved. Mug needed his head examined.

The room was dingy. The paint was peeling and had dark patches here and there around cracks in the plaster. A rusty pipe hanging from the ceiling dripped slowly into a metal bucket. The linoleum in places had worn so thin I could see the wooden floor underneath. The air inside felt extra hot and muggy. It was an old building, left over from the last century. Must be why the police brass had already moved into the newer City Hall building.

Mug showed me to a desk were an older, frowning man sat. This guy didn't wear a uniform. He wore white shirtsleeves rolled up to his elbows. His badge was on his belt. His red-rimmed eyes stared at me.

"This is Detective Bernie. You'll do what he says." Mug turned to leave.

"Where are you going?" I was suddenly feeling like I'd rather have Mug chase me around the block than deal with this red-eyed detective.

"Going out. There's lots of crime in the world, Sparky!" Off he went. This cheery Mug made me nervous. I liked the angry, chasing Mug better. The new Mug was nuts.

I turned back to Detective Bernie. He was still staring at me. Without taking his eyes off me, he picked up a stub of a cigar from a tin of paper clips on his desk. He pointed the cigar at me. "The first, most important, priority thing you will do," he growled at me in a voice that sounded like it was full of broken rocks, "is fetch my sandwich."

That's how my first day as a prisoner of the cops went.

I had to trudge my way back up Bunker Hill after the cops were done with me. I lost my roundtrip Angels Flight tram ticket somewhere. Maybe Shrimpy had it.

Nervously, I pushed open the back French doors to Creepy House's sunroom. What would Tootsie and Gilbert say? I was nothing but one disappointment after another.

What struck me was the smell. Rotted cabbage? Usually only tasty smells drifted from Gilbert's kitchen: cookies, sugar buns, fresh-baked bread.

As I wandered through the maze of hallways toward the kitchen, I heard loud wailing. That was nothing to be worried about. I knew that was Tootsie practicing her "singing" with Mr. Beele. I thought she should fire him. She seemed to think he was wonderful.

They must be in her music room that was hung with guitars, violins, every kind of musical instrument you could think of. Not that Tootsie played any of them. I followed the wailing to her music room. Carefully, I peeked one eye past the doorway. I didn't want Beele to spot me and start suggesting a beating would improve me.

Instead of one of her usual outfits with fringe and a pattern of leaping dragons or some other crazy critter, she was wrapped head-to-toe with denim bands. I knew that was the work of slimming man. From the bands oozed different colors of goo. Probably all her wackos contributed to that mess. The only parts showing were her eyes, nose, and mouth. Slimming man couldn't cover her mouth because she was supposed to be singing. She held her arms up and head flung back. That was her usual singing pose, something to do with loosening her diaphragm.

She stopped wailing when she ran out of breath. "Oh, Mr. Beele, I'm so worried my singing is not up to snuff."

Tell me about it.

"Nonsense! But, to make you feel more confident, this audition does not require singing, only a speaking voice. Rest assured that our singing practice strengthens your vocal cords and brings a youthful melodiousness. The youthful effect travels to the facial muscles, making the entire face as a fresh as that of a fifteen-year-old."

This guy was so full of baloney.

"You are such a treasure, Mr. Beele. I will need extra time with you if I get this part."

"It is assured you will have this part. If not, the studio head is a cretinous fool! You must know, I will give my heart and soul to you always. Though, remember, I will have an additional role, so my time with you cannot be unlimited."

I had had enough of this nonsense. I headed back toward the stinky smells coming from the kitchen. I hoped this other role of his meant he wouldn't be lurking around Creepy House as much. That would be a dream come true.

In the kitchen, Bobby sat at the table. I was surprised he was still here. I was so late coming back—the fault of the cops, not me—I thought he would have gone home by now. His parents kept a tight leash on him after they caught him sneaking out at night this summer to help me investigate. They didn't know about the investigating part because he didn't tattle on me. So they decided he might have joined a gang of bad boys. Bobby? Joining a gang? That would be the last thing in the world he'd join. It would interfere with his library time.

Bobby frowned at me. Uh-oh. Cautiously, I sat next to him at the table. He pulled a cloth off a green-and-red checked plate. "Your sandwich. Gilbert made it ages ago." He sounded unhappy.

The afternoon papers were scattered around the table. Bobby must have been reading them. I was on pins and needles to know if there was any new news about Bookie. I'd wait until Bobby stopped frowning at me before I risked finding stories about Bookie—Bookie not being Bobby's favorite person.

At the stove, I saw the source of the horrible smell. The goblin busily stirred a huge boiling pot. The steam reeked. Doctor stood next to the pot. "Yes, it's about right," he murmured to Gilbert. "She needs to soak in this until all those denim bands come off." I should have figured this nonsense came from Doctor.

The smell was too much for me. I stood up and opened the kitchen door for some air. This got Gilbert's attention. "Ah, Sparky! We heard the wonderful news that you are volunteering for the police! Mademoiselle said we are all much safer now with you to protect us. Our very own little police girl."

What?

In the next moment, a chill ran through me. I remembered thinking how easy it would be to rob Tootsie of her jewels, jewels that would satisfy Chum-Chum's hankering for a valuable something-something. The something-something that might be the ticket to Bookie's freedom. I felt ashamed. That thought should never have popped into my head. The Creepy House people were too nice for the likes of me. I wasn't a little police girl. I was a little criminal girl.

Doctor knew my score. He gave me a dark look. He had his own secrets to hide from Tootsie and Gilbert. I wouldn't rat him out and he wouldn't rat me out. But he could see right through me.

Doctor didn't have time to do much glaring at me. "The mixture is done," he decided. "We need to carry it up to her tub now, while it is still very hot," he said to Gilbert.

With their hands wrapped in multiple dishcloths, they hefted up the huge, steaming pot. Gilbert gripped the handle on one side of the pot and Doctor gripped the handle on the other side. Gilbert huffed and puffed as they carefully walked sideways out of the kitchen.

I heard slimming man in the hallway. "Ah! It is ready. Mademoiselle, time for the soaking phase!"

Tootsie's voice answered from further away, "Wonderful!"

As soon as Gilbert and Doctor left the kitchen, Bobby turned to me. "You aren't volunteering for the police, are you?"

"No."

Bobby could also see right through me. He pointed to the side of my jaw. I felt where he pointed. Ow. It was sore, probably because that's where Shrimpy socked me. I must have been sprouting a bruise. Oops. Not long ago, I had to go through a lot of trouble to hide marks from my run-in with Petunia, a crazy, twelve-year-old with fists like hammers.

Next Bobby pointed to my shoulder. I felt that spot. That's where the Chicago toughs tore off my sleeve when they tried grabbing me. Forgot about that.

Bobby folded his arms, frowning. "Sparky, you have to stop getting into fights."

"The thing was, you see. . . ." I tried to think of what to say without really saying anything about what I'd been up to.

He cut me off. "You weren't in school. Principal even asked me where you were. I told him I thought you might have a cold." Bobby crinkled his eyebrows together. He hated telling fibs, especially to grown-ups.

"Thanks, Bobby. I owe you one."

"If you want to pay me back, come to school tomorrow. Meet me in the library for recess like we planned."

"Everyone hates me in school."

Bobby sighed. "I know about the other kids. But that's what I am here for. We'll help each other. I'll help you study. I know you'll do well, Sparky. But you just have to show up."

Some of the other kids did call Bobby a bookworm. Though he really was a bookworm. Bobby knew they called me worse, and he felt bad for me. I felt bad for myself.

"I thought you'd be back home by now since I'm so late," I said.

Bobby frowned all over again. "I did go back home. But I was worried because you hadn't been in school. I told my parents I forgot a book over here, so came back."

There he was, fibbing again for me. I didn't deserve Bobby. I didn't deserve the Creepy House people. Who did I deserve?

As I took a bite from my sandwich, my eye drifted to the papers. There was a different Bookie mug shot. He looked younger and even crazier. He was baring his teeth. Yeah, Bookie sometimes did that.

Bobby noticed me staring at the mug shot. He jabbed his

finger on it. "This guy, this is the one you work for, the one you call Bookie, isn't he?"

"Yeah, but he didn't kill anyone." At Monkey Island, anyhow. "I should know. I was there!"

Bobby sat back and folded his arms again. Whoops. I shouldn't have let on that I was at the crime scene.

"Sparky, you need to stop hanging around that man. He's a hardcore criminal and a bad influence. You need to leave your old life behind."

Did I tell you Bobby liked to lecture me? I wished he would quit. I knew he was right. But it was hard. Bookie meant a lot to me. I didn't know why, but he did.

"Bobby, there's something real fishy going on with Monkey Island. Look at this actor in the paper." I shuffled the pages until I spotted Claude Cavalerie's photo. This was a different actor picture, where Claude regally gazed to some distant spot. "He wasn't the guy who fell down dead at Monkey Island."

Bobby blinked, curious. "Are you sure?"

"Super-sure. The dead guy was thin, didn't have a moustache, and had blond hair that was five times lighter than yours. Some kind of body switch happened." I kept my lip zipped about Shrimpy and the flophouse. That would win me more lecturing.

"Body switching," Bobby murmured while rubbing his chin. "That does sound fishy."

I took a chance: "I know you don't like Bookie, but he was framed, seriously framed. Do you know how to look up any law angles that might help him get out?"

Bobby sighed. He didn't want to help Bookie, but the fishy

business had gotten his interest. "Sparky, people study for years to understand law. I doubt the school library has law books."

"Please." I gave him big begging eyes. Because I was begging.

He said nothing for a bit, then, "Okay. I'm not sure I'll find anything. Let me think. But I have to head home now before my parents start to get suspicious."

"Thank you, Bobby!" Before I knew what I was doing, I grabbed his hand. Big mistake. His eyes got all big and happy. I should slap myself. I pulled my hand away before I made the situation any worse.

"I'll try," Bobby said in his happy voice.

He stood to leave. Suddenly, I remembered I had another question for him. "Bobby, wait. What do you think about the name that the newspapers are giving for Bookie? It's gotta be a fake name."

I pointed to Bookie's mug shot and the name printed beneath it. "Mug called him 'Hey, Sue,' which was weird enough, and now this name."

Bobby stared at the paper. "Jesus de la Cruz," he read. "Nothing strange here. Jesus is a common boy's name in Mexico. In Spanish, it's pronounced *Hey Sus*. That's what you heard Mug saying. You say the last name like *Day La Cruise*. Remember, I've told you that you need to learn Spanish for when we honeymoon in Mexico."

Oh, no. Not this again.

"Every world citizen should learn at least three languages. I'm learning Spanish. Next, I want to learn Greek, which will help me when I explore ancient ruins on the Greek islands."

"I thought you wanted to go to ancient Egypt."

"Sparky, I told you, no one can go to ancient Egypt. That's the past. We can visit modern Egypt and still see the old stuff. Yes, I want to go to Egypt and Greece and many places. You'll come with me. When we're in Mexico, we'll explore their ancient ruins together."

Then he was off to his parents' house. Bobby was in a better mood, but I'd opened that whole can of worms about honeymoons and all that baloney. Bleh.

Bookie, you have no idea what I have to do to help you.

WEDNESDAY

In the morning, the goblin was boiling onions and lemons. It was another concoction to smear all over Tootsie. "I have such a strong feeling about this audition, Sparky. I am certain this is the one," he said dreamily as he stirred his stinky pot.

I was glad someone was happy.

At least my breakfast spread this morning was top drawer. Goblin had outdone himself ordering boxes—yes, you heard me right—boxes of goodies from the bakery. Of course, I wouldn't be the only person nibbling on the goodies. Tootsie's wacky crew ate plenty of treats.

Apart from the wacky crew, there was a problem. Goblin wasn't keeping the boxes in the kitchen, so I couldn't sneak snacks whenever I felt the pastries calling. "I must hide the boxes, my Sparky. Sometimes late at night, our Mademoiselle comes downstairs to search for food. I think she is still asleep and does not know. Doctor says we must not mention it to her. Mademoiselle's nerves, you understand."

It wasn't her nerves. She was half-starved to death with her audition dieting.

I didn't say anything. At least I had some good treats to make up for the bad day at school I was sure to have. On a pink, spotted plate, lounged the fattest donut I'd ever seen. It dripped with shiny chocolate. Next to it was a square of cake crusted with a crunchy topping that melted as I ate it. Oh, nice. Then there was a mini-pie, like my own personal pie just for me. It was round with a flaky crust. In the middle were chunks of what the goblin told me were fall pears. I nearly cried as I bit into them.

I loved this bakery. I loved it so much.

Feeling better, I poked through the morning's papers. Nothing new about Bookie, just another mug shot where he looked like he was screaming. Bookie needed to take lessons from Tootsie on proper posing for pictures.

Wait a minute. Was that a photo of Knucklehead? It wasn't a mug shot. Was he standing next to "Onion Girl?" I said that last bit out loud without thinking. This got Gilbert's attention.

"Onion Girl? She is in the papers?"

Just say "Onion Girl," and you had Gilbert's and Tootsie's attention.

Onion Girl was Tootsie's archrival from their silent movie days. Her real name wasn't Onion Girl, any more than my real name wasn't Sparky. She got that nickname, which she hated, from a dramatic scene in a popular silent movie where she did a lot of crying about the tragedies of life while chopping onions. Then she ended up dying. She did a lot of serious, crying-type silent movies, so she was also called Sobbing Sally. Onion Girl's real name was Sally Smiths.

If you asked me, Onion Girl was a name with more pizzazz than Sally Smiths. But what did I know?

Even though Onion Girl and Tootsie hated each other, they wanted to know what the other one was up to.

Gilbert hurried over to the newspaper I was staring at. Quickly, so Gilbert wouldn't notice, I put my hand over the Shrimpy bruise on my jaw, like I was just casually resting my chin in my hand. After scanning the paper, Gilbert declared, "I must find Mademoiselle!" He rushed out the kitchen in search of Tootsie, leaving his pot of onions and lemons to bubble on its own.

He returned with Tootsie in tow. Her face was covered with black goo. Same with her hands. They matched her black robe with a pattern of flying white-and-black birds with long necks and long legs. Their eyes were little green rhinestones.

"He's French, a poet! This is her new man, the papers say," Gilbert explained.

"Where?" Tootsie said as she grabbed the paper. She smeared black handprints over the paper, half covering Knucklehead's photo.

Even with the photo smudged, I saw Knucklehead was still wearing his fake nose bandage, still pretending his nose was blown off for the sympathy factor. It was a different style of bandage, though. It looked like a black eye patch, but he wore it across his face to cover his nose instead of his eye, like a nose pirate. He wasn't wearing his usual rumpled brown suit. Instead, he wore a striped, long-sleeved pullover and a round cap on his head.

Tootsie pointed to the cap. "Her poet wears his beret at the wrong angle. She's lived in Paris. She should notice that."

"Ah, she probably loves his attention, whatever he may really be," Gilbert said.

"Makes her ex-husband's huge mansion feel less empty, I suppose," she snorted.

Tootsie's mansion was huge too. If truth be told, Tootsie couldn't really complain about Onion Girl and Knucklehead the French poet, because she allowed Doctor to slither around Creepy House. But I kept my mouth shut.

So Knucklehead's latest racket was pretending to be a French poet up in the Hollywood Hills with Onion Girl?

It gave me an idea. I might have to skip school for a second day in a row.

I took my bath and dressed in my school outfit as if I were going to school. I got my lunch tin from the kitchen. It was a new tin. Fortunately, the goblin had extras, and, fortunately, he didn't ask what happened to the other tin. I couldn't tell him it was in the big house with Bookie. Then I picked up my extra pencil box from my room. I didn't have my school bag and books anymore, so the pencil box would have to do for a prop.

I made my way to the sunroom's French doors. I planned to go through the overgrown jungle of the backyard and keep going down Bunker Hill and out of downtown. No school for me today.

I almost reached the back French doors, when out of the shadows stepped Doctor to block my path. He held his fedora in his hands. It was dark blue to match today's dark blue suit color. What was up?

"Where are you going?" he asked in his quiet voice, his dark eyes boring into me.

I did not expect this hiccup in my plans, but I kept my cool. "I'm going to school. Where else?" I even got a smart tone with him.

"No, you're not."

"Yes, I am!"

I tried stepping around him, but he was light on his feet and blocked me again.

"I am driving you to school."

"What about walking being good for the little children and all that? I don't need a ride."

He smirked at me. "Don't worry. I won't drive you in that boat of a car," he said, meaning Tootsie's massive gold movie star car.

I tried dodging him again, but he was too quick. I felt like biting him, but realized this was a fight I couldn't win. I was going to school today. The thought of it made my heart sink.

"To the front," he hissed. He marched me out the front door and down to a black sedan parked on the street.

The sedan didn't stand out, wasn't flashy, but something about it told me this was a pricey car. The sedan was like the suits he wore: simple but not cheap by a long shot. I didn't know Doctor had his own car. It made sense. He had to get around somehow and I didn't peg him for the sort who took the tram or walked.

He opened the passenger door. Once I was inside, he slammed the door hard, barely missing my foot. After he slid on his fedora and slid behind the wheel, he looked over and said, "Where's your school bag? Your books?"

"Somebody stole them."

He sneered at me. Then his eyes zeroed in on the side of my jaw. He'd spotted Shrimpy's bruise. "It's too late to cover that now. You have to go to school how you are." He tore away from the curb.

"Your school called all day yesterday," he spat as he drove a little too fast. "Fortunately, I was able to intercept the calls. Mademoiselle and Mr. Grossman do not know you skipped school, and we will keep it that way, understand?" Mr. Grossman is what he called the goblin.

"Yeah," I mumbled.

"The same for this police business. You are not being forced because you are a juvenile delinquent. You are volunteering because you are a good little citizen."

"Sure," I mumbled again. This explained things. Doctor came up with the volunteering story.

"We cannot allow any upsetting news to disturb Mademoiselle and interfere with her audition. This is a most critical audition. Her heart is set on it, which you don't seem to grasp. Stop being selfish. Think of others for once in your life."

What in the world? This character, who crept around Creepy House like a spider, had some hot nerve lecturing me. "I haven't done anything to mess with Tootsie's audition!"

"See that you keep it that way."

He came to a stop by the school so hard, I felt like I was about to fly out the window. "Hurry up," he said as I climbed out of his sedan.

I followed him as he marched through the front school yard. All the kids were outside waiting for the bell. They stared. The oinking kid snickered. Doctor made a dead stop, which made me almost ram into him. He gave the kid his darkest stare. That shut the oinker up.

Doctor marched me all the way to Miss S's office.

"Ah, so the wandering Sparky has returned," Miss S said with a sly grin.

"All yours," Doctor said and left.

I think you can imagine it was not a fun morning. Principal peeked out his door to say, "Not again." Miss Clark came by. She wanted to know where my books were. She didn't believe they were stolen. "It's only the third day of the school year, Miss Brown, and already you are behind in class. Goodness knows what you did with your books." She bent down to peer at the bruise on my face. "Fighting again, I see."

The replacement books Miss Clark found were worse for wear. From the stains on the pages, the last kid who had these books spilled a lot of food on them. "See that you don't lose these too," Miss Clark admonished.

Miss Clark instructed me to read certain parts of the books while I did time on the punishment chair. That's what I did or tried to do all morning. As the hours dragged by, it got hotter. Whenever I started to doze, Miss S dropped something heavy on her desk to shock me awake.

When the lunch bell rang, Miss S said I could eat lunch, but in her office in the punishment chair.

The goblin's tin of lunch was some comfort. He made the sandwich with thick, thick slices of bread from the wonderful bakery. For the treats, oh, my, another mini-pie. This one was stuffed to the brim with apple slices and crunchy brown sugar. Keeping company with the pie was another type of cookie bar. This one was dark and smelled like molasses. When I bit into it, the taste of gingerbread filled my mouth. Under the cookie bar was a third treat! This wonder was a soft, round chocolate cookie that melted in my mouth. It also melted all over my hands.

"You've gotten chocolate all over your face, Sparky," Miss S pointed out.

Whoops.

I noticed she had a sandwich and a pile of crackers for her lunch. Neither looked very interesting, but she didn't seem to care.

"When the recess bell rings, get yourself cleaned up in the washroom. Then report to the library. Your friend Bobby has kindly volunteered to help you be a better student. We don't want those chocolate hands of yours marking up all the library books."

I looked down at the books on my lap and my lunch eats piled on top of them. I'd gotten quite a lot of chocolate, apple pie, gingerbread, and sandwich mustard on them. Whoops again. I was as messy as the last kid who used these books.

Miss S shook her head. "You'll be spending the entire school year in here with me if you don't shape up."

Oh, no.

After I cleaned up as best I could, which I admit wasn't top drawer, I headed to the school library. The pet shop kid was coming out as I was coming in. He leaned close and whispered, "We can stow away on a ship across the South Seas and be so far away, no one can catch us. The other side of the Pacific Ocean is a different world. Let's talk." He gave me a meaningful look—but meaning what?—and kept going.

I wish he'd knock it off with all this ocean sailing business. But my mind did drift to the little ships on the shelf in the saloon, and I wondered.

Mrs. Bean, the school librarian, smiled at me. I hadn't seen her since I'd last been in school. She looked about the same: flowered dress, pinned-up hair that always got loose and flew around her face, reading glasses dangling from a rhinestone pin shaped like a book. She was always nice to me, even though I wasn't exactly library material.

"Welcome back, Sparky," she said. "It's good to have you with us again." She smiled nicely as she said this, like she really meant it. Who in their right mind would want to see me again?

Bobby was waiting for me, but he wasn't smiling. I thought he'd be happy to see me, but he stared at me suspiciously. "What'd he say to you?"

"Who?"

"Cornelius."

"Who?"

"The kid from the pet shop that you just spoke with."

"I didn't say a word to him! Besides, he says his name is Dr. Arcanum."

Bobby sighed. "Dr. Arcanum is the man who owns the shop where Cornelius works. The boy's name is Cornelius Lee.

"Oh."

"Some of the other kids call him Corny, which is not right. None of the kids in the advanced academic class call him that. We know better."

I guessed he was talking about the brainy kids' class. Figures it would have a mile-long name. Not like dummy class.

"Well, what did he say?"

Why did Bobby care? The kid, this Cornelius, was rude to Bobby exactly one time, and Bobby couldn't let it go. Bobby got buggy about me talking with other boys in general. Bobby was smart, but he still needed his head examined.

"He likes boats," I answered. That was basically true.

Bobby eyed me, but then decided to buy it. "Cornelius is a bit different."

That was completely true. Time to change the topic. "So did you find any law tricks to help Bookie that we talked about?"

"Not exactly. But I think these books may help." There was a pile of books on the table where we sat.

"Are those law books?" I asked.

"No. I confirmed with Mrs. Bean that the school does not have law books."

I felt myself sinking into the chair. "If they're not law books, what are they about?" I picked up one. There was a blond kid on the cover, not unlike Bobby. He was standing in front of a little yellow convertible.

"These books are about *Reginald the Smartest Boy in the World.*" He sat back and smiled.

"Is this Reginald coming to Bunker Hill to help us with what happened at Monkey Island?"

"No, he's a fictional character. He's made-up."

"That's no good," I muttered.

"But it is. You see, in every book, Reginald solves a mystery, a crime. There are dozens of books full of ideas that can help us. This book especially made me think about what might be going on with Monkey Island."

He pulled the book with the yellow car from my hands and

pushed another toward me. On the cover, there was a mountain with growling teeth and terrified horses running around. Reginald was in the mix, looking serious and driving his yellow car.

This is *Reginald the Smartest Boy in the World and the Case of Monster Mountain and the Vanishing Steeds*.

"I don't get it." I flipped through the book. Here and there were drawings of what Reginald was up to: driving in the convertible, looking serious, pointing at a piece of paper while surprised grown-ups looked on, riding a horse, scrambling up a cliff. There was a small dog running around with him.

"That's Poppy. She's the smartest dog in the world."

Everybody was smart in these books. I sure wouldn't belong in them. Still, the stories kind of looked interesting.

"Mr. Bud, a rancher in Montana, woke up one morning to find his prized herd of horses gone. Locals said the angry mountain spirit swallowed them whole. But another rancher, Mr. Mertid, accused Mr. Bud of stealing his own horses as part of an insurance scam, which caused the sheriff to lock up Mr. Bud in jail."

That sounded like Bookie's case.

"Mr. Bud does the only thing he can: he has a telegram sent to Reginald asking him to help solve the case. Reginald speeds from New York City to Montana in his future car." Bobby held up the book with the yellow convertible on the cover. "It can go two hundred miles an hour using future technology and doesn't need gas."

"Somebody's gonna steal it."

"Somebody did. A gang was behind it. They painted the future car red to disguise it. That was in *Reginald the Smartest*

Boy in the World and the Case of the Hopping Ghost and the Stolen Future Car."

"Guess he got it back and painted it yellow again, huh?" I peered at the kid standing in front of the convertible. "So how old is this kid? Twelve?" That was Bobby's age.

"No, he's fourteen. But the governor of New York gave him special permission to drive cars because he's the smartest boy in the world and helps so many people with his crime solving."

"Where's this kid get money to buy a car like this? Steal it?" Maybe Reginald had a few things in common with Bookie.

"No! The wealth is from his uncle, who was the richest man in the world. But his uncle gave all his material possessions to Reginald, making him the richest boy in the world. His uncle disappeared from the regular world to become a mystic. Every book has a clue about where his uncle is. I've made a list of the clues. Next time you're at my house, I'll show it to you."

Bobby had way too much time on his hands. "I'm not seeing how this has anything to do with Monkey Island."

"Let's go back to the missing horses. Reginald discovered that the mountain didn't have a monster that swallowed the horses. They were herded up the mountain and hidden in a secret corral. When he read papers Poppy found in the corral's bunkhouse, Bobby learned that the insurance on the horses wasn't taken out by Mr. Bud, but by Mr. Mertid. Everyone was shocked. Because Mr. Bud was in jail, his ranch was going to be auctioned off cheap. Mr. Mertid was planning to buy it for pennies on the dollar. Plus, he already had Mr. Bud's prized horses."

Knucklehead used to run an insurance scam. Hmm. But Knucklehead wasn't the one accusing Bookie of murder.

"After more digging, Reginald realized that the person who gave Mr. Mertid this idea was Reginald's other uncle, his bad uncle, who became the richest man in the world after his brother gave his money to Reginald. You see, both brothers inherited a huge fortune from Reginald's grandfather, a visionary inventor. Instead of using his money for good, like Reginald does, his other uncle uses his money for bad. The bad uncle is often behind the crimes that Reginald investigates. He was always jealous of his brother, Reginald's good uncle."

Bobby took a deep breath, like he had to brace himself for the next shock: "Reginald's mother is an inventor too, but she disappeared. It's unknown if she joined his bad uncle, her brother, on purpose, or if his bad uncle captured her and is holding her prisoner. She also inherited a fortune from Reginald's grandfather, but the bad uncle may be trying to steal it. Each book also has a clue on her whereabouts."

"So why isn't this bad uncle in the slammer?"

"He's very rich and he's always fleeing the country using the future technology he invented, because he's also very smart. Though some suspect Reginald's mom is really the inventor, and his bad uncle takes credit. Reginald vows he will one day catch his uncle because, even though he's a blood relative, he needs to be held accountable for his actions just like everyone else."

Maybe he'd be held accountable, but maybe not. Like Bookie said, the big wheels on top always came out on top.

"So where's Reginald's dad in all this? Or should I ask?"

"He's a jazz singer," Bobby said, like this character wasn't too interesting. "Sometimes he finds useful clues. But he doesn't really solve crimes or invent anything."

"Sounds like he's in the bad uncle's pocket. Probably reporting on what the kid does. Probably set the mom up to be kidnapped."

"No! He's a famous jazz singer and he tours the country, the world. When he's home, he takes Poppy for walks."

Likely story.

This was giving me a lot to think about. "So what you're saying, I think, is that someone wants what Bookie has, so set him up?"

"Exactly, Sparky!"

"Someone with deep pockets."

"Could be."

There weren't any law tricks in these books, but Bookie was set up like Mr. Bud was set up. Mr. Bud had a ranch and expensive horses. But what did Bookie have? A couple of rooms behind a ratty five-and-dime, stolen suits, boxes of cheap chocolates for floozies that were probably stolen too.

Though, if you thought about it, Bookie's rooms were part of an operation that brought in a lot of cash for Chum-Chum. Chicago was having Spots do the rounds, so they must be collecting the money now instead of Bookie. Were they muscling out Chum-Chum? And how did the body switch figure in?

I picked up another Reginald book. The cover had gleaming, pointed towers. Reginald, standing on a board of some kind, was flying around the towers. The dog was flying around on a board too.

"That's Futurium," Bobby explained. "It's built using all the inventions from Reginald, his good uncle, his grandfather, and his mom, before she disappeared. The residents are scientists, mathematicians, artists, playwrights, and poets. That's where

Reginald's dad lives when he's home. There are lots of animals too, and they roam freely."

The animal bit was something I'd like. "But I'd rather keep Bunker Hill the way it is, with the old houses and stuff."

"Futurium is not on Bunker Hill. Both the governor of New York and the mayor of New York City gave Reginald permission to use part of New York City to build it. Everyone who visits it is amazed." Bobby paused. "Of course, it's fictional. Though the writer says, that in fifty years' time, the Flying Shoes," Bobby pointed to the boards Reginald and Poppy stood on while they zipped around, "will belong to everybody. Futurium will be Present Day World."

Didn't seem likely to me. But I'd sure like a pair of Flying Shoes. I'd fly over the city, swoop low to the sidewalk, then zoom up really high. Maybe Cornelius didn't need to find a boat. He needed to find Flying Shoes to zip across the ocean.

I was allowed to go back to dummy class after library recess was up. When Miss Clark told us to write our names on a piece of paper, I realized I didn't know how to spell my real name. Maybe I used to when I was last in school. But that was ages ago, and I'd forgotten. That got me laughed at again. Then it wasn't too long before I was ordered back to Miss S (don't ask).

"You must really like me because you keep coming to visit," she said to me, eyebrow raised.

I'll let you imagine how the rest of the afternoon went.

When the end bell rang, I wasn't off the hook. Not by a long shot. I still had to do my time with the cops.

After fetching Detective Bernie his sandwich, he told me to water the plants. He pointed me to a can with a spout and handle, then told me to fill it up in a closet that was crammed with a laundry-tub-sized sink and a toilet with a cracked seat. "That's our john. If you gotta go, use that one. There's another one, but that's only for LT, so keep out of it or I'll have a problem with you."

I didn't know the first thing about plants, in pots or in the ground. So I winged it. I filled the can with water. I went to the first of about a dozen one-leafed, sad-looking plants in rusting coffee cans scattered around the space. I dumped water on top of the plant's one leaf. The water cascaded down, hit the dirt in the coffee can, and overflowed to the floor.

"What are you doing?" Detective Bernie shouted at me in his broken-rocks voice.

A cop near the splash zone called to him, "Hey, Bernie, get a handle on your girl here!"

Detective Bernie got up and walked stiffly with both knees slightly bent and his arms out like he was about to grab something. He snatched the can from me. "Decades on the force and this is what I'm reduced to," he growled.

He showed me how to pour. "Just a little direct in the dirt. Not all over the top! Pour slow. When it looks like it'll flow over, then stop. But if the dirt is already wet when you get to the plant, that means some other character here put some water in it. Don't add any more or the plant will drown on your watch. Don't let that happen. Understand?"

I nodded. Detective Bernie stiffy walked back to his desk while grumbling more about what he'd been reduced to. He called back, "Wipe up the mess you made on the floor. There might be some rags or something in the john. We run a tight ship here."

There weren't any rags in the john, so I used the hem of my sailor dress to mop the floor. A couple of cops raised their eyebrows at me but said nothing. Back to plant watering I went.

Mug had a one-leafed plant perched on his desk, so I headed there. Mug wasn't out fighting crime. He was sitting in his chair. His eyes looked at the ceiling and he had a dreamy smile on his face. I super carefully poured water into his plant, but he didn't seem to notice. I looked up to where he was staring at the ceiling. There was nothing but stains and old spiderwebs.

"What are you so happy about?" I asked.

He shook his head and kept smiling, never taking his eyes off the ceiling. "LT's something else, isn't she? She's so smart about catching crooks."

"Why does everybody call her LT? What does that mean? Shouldn't you call her boss?"

"LT is cop talk for lieutenant. Don't worry, you'll get the hang of the cop lingo soon enough. You're one of us."

Hardly.

"I'm wondering what kind of flowers LT might like best," Mug said with his dreamy smile.

"Flowers? That gal strikes me as liking shooters better than flowers if you ask me."

Mug's eyes darted down to me for a moment, before traveling back to the ceiling. He was lost in thought.

Everybody needed their heads examined today.

I was dog-tired by the time I made my way up Bunker Hill and back to Creepy House.

In the kitchen, Tootsie stood with the two face broads on one side of her, and on the other, Gilbert stood at the ready by a pot of stinky, simmering something on the stovetop. It smelled like old socks and rainwater in the gutter. (Yeah, I had to drink that kind of water in a pinch before I had a home—but don't tell anyone, okay?)

Tootsie was wrapped in white sheets today, like a mummy. I could only see one eye and half her mouth. She stood on more sheets. Slowly, Gilbert ladled stinky pot water over her head. It dribbled down her face and kept going to the sheets she was standing on.

"Take it easy. Not so fast," one of the face broads directed. "And don't miss her backside. Make sure that's soaked," the other ordered. Gilbert nodded seriously and tried to follow what the broads wanted. From my experience with the face broads, they didn't tolerate disagreement.

Bobby sat at the kitchen table, which was piled with new school supplies and a new school bag that looked nicer than the one that the Chicago kid stole. The bag was white and blue to match my sailor dresses.

Tootsie saw me. "Sparky!" she half-mumbled because her mouth was half covered. "Doctor told me you lost your school bag, so we went shopping today to get you a new one and new pencils and papers and everything you'll need."

"Thanks," I said, feeling guilty that they went through the trouble, especially with Doctor thinking I was messing up Tootsie's important audition.

"Think nothing of it! I've lost so many things myself. In

Paris, I lost a valuable bracelet in the Seine. How it sparkled as it tumbled down to the water. It may not have been such an accidental accident. I was so upset with him."

Gilbert's eyes looked worried at the mention of this "him." He didn't have a chance to worry much, because one of the face broads barked, "Hurry! It's time for the next step!" The other added, "March! Now!"

The three of them hustled dripping Tootsie out of the kitchen. "Bye, Sparky! Bye, Bobby" she called back. The goblin would have some job cleaning up that stinky water on the floor and hallway rugs. As long as it helped her audition chances, he wouldn't mind. The goblin was always busily cleaning anyway.

Bobby was in a cheerful mood today. Maybe it was our library time that did it. "These are swell school supplies, Sparky." He picked up a pencil box and admired how, when he pressed the top just so, it snapped open.

My sandwich was hiding under a dishtowel with a dancing bear pattern that matched the sandwich plate. Surrounded by the school supplies, a larger dancing bear plate displayed donuts. Oh, yes. There were dripping chocolate donuts like the one I enjoyed this morning, plus sugar-doused donuts and donuts slathered in frosting and coconut flakes.

I could tell Bobby had taken a donut by the smear of chocolate on his chin. I pointed that out to him. "Oh!" he gasped. He hopped up from his chair and took care of that smear at the kitchen sink. To Bobby, any messiness was an emergency.

Then Bobby noticed all the puddles on the floor left by Tootsie. Bobby got busy tossing dishtowels on the puddles and swishing them around with his foot. He wasn't having much luck. I watched him while I took bites from my sandwich. I really enjoyed those thick, thick slices of bread.

While he was studying what to do about the puddles, I asked, "Hey, Bobby, can I ask you a favor?"

"Sure," Bobby said. He came back to the table, though not before giving the puddles one last look like it was hard to tear himself away.

"Don't tell anyone, okay?"

"I won't," Bobby said, curious about this secret favor.

I wiped the sandwich mustard from my hands onto my dress. It was ruined from cop plant dirt anyway. I grabbed a paper from the fresh stack Tootsie bought me. I pushed it toward Bobbie, along with a new colored pencil. It was purple.

"Can you write out my name? Not Sparky. My real name, Ambrosia Brown. I forgot how to spell it."

Bobby's mouth dropped open and he blinked. But he recovered himself soon enough. "Of course." He wrote out my name in big, neat print letters and then in big, neat cursive letters. He pushed the paper and purple pencil back to me. "Just keep copying this, and before you know it, you'll have it memorized."

Good ol' Bobby. He was patient with my shortcomings. And I had a lot. He was a real friend.

"I have to head home," Bobby told me. "Since you're at the police for a couple of hours now, there's not much time for after-school studying. But we'll make it up on the weekends, and I'll see you every day for library recess. Right?" He looked at me pointedly.

"Yeah, that's right."

Satisfied, he headed back to his house.

Bobby hated to fib, but I didn't have that problem. I had no idea if I'd be at school tomorrow because I had a long journey ahead of me tonight.

I went to my room and made like I was going to bed like a good little girl. I kept my door cracked open so I could hear the comings and goings in Creepy House. I shushed the leopards. "Keep quiet. I have to listen." They didn't make a peep, though they never made peeps.

The face broads left. "Be back tomorrow." And "Same time, same place." Raw-food lady and slimming man panicked over an emergency involving lettuce but eventually left. I heard Doctor saying, "Every step in this process is critical."

Then, silence. After shushing the leopards one more time, I crept from my room. I needed to sneak upstairs to Tootsie's closets to find the right outfit for my nighttime adventure.

I tiptoed to her stairs with mismatched metal squares for banisters and more squares dangling overhead. An artist gave the squares to Tootsie when she was at the height of her silent movie fame. Once upstairs, I stepped into Tootsie's maze of hallways and rooms that were her closets.

I had a scare when I heard voices up ahead. It was Tootsie's dress lady and assistant. "We will mix sunshine beach with midnight vamp. Perfect."

Whatever.

I turned and snuck into a different part of her closets. There were always dim electric lamps burning in the rooms. Because the window panes were colored glass and the clear glass transoms above them were small, even during the day it would have been shadowy without the lights. Maybe Tootsie wanted the lights so she'd be able to see her old costumes whenever the mood struck. The lights probably also kept her from tripping over the shoes, bows, and hat boxes. Whatever the reason, she sure didn't worry about the electric bills.

I found a pony outfit. Nah. I was done disguising myself as animals. A nurse outfit? Interesting, but not quite right. Here was a roomful of Tootsie's old vamp flapper dresses. Yes! Since I was going into the Hollywood Hills tonight, I needed to dress Hollywood-style.

The dresses were thick with sparkles: green sparkles, gray sparkles, white sparkles. They looked new. All of Tootsie's costumes were in good shape. That's because the goblin took such good care of them. He even managed to repair the ones I borrowed, unless they got completely destroyed, like the dog-goat outfit this summer. Hey, that wasn't my fault. The police dog did it.

I found a particularly snazzy flapper dress with purple sparkles that came with a matching purple fake fur jacket. The jacket would come in handy because, with the sun down, it would get chilly soon.

Tootsie's vamp dresses fit me perfectly because, even though she was taller than me, she was really skinny. The purple dress went down to just above my knees, and its sparkling fringe hung down to just past my knees. With Tootsie being taller, these vamp dresses must have been really, really short on her. She once laughed and told me that was the point. I guess.

I was tempted to go barefoot, but that wasn't the Hollywood look I was going for. I found a pair of sparkling purple shoes with flat heels that matched the dress. They were as long as my foot, but lots narrower. My feet were on the big side anyhow, from running around Bunker Hill barefoot in my street-kid days. Not that Tootsie had small feet. She told me the trick was to shove the big feet into the little shoes and just live with the pain. I had more than a few ouch moments shoving my feet into them. This movie star business was for the birds.

I dodged the dress lady and her assistant again. I tiptoed down the stairs without bumping into Doctor or the goblin. Moving quickly, I was out the sunroom French doors and through the back gate.

I got stares on the Red Car train going to Hollywood. I ignored them. I hopped off near the street I remembered that turned up into the dark Hollywood Hills where Onion Girl lived. Now that I was here, I wasn't sure what to do next. I hadn't thought about how I'd actually get up the dark street that twisted into the Hills.

There was no choice but to hoof it in those painful shoes. The road quickly became narrow and turned into unpaved dirt. A cliff rose up steeply on one side and dropped down steeply on the other side of the road.

I heard the rumbling of an auto coming up behind me. Quickly, I flattened myself against the cliff so the car wouldn't squash me.

Out of the shadows came a sporty yellow convertible, top down. It reminded me of Reginald's future car, except it was longer. The man at the wheel stared vacantly ahead. Did he even see me? As the convertible passed me, it sharply slowed to take a hairpin turn up ahead.

This gave me an idea. I had to act fast before the car sped up again.

Crouching low, I ran and then hopped onto the convertible's fat back bumper. The car dipped from my weight. If the driver noticed, he never turned around.

After the car rounded more bends, I recognized the hillside glowing with light coming down from Onion Girl's house on top of the hill. Suddenly, the convertible turned to the right, up another road. Oh, no. I had no idea where this car was heading. I jumped off the back bumper and rolled in the dirt.

I was not doing Tootsie's vamp costume any favors.

I watched the convertible as it motored up the other road for only a short distance. Then it veered to head up a steep drive-way dotted with small lights. The drive led to a mansion half-hidden behind a row of palms and tall bushes. When the car reached the top of the drive, it pulled to a stop. The man shut off the convertible's lights, but he did not get out of the car. He just sat there in the dim glow from the driveway lights.

Strange, but none of my business. Like Bookie said, the world's a strange place, so don't waste time trying to figure it out.

Onion Girl's driveway was a short walk away. I forgot she had a gate at the bottom of her drive. It was locked. There was no fence, so I would be able to scramble around the gate. Not that it was easy. The hillside rocks and scrubby plants tore at Tootsie's vamp dress and jacket. One of the purple sparkle shoes got caught in a branch and disappeared somewhere.

Once around the gate, I circled back to the drive. It was steep and made of gravel, so I had to be careful not to slide. The air was cool by now, which made the climb up a little easier, but not by much.

I hadn't planned on what to do exactly when I got to Onion Girl's place. I was wondering if this was the stupidest idea I'd ever had, and I'd had quite a few, when my answer came echoing down the hillside: "My bounty is as boundless as the sea. My love as deep—as deep as what? I don't get it. The more I give to you—no, I give to the—give to the? What? I thought this guy was famous. This poem is stupid. Anyway, where was I? Oh, yeah. The more I have, for both are—I don't know how to say that word. Ah, nuts."

Knucklehead.

His loud voice was easy to follow. He kept repeating this same poem over and over with lots of complaints about, "How am I supposed to memorize this?"

I followed until I saw his gangly form in the pools of light streaming from the mansion's many windows onto the vast stone-tiled patio in front of the house. Onion Girl didn't seem to care any more about her electric bill than Tootsie did. Movie stars.

The scrubby hillside plants and dirt disappeared, replaced by a sea of green lawn. I stepped off the gravel drive onto the grass. Between the lawn and the patio was a short hedge of blooming white rose bushes. Perfect. They'd give me cover until I decided what to do. I crawled up to them and peeked through the petals.

Knucklehead still wore the striped shirt, cap, and nose bandage that I saw in the newspaper photo. He was reading from a small book. The cover said something like, *Tried and True Love Poems*. Knucklehead's little white poodle scratched itself at his feet. He acquired the pooch recently, after Whisper-Whisper and his two kid cops were done using the dog as a prop for their last scheme. Knucklehead did say the pooch would help him get a sugar mama. Must have worked.

Suddenly, the dog's head shot up. It sniffed, then stared hard in my direction. Its lip curled. It growled. Then it stood up and let loose a booming bark. Surprising for such a small dog.

Knucklehead lowered his book. "Well, what are you waiting for?" he said to the dog. "If it's a rat, go get 'em!"

The pooch charged the rose bush I was hiding behind. I jumped up. "Wait! It's me! Sparky!" I pulled off my one remaining purple shoe and threw it at the dog. It caught the shoe in its teeth and swung it back and forth, growling.

"What are you doing here?" Knucklehead asked, clearly shocked to see me.

"You need to help me help Bookie."

Knucklehead held up a hand and shook his head. "I didn't have anything to do with what's going on with Bookie. I've been up here with my new lady. And if you don't mind, I need you to scram before the lady comes back. I got a sweet setup here, and I don't need a ratty kid showing up and messing with my plans."

I folded my arms and gave Knucklehead my hard look. "If you don't help me, I'll tattle to Onion Girl that you're no French poet, and the only poems you know, you stole from that book."

The pooch settled down on the tile to take its time destroying Tootsie's vamp shoe. Knucklehead stared at the dog, stared at me, and chewed his own fingers for good measure. "Okay, get inside. I don't want nobody seeing you."

As we walked toward the house, I heard scrambling sounds from behind a painted white fence and gate at the side of the house. That gate must lead to the back, where I knew there were more white rose bushes, stone tile, and Onion Girl's pool. The scrambling got louder until whatever it was slammed against the gate. Angry barking exploded.

This got the little white dog's attention. It dropped the shoe, tore to the gate, and added its own barking to the dogs on the other side.

"Guard dogs," Knucklehead grumbled. "She got in her head she needs 'extra security,' so she dropped a fortune getting a pair of those crazy animals. Me and guard dogs don't have the best history, if you know what I mean. These dogs smelled my number right off the bat. She says I just need to make friends with them." He shook his head.

He took me to a set of French doors with mini potted orange trees on either side. I snatched an orange from one.

"Hey, watch it!" He tried grabbing the orange from me, but I held it behind my back.

"I'm hungry. Do you even speak French? Maybe I should ask Onion Girl that when she comes back."

"She's not Onion Girl. She's Sally." He pulled open the doors. "Quit being a monkey and get in."

We stepped into a room much different from the blue-and-white parlor that I'd seen during Tootsie's visit. This room had a brown tile floor and dark red wallpaper going up to a high ceiling painted an even darker red. Black metal chandeliers hung down from the ceiling. Their bulbs weren't strong, which made the room shadowy.

The light was enough to give me a good gander at what was inside: paintings in gold frames that had a valuable, antique look about them, plus shelves full of more old, expensive-looking vases, bowls, doodads.

Knucklehead caught me staring. "Don't you get any ideas, Spark. I catch you swiping any of the lady's finery, you'll be really sorry."

"Yeah, you'll be sorry if you don't start talking. How come the dead guy in Monkey Island turned up in the same flophouse that the Chicago people have been hanging out in? Then the dead guy conveniently disappears. Where is this body now? Huh?"

From the way Knucklehead paused and scratched his fake nose bandage with his poem book, I could tell he didn't know specifics about the body in question. But he'd spent his life being a crook, so he had to know something. I hoped.

"I don't know much, okay?"

"I'm not buying that."

"Take it easy, Spark. I do know there was talk about Chicago showing up in town, hanging out in the flophouse, the one with that girl Shrimpy."

"Met her."

Knucklehead raised his eyebrows and chuckled. "I'll bet you did! Shrimpy owns that place, you know."

"That flophouse?"

"Yeah. Inherited it from her great-aunt or something."

"So who's the drunk at the check-in counter? Her dad?"

"Nah, that's her older brother. He's deep in the red to his

little sis for a lot of dough. She'll collect it from him too, if I know my Shrimpy." He laughed. "She must be renting space to Chicago. I'll bet she's charging double 'cause they're from out of town and don't know better."

He grinned and added, "Listen, I don't know facts for sure, but they told people they were checking Chicago's California operations, specifically orange groves and orchid flowers. Just routine. Nothing to worry about. But rumor has it they weren't too happy about how Chum-Chum's operation got a little, how can we say?—disorganized—while he was locked up. Is that why Chicago is in town? Or is that baloney? Who knows?"

The barking dogs outside reached a new pitch. Knucklehead leaned out the door and yelled, "Shut it up!" Didn't help. He closed the French doors, which didn't help either.

"Crazy guard dogs driving me crazy. Anyway, where was I?"

"Orange groves and orchids. That guy buried there?"

"What? No, I mean, maybe. But he could be in the body exchange."

I looked at him blankly.

Knucklehead chuckled and waved to an antique-looking sofa with spindly legs. "Take a seat and let me educate you."

One thing I could count on was Knucklehead being a blabbermouth. Hopefully, he blabbered something useful.

"If you head west to the edge of downtown, like you're going to Echo Park Lake, but not quite that far, you see these abandoned tunnels that were supposed to be for more trains or something, but never got finished. I know you know what I'm talking about. All the bad kids mess around in those tunnels."

That did ring a bell. "It's the older kids that go there. Not me. But, yeah, I know the place."

"Now we're getting somewhere." He was on a roll in his cheerful explaining mode. "If you have a body you shouldn't have, then you can exchange it for another one. The exchangee, as it were. This exchangee is dumped in those tunnels." He raised his eyebrows.

"Okay, keep going."

"To find a body you want to use for the switch—the exchangee—you look in the papers, in the obituary columns for someone that's been freshly planted. That means the dirt is less tamped down, which means it's easier to dig up. You've found your exchangee. If possible, you want to look for bodies in the nicer cemeteries, where movie stars are planted, people like that. While you're going through the trouble, you want to pick up some nice rings, a watch if you're lucky, right? Then your problem body— your exchanger—is dumped in the nice cemetery plot, and your dead swell—minus watch and ring—is dumped in the tunnel. No one's ever gonna dig up that swell's plot. Why would they? Only crooks and juvenile delinquents go to those tunnels, and they don't ask questions. So your problem is solved."

"This body wasn't dumped in a nice cemetery. It's moving around. Shouldn't the cops still have it?"

Knucklehead swayed his head back and forth in a maybe-maybe-not kind of way. "The morgue—that's where a body is kept on ice until the cops and judges are done with it. If the morgue is involved, that means palms had to be greased, strings pulled. Chum-Chum ordinarily would do the greasing to get the proper strings pulled. But this seems to be a Chicago situation. What they're doing, who knows?"

"So you're saying somebody pulled the body out of the morgue. But why keep it at the flophouse?"

"Sparky, you're not paying attention. You can't just do body exchanges any ol' time. You have to wait for dark, make sure cemetery bulls aren't prowling around. By now, the body could be in a nice cemetery with a fountain and sobbing angel statues and the whole bit. But sometimes things get dicey, emergencies happen, and there can't be an exchange. The body, inconvenient or not, has to end up in the tunnel. Or Echo Park Lake. Or the ocean. The possibilities are endless."

He must have seen my face sinking. "Most likely you'll have luck if you look at the obituaries, the ritzy cemeteries, the tunnels. But ask yourself, if you find the body, how does that help Books? In a murder situation, a body is nine-tenths of what the hangman needs in order to prove the case. No body might be better for Bookie."

"Bookie is still in jail, still facing murder, even though this body up and disappeared from the morgue. The papers say some actor is the dead guy, but this actor doesn't look a drop like the real dead guy. The cops don't believe me. If I find the body, I could find something else that proves Bookie is innocent. I could figure out who's moving the dead guy around and why."

Knucklehead eyed me. "You shouldn't talk to no cops, Spark. That'll make anything worse."

Oops. I said too much. Better not let Knucklehead know the cops also had me working for a detective, if you could believe it.

"Sparky, it sounds like something all around kooky is going on. Maybe the body will help, but it's a hopeless wild goose chase if you ask me."

"Some friend of Bookie's you are."

"Listen, Books had a good run, but stuff happens. Sometimes

you just have to let it go. Think of yourself, Spark. If you get picked up by cemetery bulls for digging around after disappearing bodies, you could be blamed for helping Bookie murder that guy. You just dodged a murder charge this summer. I'm sure you don't want to go through that again."

"But I have to try!"

"Think about it: Bookie probably did knock that guy off. Bound to happen eventually."

"No, he didn't!"

"There's a reason Books is known as Hothead. He probably got into it with this guy and things got outta hand."

I was about to turn into a hothead at Knucklehead, but suddenly, the dogs went quiet. Knucklehead lifted his finger to my lips and cocked his head to listen.

A scratching sound. The white pooch's paws were on the French doors' glass panes. Then the dog darted away. I heard it happily yipping. The guard dogs whined in a hopeful way. Was it Onion Girl? If so, she must give them treats.

"She's back. Run, hide. Now!"

Outside, I heard the solid clunk that only doors on huge movie star sedans could make. "Yoo-hoo! Pierre, my love! I'm back with Mr. Beele!"

Knucklehead pushed me off the sofa. "Hide!"

I zipped around the corner, then peeked back to see the action.

Knucklehead tried jamming his love poem book under the antique sofa's cushion, but the cushion was attached to its spindly frame. The cushion ripped. "Ah, nuts." Knucklehead shoved the poems into the rip and tried to pat the fabric back in place. "Good enough."

"Pierre!"

Knucklehead threw the French doors open and bounded outside. "Oui! Oui! Amore! Amore!"

Even though Knucklehead threatened me, I wasn't done here yet. A particular shiny doodad caught my eye. Chum-Chum said he needed something nice. This doodad was more than nice.

I crept away from my corner and back into the room. My hands wrapped around a silver statue of a seated fluffy dog with its tongue hanging out. It was about the size of a puppy. When I picked it up, I nearly fell forward. It was a lot heavier than a puppy. From the hole on the bottom, I realized it was hollow. Still, it was thick metal.

I shuffled the dog doodad around in my arms until I had a solid hold on it, while still being able to clutch my orange. I was mighty hungry and planned to peel that orange as soon as I got out of this red-hot situation.

"We've had such a success with practice today!" I heard Onion Girl enthuse through the now open French doors.

"Practicing in a proper soundstage will give you the extra edge in the audition." That was Beele's voice. Odious Mr. Beele, helping Tootsie practice one minute, then turning around behind her back and helping her arch-enemy Onion Girl the next. I wondered if Onion Girl and Tootsie had the same audition.

I didn't have time to think too deeply about this. I had to make tracks. I moved toward the back of the house, through hallways and more rooms. I had to find the blue-and-white parlor where Tootsie had tea when we visited. It also had French doors, and those led out back. True, the guard dogs were out back. I hoped they were too busy whining for Onion Girl to notice me.

There! I spotted the blue-and-white room. I was able to push the French doors open with my shoulder. I was out.

Not so fast. I heard that little poodle yowling and the yowling sounded like it was moving through the house. Moving straight toward me.

The guard dogs heard the poodle's yowling. Their hopeful whining turned into aggressive growls.

Then I saw two guard dogs bounding from the side of the house, and the white dog tearing through the French doors. They were on a collision course with me.

I didn't have another shoe to throw. My only weapon was the orange. Not much but I had to try. I raised it up.

Suddenly, all three dogs stopped barking. Instead, they pranced about, tongues hanging out, eyes fixed on the orange.

A ball. The dogs thought I was throwing them a ball. Okay, fine.

I threw the orange as far away from me as I could, which wasn't easy with the heavy metal dog I was balancing in my other arm. The orange landed in the pool. On top of it landed the three dogs with a splash. Of course, they had to start fighting over it.

I took my chance to scramble toward the other side of the back area, where I knew the garages and driveway were.

The angry growling and barking grew louder and louder. Through the mansion's many open windows, I heard Onion Girl's cries as she ran through the house toward the back, "My babies! My babies! Who is attacking my babies?" I heard Beele shout, "A bear attack!" And Knucklehead, "Oui! Oui!"

I had to quickly duck into shadows at the side of the house when lights popped on in the windows above the garages. Out came Onion Girl's housekeeper. She must live up there. "Madam! What has happened?" She ran down the steps at the side of the garages.

Since everyone was rushing to the dogfight, I had a clear shot to the driveway. I ran. As the gravel drive began to travel steeply downward, I started sliding. Then I was rolling. I picked up speed until I slammed to a stop against the closed gate at the bottom. At least I got down faster, and I still held the metal dog tight in my arms.

I picked myself up. My legs were banged up. Funny thing, the fake fur jacket acted like padding and the sparkles on the dress acted like a suit of armor, keeping me from being banged up even more. Though, the dress sacrificed a lot of sparkles and fringe on the way down, and the jacket didn't look so new anymore.

I scrambled through the brush to go around the gate. The poking branches tore off even more sparkles and ripped more holes. Finally, I was back on the dirt road. There was no way I could walk down this twisty, dark road with the heavy dog. I decided to go as far as the house where the convertible was parked. I'd find somewhere to hide there, get some shut-eye, and figure out what to do in the morning.

Yeah, I knew morning meant school. I'd figure out what to do about that later.

All that mattered was that I didn't have to scour the town for a missing dead body. In my clutches was exactly what I needed to persuade Chum-Chum to work his magic to get Bookie out: a dog made of real silver.

I was dead beat by the time I marched up the steep drive to the convertible house. The night air was extra cold up here.

Breezes came down from the Hills, poking through the rips in the fake fur jacket. I shivered. The convertible was still parked in front of the mansion. The man no longer sat inside. The convertible's top was still down, so I looked inside. I saw a back seat with a comfy-looking plaid blanket.

It wouldn't hurt to curl up under that blanket, get warm, and get a few winks. So that's what I did.

Thursday

The next thing I knew, I woke to light filtering through the plaid blanket. I smelled fresh, salty air. I'd only smelled that once before, when Bookie drove me to the ocean.

I whipped the blanket off my head and sat up.

The air was hazy, so it was still early. Away from buildings and hills, the sky was vast. What was even more vast was the mass of water that started where a long stretch of sand ended. The Pacific Ocean, the one Cornelius, the weird pet shop kid, wanted to cross.

My eye caught someone standing by the car. My heart froze. The man wore a straw boater hat.

No, it was a different straw boater. The weave looked finer, more expensive. The band wasn't dark but a light color that matched the man's suit. This guy must be the convertible's driver I saw last night.

He was faced away from me, watching the ocean. The light-colored suit he wore had a soft shimmer and a nubby texture. It reminded me of a tie Bookie used to own. He said it was raw silk. He let me touch it, but only really quick, because, "you don't know how to keep your hands clean."

Bookie's raw silk tie was dark red with random black-and-dark-green squares. When the convertible man turned, I saw his tie also looked like raw silk. It matched the color of his pale cream suit and had a soft pattern of coral swirls. His shirt, which I'd bet was also silk, though was too smooth to be raw silk, had the same cream color. His shoes too! He almost blended into the sand.

As he turned, his blank, pale face and empty hazel eyes saw me. He stared for a moment. Suddenly, his eyes sparkled with life, and a broad smile with the most beautiful white teeth I'd ever seen filled his face. It was like the sun came out, even though the sky was still gray with haze. I couldn't believe how he'd changed.

"Do you want my autograph?" he said, smile beaming.

Okay, I got it now. I was dealing with another actor like Tootsie. He'd probably been out of work and forgotten since the pictures started talking.

This actor's face rang zero bells for me, but he'd deflate like a popped balloon if he figured that out. From my dealings with Tootsie, I knew what I needed to say.

"Oh, yes, mister! Please!" I put on my excited little kid routine. If he thought it was strange that I was wearing a ripped, purple fake fur jacket and flapper dress with most of the sparkles gone, he didn't say anything.

"Of course." Then his smile suddenly faltered. "I used to carry photos in my trunk in case, but then no one. . . ." He trailed off. I could see the balloon deflating.

"Could I just be by you! Please! I'll die if I can't!"

The sun came back. "Ah, my little fan, you've gone through such trouble to find me, of course! We shall go to breakfast together. I know just the place. And please," he said winking, "you must ride up front with me."

I clamored over the seat to the front, being careful not to drop the silver dog. I left dirty bare footprints all over his cream upholstery that also matched his suit. He didn't seem to notice or care about my footprints.

As he slid into the convertible, he did notice the dog in my arms. "I gave someone a dog like that once," he said, his eyes drifting to the past. "I think we all had too much money back then."

I tensed, waiting for the *Hey, kid, where'd you get that valuable dog anyhow* remark. It never came. This guy, whoever he was, lost interest in the dog, and drove his convertible away from the beach. I hoped wherever he was heading, it was closer to downtown.

His face settled into a happy place. His smile wasn't as broad, but that would have been a strain to hold in place, even for an actor. I must have made his day. As long as no cops were being called, that was fine by me.

The restaurant was in Hollywood, which worked for me. I could catch the Red Car back downtown.

He pulled the convertible into a parking lot behind the restaurant. I panicked when I saw uniformed staff appear to park the car for him. Quickly, I pulled off the ripped jacket and wrapped it around the silver dog. I couldn't risk any more eyeballs seeing it.

One of the uniforms opened the passenger door for me. He kept his face straight, though I did see him glance at me with a quick *What in the world?* look before his face went straight again. In the sunlight, I saw my legs were dirty and covered with scabs and scratches. Fortunately, my arms were okay thanks to the fake fur jacket protecting me when I rolled down Onion Girl's hillside.

Inside the restaurant, it was dim with dark wood and round booths in the shadows. The waiter who came forward was dressed like a formal gent in black tie and white jacket. He knew the convertible driver and bowed like the man was some kind of big deal, which he must've been. The waiter eyed my dirty bare feet. From the look that passed his face, I could tell he wanted to sneer and kick me out. But I was with Mr. Important. The waiter's look lasted only a half second before he switched to a smile. He bowed to me and said, "Mademoiselle." Funny, that's what everyone called Tootsie.

The waiter showed us to a big, round booth in a back corner. I positioned the jacket-wrapped dog close to me on the seat and angled it so passersby would have trouble seeing it. The shadows in this dark place also helped me hide it from prying eyes.

As I leaned against booth, I felt hard sparkles on the back of the dress. How about that? Some sparkles had survived my roll down Onion Girl's drive, thanks to the jacket. I was proud of myself. I hadn't completely ruined Tootsie's vamp dress. Okay, I'd mostly ruined it, but I hadn't meant to. When I shifted in my seat, I felt some of the sparkles come loose and tumble down. I twisted around to find them in the booth, but it was too dark to see. I heard a couple of sparkles ping to the floor. Oops.

The convertible man seemed familiar with the restaurant's show. He said quietly, "Thanks, Sarge. The usual, please."

Sarge, the waiter looked at me. Before anybody could say anything, I shouted, "Ice cream!"

Sarge smiled like I was so cute, but behind the smile I could sense the bottom of his shoe wanted to kick me out on my fanny. This waiter was a pro and kept his cool. "Of course, Mademoiselle."

The actor laughed in a quiet kind of way. "Whatever she wants."

Sarge bowed. "Certainly."

After keeping us waiting for a good long while, which the man didn't seem to mind, like it was normal, Sarge came back with a big silver tray. On it was a glass of water with a slice of lemon jammed on the lip. "Careful, sir, it's hot.

When the man saw me staring at it, he said, smiling, "Have to watch my waistline."

Sarge was back in a flash with my ice cream. Let me tell you, it was no Monkey Island ice cream. This came in a glass dish with a pattern of swirls cut into the glass. Inside this ritzy dish were not one, not two, but three scoops of ice cream: one chocolate, one vanilla, and one pink. If that wasn't enough, the scoops were topped with a pile of whipped cream. On top of the whipped cream oozed liquid chocolate. On top of that were smashed nuts and red cherries, redder and fatter than the ones at the downtown saloon. And wait, what was under this dream? Sliced bananas. "I can't believe it!" I said before I could think, which Bookie said I did a lot.

Convertible man chuckled. Sarge vanished.

I dove in, snout first. Then I discovered a spoon with an extra-long handle next to the glass dish. I used it like a shovel. I went to town until I was nearly exploding. Still, I'd only gone through half of that wonder. I leaned back in the booth to take a breather.

"I think you like it," the actor smiled.

I noticed he hadn't touched his hot water. He stared toward the front windows and door. When people came in, sometimes they saw him and nodded or waved. One man came to the back and said, "Nice to see you," and wandered to his own booth. Others came in but didn't notice the guy. When people saw him, his face brightened, and he flashed his sunshine smile. When people didn't notice him, his face went blank.

He really was a lot like Tootsie.

"Hey, do you know Tootsie?" I asked.

His eyes moved from the door to me. He looked hopeful but said nothing. Did he want an update on what Tootsie was doing?

"She's going for an audition," I said. In the next second, I realized this audition might be a secret. I remembered Doctor's lecture about how I was ruining Tootsie's important audition. Me and my big mouth.

But convertible man didn't seem surprised. "Yes, the audition." He smiled. "I'm so happy for her."

Was he going on this audition too? Him, Onion Girl, Tootsie, all the silent stars must be trying out.

The man did manage to take a couple of sips from his glass of water before he lost interest. After a while, Sarge came by and took his glass of hot water that wasn't hot anymore.

When Sarge's hand touched my dish, which was a melted ice cream swamp by now, I howled. The snarl flashed across Sarge's face for an instant, but then he went back to his isn't-it-so-cute mask.

Convertible man smiled. "How about bring the young lady a bag of cookies and things?" He turned to me. "Will that help?"

I was dumbfounded and then some. So I just sat there with my mouth hanging open.

"Very good." Sarge smiled in his careful way while he snatched my ice cream dish and vanished with it behind swinging doors that must lead to the kitchen.

Sarge returned with two bulging sacks. They smelled of sweet goodness. My arms went around the sacks as I breathed in deep.

Suddenly, the actor said cheerfully, "Sarge, I have an idea. Please bring me a pencil."

Sarge was back in an instant with the pencil.

Pencil in hand, the actor pulled one of the sacks from me. I was about to holler until I remembered he was paying, and I had a valuable piece of stolen merchandise next to me. I needed to mind my manners, which Bookie told me I did a bum job of minding.

With a flourish, the actor scrawled something large and loopy on the sack. He turned and smiled at me in an expectant way.

Oh, right, the autograph. I was supposed to be a fan wanting his mark. No problem. I knew what to do to earn my ice cream and cookies.

I squealed extra loud, bounced up and down in my seat, and clapped. All eyes in the restaurant turned toward him. He gave the biggest smile in the world to all of them. I knew what he was saying: *I have a fan and you don't.*

He glided like walking on air as we left the booth. Sarge grinned and said something about "such a darling little fan." Sarge snapped his fingers, and one of the uniforms appeared to take the cookie sacks to the convertible.

The uniform also tried to take the jacket-wrapped dog, but I wouldn't let him touch it.

As the actor pulled his convertible away from the restaurant parking lot, he asked, "Now, where should I take you?"

"Downtown, if you don't mind."

"Of course. It's a beautiful day for a drive."

It was. The morning haze had cleared away, leaving blue skies and puffy clouds. It wasn't too hot or too cold. In my arms, I had just what Chum-Chum wanted, plus two sacks of cookies that I suspected would be a dream to chow down, thanks to this actor who was as happy as the blue skies because he had a fan.

I asked him to stop a block from Chum-Chum's storefront. No need for Chum-Chum to see a snazzy, expensive yellow convertible dropping me off.

He hopped out of his convertible, opened my door, and helped me out. It still was a struggle to hold the sacks and the dog at the same time, but I managed. "Gee, thanks," I told the actor.

He gave me his warm, happy smile. "Thank you for this day. Fans are the most important people in the world."

"Tootsie would agree with you there."

"Please say hello to her for me, will you?"

"Sure thing!"

Then he was gone.

I couldn't say hello to Tootsie for him because I still had no idea who this man was. Even if I did, I couldn't say hello because that would mean explaining why I was creeping around Onion Girl's house late last night instead of being tucked safe and sound in my Creepy House bed.

With my arms loaded down, I managed to push open Chum-Chum's glass storefront door with my shoulder and squeeze through. I had to step carefully over a new doll's head propping the door open.

Chum-Chum sat at his desk. Today he wore a deep green silk robe patterned with glamorous goldfish wearing purple evening gowns. He studied a hairless, one-eyed doll's head in his hands, turning it slowly around, like he was thinking. Rosie turned in her bowl and blew a bubble at me. Chum-Chum's eyes darted up. He eyed me darkly.

"I have the something," I said nervously.

He said nothing and kept staring.

Bookie always told me to never, ever get within grabbing distance of Chum-Chum. But I had to give him the dog. I stepped to his desk and carefully maneuvered the heavy dog onto his desk, which was no easy task with all the envelopes, piles of fifty-dollar bills twisted into bow tie shapes, and other junk crowding his desk.

Chum-Chum looked at the dirty, ripped jacket with disgust. He peeled the fake fur back with thumb and forefinger like he was peeling back slop bin trash. When the jacket fell away, revealing the dog, Chum-Chum gasped. He fell back against his chair and breathed fast in and out.

Then his eyes darted to the two sacks I still clutched. He stared at them, hard.

No. These were my cookies. Mine! But what Chum-Chum wanted, Chum-Chum got.

Feeling defeated, I squeezed the sacks onto his desk between the dog and the fifty-dollar bills.

Chum-Chum pulled at the sack with the autograph. He noticed the signature, blinked, then his eyes bugged.

"Oh, Rosie!" he gasped to the goldfish in his little girl's voice. "What have we here! Oh, my. Oh, my, my, my!" He hardly knew which to hug first, the silver dog or the autographed cookie sack. He must have been a real fan of that actor, not a fake fan like me. Rosie shared his excitement and swirled around and around in her bowl.

With arms around his prizes, his eyes traveled back to me. His face darkened. "Get out," he snarled, and not in his little girl's voice.

I scrambled backward, tripped over the doll's-head doorstop, and ran.

I ran for a few blocks before I stopped and sat at the curb.

Bookie was safe.

From how Chum-Chum reacted to the dog and the autograph, they must have been the right something-somethings to buy his help. That's all that mattered.

I looked down at my dirty feet, scratched legs, and Tootsie's tattered flapper dress. I sure couldn't go to school like this. I decided to park myself with the two gorillas in the saloon where they now worked and spend the day with them. Yep, today was a good day.

Just when that thought wandered into my head, a sedan screeched to a stop in front of me.

It was Doctor's black sedan. Oh, no. He was inside. His suit and fedora were as black as his sedan today. His face looked like thunder.

I took off running but Doctor was quick. He flew out of his car, chased me, and blocked my path. "Don't run from me," he hissed. His eyes looked me up and down. He must have realized the ragged dress I wore was one of Tootsie's because he clenched his fists until his knuckles were white. When his eyes reached my feet, he bared his teeth. "You cannot go to school without shoes."

Before I knew it, Doctor pulled off his shoes right there on the sidewalk, bent down, grabbed one of my feet, and shoved it into his shoe.

"I can't wear these! They're ten times too big!"

He looked up at me with his cool little smile. "Oh, I'll tighten them."

He shoved the other shoe on my other foot, then yanked the laces, tightening them as far as they would go. They were still clown shoes on me.

A woman passing by chastised, "Those shoes are not for girls, sir."

Doctor looked up at her with his blackest, coldest stare. He bared his teeth. "My goodness!" the woman gasped as she scampered away.

"Back to the car," he said in his whispery voice. "And don't try anything or I will have to drag you."

My school bag was on the front passenger seat. I looked inside and saw my new school supplies, books, and, most importantly, the goblin's lunch tin. As he pulled his sedan from the curb, I pointed out, "I have to go back to. . .," I almost said Creepy House, ". . .home and change my clothes. I can't go to school like this."

"Oh, yes, you can."

"But the kids there will go crazy. They already oink at me and. . . ."

He cut me off. "I've been driving for hours in Bunker Hill and downtown, hunting for you. I left very early in the morning with the story that I was driving you to school well before the bell because you are such an eager student. I prescribed a particularly elaborate deep soaking treatment for Tootsie so she, Mr. Grossman, and all her people would be too preoccupied to notice that not only was I leaving without you, but you weren't even in the house."

"But. . . ."

His cold, whispery voice cut me off again. "When you come back from your," he paused, "police assignment, go directly to your room. Change into your usual school clothes. Hide what is left of that dress and my shoes in back of the bottom drawer of your dresser. Then come out to the kitchen like you usually do and pretend that you went to school early like a good little girl in your little girl's sailor dress."

"The thing is, there's this oinking kid and. . . ."

"I will retrieve my shoes, which you better not ruin, and Mademoiselle's dress before Mr. Grossman finds them. Of course, he will notice this costume is missing from her closets. I will tell him moths got into it and the damage is such that I deemed it best for a specialist to repair. I will have to find someone to recreate the dress, as well as the jacket and the shoes, which I see you have lost. You have caused a great deal of trouble. I pray he will fall for this ruse."

The goblin did have a knack for finding costumes and clothes I ripped and dirtied up no matter where I hid them. He also had a knack for cleaning and fixing most of them so they were like new. There was no repairing this flapper dress.

"You had to pick Mademoiselle's most famous costume from *Baby Vamp and the Dancing Boys,* didn't you? I cannot allow Mr. Grossman to see how you've destroyed it. It would break his heart. I don't want to think about what it would do to Mademoiselle."

That made me feel like a crumb. How could I know it was a special dress? She had lots of sparkly dresses. It was just one of many. I sunk down in the seat. It was softer than the seats in any of Bookie's sedans. Yeah, this must be an expensive car.

I felt more sparkles on the back of Tootsie's dress come off. I reached my hand around behind me, felt for the sparkles, and shoved them in the seat crevice so Doctor wouldn't see them.

I stared down at Doctor's clown-sized shoes on my feet. They looked different from other men's shoes. Were they the handmade, custom type of shoes Bookie dreamed of owning one day? "All the top Chicago bosses would rather go naked and barefoot than put on anything other than custom shoes. They know style in Chicago, Sparky," he told me.

Chicago was also switching bodies around. But Chum-Chum had his silver dog and actor autograph, so Bookie would soon be a free man and he could kick all those custom-shoe Chicago people out of his office.

Luckily, it was lunchtime, so the school yard and halls were empty of kids. I followed Doctor inside. He walked in his socks. I struggled in his shoes that clunk-clunked on my feet. I looked down at the dress. With most of the sparkles gone and fringe torn off, it looked like a rag I fished out of a cleaning bucket.

"You know, I really can't go to class like this and. . . ."

"Shut up."

Doctor started pushing open the frosted glass "Principal's Office" door. Suddenly, he froze. Through the cracked-open door, I saw Miss S. She was talking with LT, the tough-broad police lady.

Doctor pulled his fedora low over his face, backed up quick, and walked away before they saw him. Interesting. I knew Doctor led a double life, so no surprise he didn't want a police lady seeing his face. I didn't know much about Doctor's history, and this made me wonder even more.

I pushed the door open wider and stepped to my doom.

Both the broads stared at me. LT's straight face did not change. Miss S said with a devious grin, "Well, look what the cat dragged in."

Principal peeked out of his office, saw me, declared, "Unbelievable," and shut his door.

I sat in my usual punishment chair while the two of them went back to talking. I realized they were doing more than talking. LT was showing Miss S a shiny silver pistol with fancy patterns etched into the metal: whorls, swirls, and even little flowers. The pistol looked old-fashioned. It must be an antique. Probably worth a pretty penny.

"He gave it to me all right. Just this morning," LT stated, her straight face never changing.

"Nice," Miss S said, her fingers running along the designs.

Was the "he" Mug? Did he take my advice and give her this pistol rather than flowers? Must have. He got it for her so quickly, I suspected it must have come from his own private stash. How about that? Mug gave LT a fancy antique pistol. He must be seriously sweet on her. Yikes.

Without looking at me, Miss S said, "I don't have time to deal with you being underfoot all school year. Me, your LT, and Mrs. Bean have been talking about your situation."

LT leaned back, slipped the fancy shooter in the belt of her cop dress, and eyed me. She said nothing.

"You'll report to the library, to Mrs. Bean." Miss S paused, then barked, "Now!"

I flinched.

"And don't think about running off and being a truant again, or my friend here might have to hunt you down, and she won't like that much." Miss S gave me her smile she only gave when she knew she had me in a tight spot. LT gave me a hard look.

A chill went over me. What new horror now? Were they going to shoot me with Mug's fancy pistol? Shoot me and bury me under books in the library, never to be seen again? All I could do was give them a trembling nod and hurry out into the empty hall.

I started making my way super slowly to the library, dragging my feet in the clunking shoes. A rotating magic lantern show of the terrors that could happen flashed in my mind. I heard the click of the Principal's door open behind me. I turned. There was LT, arms folded, the pistol boldly shining from her belt, the hard look in her lava eyes. I took off running.

I tore the library door open, skidded inside, and shut it behind me. The library was as empty as the halls. It would be because it was lunchtime.

"There you are, Sparky," Mrs. Bean said cheerily. She held no pistol, no axe, no meat hook. She did hold up a book.

The cover had a cowgirl on it with a horse. The cowgirl was holding up a lantern outside a cave. Both looked scared. I wondered what they were scared about.

"This is *Wild West Carla and the Mystery of the Lost Treasure Map*. I thought you might like it a little more than the books about Reginald that your friend Bobby enjoys." She winked as she handed it to me.

My finger moved over the cover. I didn't like the dress Carla wore because I didn't like dresses. Though this cowgirl dress wasn't too terrible, with fringes on the sleeves and beads on the front. Her cowboy hat and boots weren't too bad either. My finger moved over the horse next to her. It was all black.

"That's Midnight, the Wonder Pony," Mrs. Bean explained. "She helps Carla, and Carla can understand Midnight's neighing."

I think this librarian spent too much time reading these books, but they did sound interesting. Midnight must have been a nice horse, unlike Marigold's Dodger that always wanted to bite me.

"Why don't I check that book out for you? Take your time

with it, and when you want another, let me know." Mrs. Bean winked again and smiled. She paused. "Sparky?" she asked. "Do you have any lunch? I have some things to eat, if you're hungry."

I stared at her. I think my mouth was hanging open. Eating anything, even air, was a no-go in the library. That would get you more than Miss S's punishment chair. That would land you in Principal's bad-kid chair. "I have a lunch tin, but I'll wait."

Mrs. Bean held her finger to her lips. "I won't tell if you won't. Go on, have something before the other children come."

I was nervous about this library rule-breaking. Would LT charge in and slap me in cuffs? But I was extra hungry. This morning's ice cream wore off long ago.

I pulled open the goblin's lunch tin, trying not to make noise, even though I was the only person here besides Mrs. Bean at her desk. I had to keep from shrieking in happy surprise when I saw that, next to my sandwich, the goblin had stuffed two fat, round buns, each with a different filling bulging out of the top. One filling was a deep purple so dark it was nearly black. I bit in. It had a sweet crunch to it. I'd never tasted such a thing before. The other bun's filling was orange. I bit into that. Sweet but different than any other fruit I'd tasted.

I had to know what they were. I took both buns to Mrs. Bean's desk. She was the librarian. She must know pretty much everything in the world. "What is this stuff in these buns?"

She smiled and brushed away her hair that was always flying loose. She pulled her reading glasses from where they hung on her book-shaped pin. She slid them on and studied the buns. "Oh, the dark one looks like a fig filling. This orange one is definitely an apricot filling. What a special treat. I don't think

I've ever seen a student or teacher come to school with a lunch like that."

She found me a book that explained figs, apricots, and lots of other fruit. It had nice pictures, but I was more interested in what Carla and Midnight were up to.

Being extra careful not to dribble crumbs on the pages—which was a challenge for someone like me—I opened *Wild West Carla and the Mystery of the Lost Treasure Map.*

There were drawings here and there inside. I stopped flipping the pages when I saw a drawing of the treasure map. It looked torn and had pointing arrows, dotted lines, plus "Danger" written on it. A few pages later, another drawing showed a slumped-over skeleton wearing a cowboy hat. The skeleton clutched the same treasure map, like he'd died trying to figure it out. Carla and Midnight were there too. They looked even more scared than on the cover. Carla held her lantern up high so they could see the map. They were inside a cave, probably the one on the cover.

I wondered if this book might have a clue about what Chicago was up to with Straw Boater and framing Bookie. Though it didn't matter now, right? Chum-Chum would soon get Bookie out of the slammer.

The bell rang, signaling the end of lunch and start of recess. I jammed what was left of my buns and sandwich into the tin and slid it in my school bag. I didn't want any tattletale kids to know I was eating in the library. I especially didn't want Bobby to know. He'd never tattle on me, but he would lecture me.

I heard rushing kid feet. Most of them charged outside to mess around for recess. A few, like Bobby, would soon come into the library.

Quickly, I slammed Carla's book shut and slid it into my book bag. I decided to keep it a secret from Bobby.

Bobby was the first kid in the library. "Sparky! You're early!" But his smile dropped when he realized I looked like, as Miss S said, something the cat dragged in.

He sat at the library table next to me. "Are you wearing Doctor's shoes?"

"I, ah, lost my shoes, so. . . ."

He didn't wait for my excuse. "Sparky, tell me honestly, were you out all night?"

"You see, the thing was, because, you know. . . ." I was trying to dream up a story.

Bobby's eyes darted to Mrs. Bean at her desk, then darted to two girls who came in. They saw me, then started giggling to each other. Cornelius came in, did a double take when he saw what a mess I was, but then gave me his little smile through his fringe of hair.

Bobby was so annoyed he forgot to glare at Cornelius.

He whispered, "There's too many people around. We'll talk later back at your house."

He didn't mention Doctor's shoes or the ratty dress again, but he was extra lecturing. When he noticed the fruit book, he wanted to know what that was about. Of course, the last thing I'd tell him was why Mrs. Bean gave me the book and my top-secret library eating. So I said, "I like the pictures."

"Sparky, books are so much more than pictures. I need you

to start focusing on the words. Let's go over your reading level today."

That's how library time went. When the bell rang, I hoped I'd be imprisoned in the library for the rest of the afternoon, but Miss Clark came by to fetch me.

I don't want to talk about how that went. Let's just say I have a new nickname: Clown Shoes.

Yeah.

I wanted to go back to Creepy House to change, but LT had a set time for me to arrive. I was too afraid I'd have a date with her fancy shooter if I came a minute late.

Detective Bernie's cigar fell out of his mouth when he saw me. "Just when I thought I'd seen everything." He shook his head.

I fetched Detective Bernie's sandwich, as usual. As I walked back toward his desk, I nearly dropped his sandwich when I nearly slammed into Spooky. Spooky stood, not moving, like a ghost, like he usually did. Though I usually saw him leaning his forehead against a certain lamppost on Bunker Hill.

"Hey, Spooky," I said. He didn't reply, but that was normal for him. I liked Spooky. He was a strange cop, but he was first-rate. He helped me out when I was in a tight spot this summer.

Back at the Detective's desk, I pointed out, "Spooky's not at his lamppost on Bunker Hill. I've never seen him anywhere else."

Detective Bernie waited until Spooky drifted away, out of the large cop room. "He lives here."

"Here? Why?"

"Watch it. This isn't such a bad place. I've worked most of my career outta this place. I'd rather be in this tatty building than that shiny new City Hall with the brass breathing down my neck."

"Sorry, I meant. . . ."

"Forget it. I knew what you meant. Spooky thinks this is his barracks. He thinks he's still back in the War. He had a hard time over there, Sparky. He wasn't the same when he came back. So the chief, all of us, do what we can to help him out. Us cops have to look out for one another. If we don't, no one else will." He pointed his cigar at me and gave me a long look.

"Okay, sure."

That settled, Detective Bernie gave me my new task. "Clean up after Officer Bun-Bun."

Sounded like a problem cop. Probably barfed all over his uniform, then passed out drunk somewhere, and they expected me to clean him up. Figured.

"Where is this guy?"

"Guy! She's a rabbit. Haven't you noticed there's a rabbit in here? What kind of detective will you make if you don't pay attention."

I couldn't do anything right.

Since Detective Bernie didn't like standing up or moving around, he waved over a younger, friskier cop to show me this rabbit. The young cop led me to a back corner where desks were arranged like a barricade. The cop, arms akimbo and staring hard at me, said, "This is confidential police business. No talk about Officer Bun-Bun anywhere outside this room. Especially not to any brass. Understand?"

Geez. What was with these people? "Sure, okay."

Behind the wall of desks was a spacious wire pen on the floor. It was larger than the pen where the mathematical rooster and guinea pig lived in Cornelius's weird pet shop. It was about the size of four of the cop desks.

The cop showed me the stack of newspapers for lining the pen, and the sack of sawdust I needed to pour on top of the fresh newspapers. Then there was a crate of lettuce, carrots, and cucumbers, which reminded me of the saloon Spots took me to. A big metal barrel was there for me to fill with Officer Bun-Bun's pooed-on newspapers and sawdust. All of this was hidden behind the barricade. I noticed a coat rack, a file cabinet, and a couple of typewriter stands were also part of the fortifications.

"Make sure Officer Bun-Bun's office is ship-shape, corners squared, not a speck of sawdust out of place. LT comes by here to discuss cases with Officer Bun-Bun, so you'll hear about it if it's not per standard."

Then he left me with Bun-Bun. The black-and-white splotched rabbit gave me the same hard cop stare as the rest of them. The rabbit could smell crime on me. I noticed the rabbit had a real police badge hanging from its wire pen. The badge even had "Bun-Bun" stamped on it. I'd bet the brass didn't know about that.

"Okay, Officer Bun-Bun, let's get going."

It was tough work scooping up the newspapers and sawdust. Every step of the way, Bun-Bun watched me, making sure I didn't mess up.

When I was done, the young cop informed me that I wasn't done. I had to haul the metal barrel down the stairs. It clanged as I pulled it because there were metal treads on the wooden stairs. Outside, I had to pour the newspapers and sawdust into another barrel, then haul the empty barrel back up to the second floor. The barrel went clang, clang, clang. Doctor's shoes went clomp, clomp, clomp. I was a regular one-girl band in the most ridiculous clown band in the world.

By the time I dragged myself back to Creepy House, I felt like I'd been run over by a truck.

I nearly forgot about Doctor's orders about changing in my room and hiding the evidence of Tootsie's shredded dress. The clomp, clomp of Doctor's shoes reminded me.

I stuffed the dress and shoes into my bottom dresser drawer, like Doctor said. I tried not messing up his shoes, like he warned me not to do. They were in pretty good shape. Sure, there was some sawdust on them, and maybe a Bun-Bun poo or two. I was too tired to worry about that. They were good enough.

I stared at myself in my room's mirror. My face was dirty and my curly hair was worse than it usually was. It flew all around my head like a strange, hairy halo. Shrimpy's bruise looked better, but it was still there. I tried pulling my hair in my face to cover what was left of it. I should have gone into my bathroom to tidy myself up. But I was too tired. And hungry. I looked good enough.

Doctor was stationed in the kitchen next to Gilbert, who was stirring another stinky pot. I could tell Doctor was waiting for me, making sure I'd followed his instructions. He eyed my dirty face. "Police work takes you to some filthy places, I see. You are so very dedicated," he said in his cool whisper. His eyes were not friendly.

Gilbert turned around. "We are so proud of you, Sparky! You work so hard. Such a good little citizen. After Mademoiselle's audition, I shall be back to baking many wonderful delights for you. I am ashamed to give you bakery goods. But we will remedy that soon."

The bakery goods were first-rate, but I wasn't arguing with the goblin. His baking was also something else.

I sat down at the kitchen table to my sandwich hiding under a dish towel, like usual. In the middle of the table was a pink-and-white plaid printed plate that matched the towel. On the plate was a partly eaten stack of cookies of all sorts.

I should have been excited by the cookies, but sitting at the table with me and the cookies was Bobby. He frowned at me. He knew there was a switcheroo with my clothes, and this story about being a dedicated police girl was a pile of bunkum that clearly Doctor was in on.

Bobby couldn't quiz me because the goblin was still there, plus a parade of Tootsie's people kept coming in and out. Slimming man stopped by to be upset about a carrot situation. Raw-food lady came by shortly thereafter to apologize for slimming man, while still saying he was absolutely correct to be upset. The avocado-hair lady needed more avocadoes of only a certain type. "No, those are the wrong ones." Dance teacher arrived to announce, "I'm hungry."

Gilbert paused in his pot stirring to make him a sandwich. The dance teacher sat down at the table with me and Bobby. He stared at the book Bobby was using to try to help with my reading.

"You should study the arts," the dance teacher informed us. "The arts are the foundation of all learning." Then he talked about something he did at something called the Sorbonne, which didn't make any sense. "Yes, I have a reputation for being difficult, but that is who I am."

By the time he finished his sandwich and popped up to leave, Bobby also had to go home. Before he left, Bobby whispered in my ear, "You need to tell me the truth, Sparky."

I did need to tell him the truth.

But I couldn't.

I went to my room fully intending to go to sleep. Before I changed into my pajamas, I sat with Clara Bell and her boyfriend, the flat leopard. They always understood.

"How can I tell Bobby I was sneaking up in the Hollywood Hills, talking with Knucklehead, stealing Onion Girl's silver dog, and giving it to Chum-Chum? Besides, I don't think Bobby even wants Bookie outta the pen. He thinks Bookie is a crook. Okay, he is a crook, but I can't talk to Bobby about that."

The leopards didn't say anything, but they never did. I leaned back against my bed. I needed to talk with someone.

It's then that I made my decision. Sure, it was late and I was beyond tired. Even so, I'd sneak to the weird pet shop and visit Cornelius. Hadn't he said he wanted to talk?

This was something I really couldn't tell Bobby.

The basement pet shop was open, as always. At the bottom of the building's exterior stairs, a sign painted on the shop's glass-paned door warned: "Poisonous Beasts Inside. Step at Your Risk Please." Through the door's gauzy curtain, I saw Cornelius, pencil in hand, bent over books at the front counter.

Probably doing homework. When I came here this summer, he was always reading some weird book with a strange symbol on the cover. With books, he was exactly like Bobby.

I pushed the door open. His head popped up. Through the fringe of his black hair, I saw his dark eyes pop. Then, in a second, he smoothed back into his cool look and his eyes disappeared behind his hair. "I knew you'd come."

I didn't like anyone guessing my moves, but he had me there. I'd come.

I'd planned to talk about Bookie, Monkey Island, all the crazy business I'd been through while trying to get Bookie out, and how happy I'd be when things were back to normal, and Bookie was back in his five-and-dime.

Now that I was here I realized I couldn't talk about that. Cornelius didn't know I ran for a crook named Bookie. He suspected I'd done some second-story work "borrowing" jewels. But he didn't know the half of it. I also remembered Bookie and Chum-Chum didn't like old Dr. Arcanum and his pet shop. There was history between them from back in their carnival days. That history was a mystery to me. What I did know was Bookie and Chum-Chum would be mighty mad if they found out I was talking about them with this kid in this particular pet shop.

I hadn't thought about that. Now I wasn't sure what to say, what to do.

So I looked at my toes and mumbled, "Tell me about this South Seas business."

I could tell he was trying to keep his cool, mysterious air, but he was too excited. "Come this way." He waved for me to follow him to the back of the store.

The bald monkey, who always wore a boy's sailor suit, pulled its eyes away from the peephole in the wall above the high shelf where it liked to perch. The monkey chattered quietly and watched us curiously. I knew that the owner of the shop, the real Dr. Arcanum, was behind the wall. Was he asleep? Was he out somewhere? Would the monkey tell on us?

As if reading my mind (or did he read my mind?), Cornelius said, "Never mind the monkey."

We walked by the sawdust-filled wire pen on the floor in back where the guinea pig and rooster and their math books lived. Both were busy making notations on paper, with the guinea pig clutching the pencil in its mouth and the rooster in its beak. It was obvious Cornelius spent a lot of time training the pig and rooster to do counting tricks. He denied it. He said their mathematical achievements could not be explained by science, or some baloney like that. He also called the rooster Dr. Arcanum, and he called the guinea pig Professor Mysterium. It was a weird shop, and the kid was just as weird.

Beneath shelves filled with glass pens housing scuttling spiders, lizards, and creatures I couldn't quite see hiding under rocks, was a hefty old trunk. Cornelius grabbed it with both arms and used all his weight to wiggle and slide it out from under the shelves.

Then he pulled out a slim chain that was looped around his neck and hidden beneath his black shirt. At the end of the chain was a heavy old key. Without taking it from the chain, he bent forward and put it into the rusted padlock holding the trunk shut. He struggled and waggled the key here and there. I could have offered to pick it for him. Would have taken me two seconds for an old lock like that. But I wasn't in the mood. Let him figure it out.

With a few more waggles mixed with angry muttering, the padlock popped open. Cornelius slid the key beneath his shirt again. He pulled the trunk lid open. "My grandfather's stuff. Plus, my own research."

Inside were piles of yellowed paper with strange, black writing on them, a model ship, lots of maps, brightly colored boxes. That's only what I could see on top.

"My grandfather was a powerful, mystic warrior prince in Korea. He had many jealous enemies, who forced him to flee to America."

My first thought was bill collectors were probably the enemies on his tail. But maybe that was just me.

"These are his writings. You see, he went back to Korea with my dad to reclaim their lands and positions. Unfortunately, their enemies captured them. Right now, they are being held captive. Luckily, everything here is a clue. My goal is to put it all together, then stow away across the ocean, rescue them, and reclaim my rightful place as well. I am a prince too."

He looked up from the papers, swished the hair from his face, and looked me boldly in the eyes.

This was all very interesting but sounded kind of hinky to me. But maybe that's just me. "So did you hear anything from them after they left for Korea?"

"No. I told you, they're captives. They were ambushed at midnight and captured after a long sword fight."

"So how do you know all this, then?"

The kid rolled his eyes up and sighed like I only had two brain cells. Though, a lot of people thought I only had two brain cells.

"Did Dr. Arcanum tell you that?"

"Partly. He gave me the trunk."

I thought for a minute. "Dr. Arcanum is your other grandfather?"

The kid didn't answer and seemed more annoyed than ever. That was a touchy subject. I'd best move on to something else. I pointed to the weird writing. "You know how to read that?"

He liked this question better. "I'm learning, and I am getting better at it."

"Is this stuff your dad wrote?"

"No. As far as I can tell, these are advertisements for work in America. But there's more books here about philosophy that I think he wrote."

Maybe his grandad did write highbrow books and was a prince. Or maybe ol' granddad came to America looking for work, hoping to escape bill collectors. Then he realized the streets weren't paved with gold. When he scraped together enough dough, he and his grown-up son, Cornelius's dad, took off without a word, leaving the boy with his other, weird pet shop granddad, who was good at telling stories.

But maybe that's just me.

I kind of felt bad for him. I was tempted to ask where his mom was, but that would likely be another hornet's nest. She might be on to husband #2 or #3 or whatever. All the kid had was his granddad, Dr. Arcanum. Cornelius was sort of like me. I had a fake family nowadays with Gilbert and Tootsie. But actual family? Nah, not since my mom died a few years back.

"What does Dr. Arcanum think about you leaving?"

The kid moved his eyes away, thinking. "He said that I should wait until I'm grown up before going to Korea because, that way, I can get an actual job as a sailor and get paid for it.

He said if I stow away, they'll make me work for free when they catch me. But I don't care. It won't really be working for free because I'm trading for my passage across the ocean."

This whole going-across-the-ocean business was sounding more dicey by the minute.

He sensed my doubts. "Listen, I'm getting better at reading Korean. Soon, I may be able to read well enough to put all the clues together from this trunk. There's an old Korean guy who is teaching me Korean. In trade, I let him try to stump Dr. Arcanum and Professor Mysterium with math problems he comes up with."

"I guess. Is Korea far away?"

"Very far! But there's lots of stops on the way. There's tropical islands with warm beaches and coconut palm trees, like Hawaii and the Philippines."

That sounded pretty good to me. "Korea is tropical too?"

"No. It's cold. It snows a lot."

What?

"Enduring the cold is what strengthens a stoic mystic prince."

I felt myself slumping. If I went with him, and that was a huge "if," I could jump ship in Hawaii and let Cornelius keep on going. He could hunt down his runaway dad and granddad on his own. They'd probably just hit him up for money if he ever found them.

This was silly wishful thinking for me. First of all, Bookie would never allow me to stow away to Korea or Hawaii or anywhere else. He expected me to stay on Bunker Hill and work for him.

The kid prattled on about Korea and the Pacific Ocean as he pulled out maps. He pointed out important things to remember about sailing by using the model ship.

I decided to ask Bobby about Hawaii and the Pacific Ocean tomorrow. Even though I'd never go, I'd ask, just for the heck of it. Bobby was always saying I needed to learn things, right?

I told the kid I had to go. It was getting late. He looked me in the eye, gave me a top-secret smile, and said, "We'll talk more later."

Yeah, later.

I was so wiped out by the time I snuck back to Creepy House, I didn't have the energy to change into my pajamas or crawl into bed. I fell asleep on the floor next to Clara Bell and her boyfriend.

I slept well because I knew tomorrow morning, Bookie would be free.

FRIDAY

was shocked awake. It was morning. Someone was kicking Clara Bell. That's what woke me. I rolled over to see who it was.

Doctor.

"I won't ask you where you crept off to last night. But I will ask you to get up and I will drive you to school. Off the floor, now. Get into the kitchen." He turned and walked out of my room.

Doctor wasn't going to ruin my mood today. This was a great day because Bookie was getting out.

I bounded to the kitchen. I didn't even bother changing into my pajamas so I could pretend I fell asleep in my bed. I figured Gilbert would be busy with audition business and wouldn't notice.

I was right. His face was red with concentration as he shredded orange peels. All the while, hair lady #2 looked over his shoulder and insisted, "Thinner, thinner. These peels must be as thin as a slice of air."

Doctor reappeared, lurking around the kitchen doorway to make sure I didn't skip school today. I ignored him.

I was so anxious to look through the morning newspapers I almost didn't notice the round cake in the middle of the table. It was golden brown and flecked with spices. Its center was piled with chunky strawberry jam that shone with sugar. The goblin had already left me a big slice on a plate with a strawberry pattern that matched the cake. It smelled amazing. I stuck my nose so close, it got smeared with strawberry jam. Next, the jam and cake were in my mouth, where they just about melted. Yes, today was a good day.

Back to the papers. As I chewed more bites of cake, I flipped through the pages. My smile started to falter as I saw page after page had nothing about Bookie being innocent. In fact, there was nothing at all about the Monkey Island murder, as the papers were calling it. The only mention of Monkey Island was a bit about the city shutting it down because it was a danger to health or something like that. There were more close-up photos of the new Mayor snarling at the camera and headlines about him "Cracking Down on Crooks." But no Bookie.

I went through all the papers a second time. Again, there was nothing. I realized Doctor had crept closer and was watching me, curious. "Looking for something?"

"No!"

"Good. Then take your bath. You're filthy."

Maybe Chum-Chum needed more time. That was it. With Chicago in the picture, everything could be more complicated. I had to believe in Chum-Chum, trust him.

Though Bookie always told me never to trust Chum-Chum.

I was so worried about what was taking Chum-Chum so

long, I barely heard Doctor complaining on the drive to school about the sparkles I'd jammed in the seat crevice, and the rat turds I'd left in his shoes.

I was about to tell him they were bunny turds, until I remembered the young cop ordered me not to tattle about Officer Bun-Bun because she was a cop secret.

In class, there was another drawing on my chair. I think it was supposed to be me in clown shoes. "Where's your clown shoes, oinker girl," a boy whispered as he passed my desk. He wasn't oinker boy, my usual tormentor. That meant more kids decided the oinking nonsense was funny and wanted to join in. Just what I needed.

There was more snickering and tittering. Miss Clark had to do a lot of ruler banging on her desk. All the while my mind whirled over Chum-Chum and Bookie. Did Chum-Chum double-cross me? Did he take the silver dog and actor autograph and abandon Bookie? No, he couldn't have. Or could he?

Then I was dreaming of Chum-Chum laughing at me. He had a ruler too, and he was banging it on my desk. Only it wasn't Chum-Chum, it was Miss Clark.

"Young lady, class is not the place to take a nap."

Lots of snickering from the real clowns in the back row.

"I wasn't sleeping!" That got a big laugh. It also got me sent to Mrs. Bean.

Mrs. Bean wasn't annoyed, but smiled like seeing me was good news. "Let me round up more books about Carla for you to look at."

As I poked through the stack of books, I realized me and Carla had something in common. She had a lot of people out to get her, kind of like I did.

There was the bad cowboy who chased Carla and Midnight while flying his airship mounted with machine guns. Luckily, Midnight could run fast. There was the rich rancher lady who stole everybody's water and prowled in a submarine through the underground rivers and lakes filled with the stolen water. The submarine had mechanical attack alligators the rancher lady sicced on Carla and Midnight. Luckily, Midnight could swim fast. Then there was the evil professor who was jealous of the nice schoolmarm who helped Carla and Midnight by using clues from books. Hmm. Maybe that's why Mrs. Bean liked these stories. When the evil professor wasn't trying to kidnap the schoolmarm and force her to marry him, he built robot horses to go after Carla and Midnight. Luckily, Carla and Midnight disguised themselves as robots and tricked the evil robot horses.

Okay, maybe I didn't have robots after me, but I had Doctor and LT and the oinking kids at school.

Carla and Midnight also got help from Flash, a wild stallion and leader of the wild horse herd that Midnight originally came from. The wild horses kept an eye out for anything suspicious, like airships or robots. When Carla and Midnight saw Flash standing on Signal Cliff, they knew he had something to pass along. Midnight ran to Flash to get the news, then ran back to tell Carla, who understood horse talk perfectly. Flash couldn't tell Carla anything directly because of something I couldn't figure out, so asked Mrs. Bean to read it to me: "The sacred oath of all horse ancestors going back down through the depths of time unknown forbids wild horses from sharing horse words with humans." I still couldn't figure that out. Maybe since Midnight wasn't wild anymore, he could talk with Carla? If I could read better, it probably would make sense.

I did like these books, even though they were books. I wondered if Cornelius was heading in the wrong direction with his plan to cross the Pacific. He should travel the other way to the Wild West. It seemed more interesting.

After the lunch bell rang, Mrs. Bean told me I could sneaky-eat my lunch in the library again. When I popped the lid off the tin, I nearly passed out. Along with my sandwich, the goblin had packed a giant slice of chocolate cake with thick, thick creamy frosting. I showed it to Mrs. Bean.

"I think whoever packs your lunch loves you very much," she smiled.

Really? Was that what this cake meant?

I felt stunned and just sat in my chair, nibbling the cake and considering this, until I felt myself drifting to sleep again. The clanging bell for recess woke me up with a jerk. Quickly, I closed my lunch tin and hid it in my school bag. I shoved the stack of *Carla* books onto a chair so Bobbie wouldn't see them. I slipped my favorite, the one about the treasure map, back into my book bag.

Cornelius strolled in. He gave me his meaningful look before going to his usual table in the corner of the library. Bobby came not long after. "You weren't at lunch again."

Before he started lecturing me, I got my question in: "How long does it take to go across the Pacific Ocean? Is it like from here to Pasadena?"

Bobby blinked at me, then said, "No. The Pacific Ocean is vast. If you took a train from Los Angeles to New York City, it still wouldn't be as far as traveling across the Pacific."

"What about Hawaii? Is that as far as Pasadena?"

This prompted Bobby to get books with maps and pictures so he could point out how absolutely wrong I was about how far apart things were in the Pacific Ocean. "Fortunately, in modern times, ships have engines, so it doesn't take as long to cross the Pacific as with the old sailing ships. Still, it's a long, long way from here to there."

I wondered if Cornelius realized that. At least my Pacific Ocean questions made Bobby forget that he wanted me to tell him the truth about what I'd been up to. He'd remember soon enough, but I'd worry about that later.

I fell asleep again in class, so got sent back to Mrs. Bean. "Well, hello, again, Sparky," she smiled.

I returned to Carla and Midnight until I fell asleep in the library.

The bell woke me up. I felt groggy but it was time to report to the cops.

After fetching Detective Bernie's sandwich, I was back to dealing with Officer Bun-Bun. It was Friday, which meant I was supposed to organize all her supplies and make sure the barrier around her pen was "so tight, not even brass eyeballs can get through it," as the young cop ordered.

When I was pushing the typewriter stands closer together, I

noticed the rabbit was standing on her hind legs and twitching her nose. She stared at me.

Suddenly, the young cop was behind me with his arms akimbo and hard stare. "You haven't given Officer Bun-Bun her apple slices."

"What apple slices?"

He paused so long I thought he'd forgotten about me, until he said, "An officer in the field must take initiative. I cannot follow you around to tell you every single thing to do."

Still, he showed me every single thing to do with the apples. It turned out they were in a sack next to the crate of lettuce and cucumbers. In the sack was a little knife. With the little knife I was supposed to cut the apple into slices that had to be "per standard."

When I dropped the apple slices in Bun-Bun's special apple bowl, she hopped and ran in circles around her pen before she settled down to dig into the apples. I guessed that meant she liked them. This satisfied the cop and he wandered away.

One of my organizing jobs was to sort Officer Bun-Bun's newspaper supply into "neat stacks per standard." There were a lot of papers. One pile toppled over as I was trying to straighten it. When I bent down to pick them up, I noticed one paper had flopped open to the obituary page.

Wait a minute, Knucklehead had said to check the obituaries for swanky cemeteries with freshly planted bodies. Here in Officer Bun-Bun's papers was exactly what I needed. I admit I made a bigger newspaper mess by digging through the stacks for the obituary pages. The problem, I soon realized, was there were a lot of dead people, and I had no idea which cemeteries were for the high rollers and which were for the working stiffs.

I was about to ball up the obituaries and throw them against the wall when I spotted that name: Claude Cavalerie. The washed-up actor, the one who wasn't the dead man in Monkey Island, despite what the rags said.

His obituary was short. Basically, Claude Cavalerie keeled over on the Red Car to Hollywood over the weekend. His claim to fame was playing "Reverend Dullness" in different silent movies. *Country Boy and the Flappers* was the most famous. Never heard of it, but maybe it was a big movie back in the day. No family, no photo.

The story was clear to me. This guy had been out of work for a few years since the talkies showed up. He'd never been a big star, so had no mansion or money stash to keep him afloat. He couldn't pay his rent and ended up living on the trains with a bottle of bathtub booze for company. The rotgut probably did him in. Another sad story.

What was most interesting to me was the date on the paper and in the obituary. The paper was Monday's morning edition, the Monday Bookie took me to Monkey Island. The obituary said "weekend," which meant Saturday or Sunday.

Claude Cavalerie was dead before Bookie set foot in Monkey Island. Was Claude picked for the body switch because he had no family, no neighbors, no friends who might question what was going on with his photos suddenly showing up in the papers along with stories claiming he really was murdered on Monday?

Who picked Claude Cavalerie? Was it Chicago? Chum-Chum? Did Whisper-Whisper have a hand in the goings-on?

I still hoped against hope that Chum-Chum would come through and help Bookie. But I worried more and more that he had double-crossed me.

The obituary mentioned there was no memorial service and he was already buried in a certain Hollywood cemetery.

That's where I needed to start.

I should have gone back to Creepy House, made an appearance, satisfied Doctor's suspicions, told Bobby something to get him off my back.

I didn't. I couldn't wait. After the cops were done with me, I headed straight to the pet shop.

When Cornelius looked up from his homework book, I announced, "I got a favor to ask you."

Cornelius was bouncy in his seat on the Red Car train to Hollywood. He could hardly believe we were going grave robbing, as he called it. "You're a really interesting girl, Sparky." He kept grinning.

I told him we were investigating a body switcheroo, not grave robbing. At least he was helping.

There was no need for me to drag a bunch of books to the cemetery, so I left my school bag at the shop. Cornelius found a shovel and a pickaxe in the yard behind the pet shop building. We brought those on the train with us. That got us some stares, but, otherwise, the passengers ignored us. Cornelius also grabbed a couple of canvas sacks "for the body." They weren't big enough for anything larger than a cat. I realized I hadn't thought about what we would do if we found Straw

Boater's body. I decided to worry about that when we found him.

I didn't want to tell Cornelius everything. Like I said, his granddad Dr. Arcanum was on the outs with Chum-Chum and Bookie over something that happened when they all ran with the carnivals. So I kept the story vague about why exactly we needed to go digging in this cemetery. I stuck to what the papers said about the Monkey Island murder, except that the guy who was supposed to be murdered, Claude Cavalerie, wasn't really murdered. It was another chap in a straw boater hat.

"It's *Cav Al Air Eee*, not *Cave Larry*. You're pronouncing Claude's name wrong. It's French," he said.

"Oh." I felt like a dummy, again. How come Bobby didn't tell me I was saying it wrong? Maybe Bobby only knew Spanish and was clueless about French.

Apart from how Claude's name was pronounced, as soon as Cornelius realized this favor of mine involved him going to a cemetery after dark and digging up graves, any details went in one ear and out the other. Whatever the reason for it, he was all in. Cornelius was a weird kid.

But if he was weird, what did that make me? I was the one who asked him to help me dig in graves.

Cornelius knew roughly where this cemetery was. When we got off the Red Car, we wandered the sidewalks looking for it. The pickaxe was heavy, so I started dragging it. The dragging metal made a loud noise on the cement sidewalks. Cornelius offered to carry both. Then he got tired and started dragging the shovel and the pickaxe. I think anyone could hear us coming a mile away.

I was about to tell him that we should just ditch the shovel and pickaxe, when we saw a high brick wall at the next street corner. The wall continued for several blocks along the main street, and continued even farther up the side street.

"This is it!" Cornelius announced.

Before I could stop him, he ran across the side street, reached the wall, then jumped and shoved the pickaxe over the wall. He jumped two more times before he was able to push the shovel over. I heard crunching like they landed in bushes on the other side.

When I reached him, he said, "I'll boost you over."

"That's okay. I can get over." I wasn't a primo second-story girl for nothing.

I backed up, took off running, jumped, got the toe of one shoe in the gap between the bricks, got my other shoe in a gap higher up, then boosted myself up to the top of the brick wall. The trick was to get enough running speed, and that would shoot me to the top. Of course, it would have been easier with bare feet, but I managed.

Being careful not to fall off the wall to the other side, I swiveled around and held one hand down to him. "Get a running start like I did and jump like you did a second ago; then grab my hand."

Cornelius didn't quite have the knack. He did run, jump, and grab my hand, but he nearly pulled me down. Fortunately, he was taller than me and managed to slap one hand on top of the wall with a second jump. After a bit of struggle, we both tumbled down into the cemetery's shrubbery.

"We're in!" Cornelius said.

"Keep it down. There's gotta be cemetery bulls around."

"Who?"

"Guards looking for prowlers like us." I suddenly realized I should have gone back to Creepy House to raid Tootsie's closets for dark clothes. In my white sailor dress, I must have stood out in the dark like a spotlight. At least Cornelius always wore black.

"Got it. Cemetery bulls." He grinned. This was fun for him. For me, it was high stakes. Bookie's neck was in a noose.

But, like I said, at least he was helping.

The pickaxe had jammed itself into the bushes, so we left it. The cemetery was mostly grass, so the shovel made less noise as Cornelius dragged it, unless it bumped over a flat stone marker. Clang!

The cemetery was huge. There were sobbing angel statues and fountains like Knucklehead mentioned, a few trees, headstone after headstone of all sizes, and little stone houses for the really high-end customers. "Where do you suppose he is?" Cornelius asked. He pulled out a cigarette lighter and flicked it on. Didn't help.

So we wandered. As we turned the corner of a particularly large stone house, we came upon a man sitting on a stone bench in front of a row of headstones.

He turned when he heard Cornelius's shovel bang on the stone pavers alongside the stone house. I was about to turn and run for it when the man said, "Ah, my little fan! You do follow me everywhere."

It was the actor from yesterday morning who bought me ice cream and cookies and gave me the autograph that Chum-Chum now had in his grubby hands. Tonight, he was dressed in fancy formal gear, complete with white gloves and top hat.

"I was just telling my friends the good news," he said to me. "The audition went well. I got the part!"

There weren't any friends, only tombstones. But none of my business. I felt Cornelius freeze behind me, unsure what to do.

I knew the part to play. "Oh, wow! Of course, you did well! You're the best actor in the whole world!" I jumped up and down for good measure.

Even in the cemetery shadows, I could tell he lit up with one of his huge sunshine smiles. Then his attention drifted to the headstones. "Fans, they are such a handful. I miss them so much."

He sure wasn't talking to me. Before he got too involved in conversing with the dead people, I asked, "Say, I'm hoping to pay respects to an actor who passed just a few days back, Claude Cavalerie." I was careful to pronounce his name how Cornelius said it. "Do you know him?"

His head turned quickly back to me. For a second there I worried he'd get catty and huffy that I was asking about some other actor besides himself, but he seemed sad. "He's no longer with us? I didn't hear. He turned to the headstones. "He was such a friendly fellow. Quite a talented dancer, but would never get cast in those roles because he was a little on the hefty side. He mainly played reverends, poor thing."

"Do you know where he might be in this place?"

He looked back toward me. If he noticed the kid in black standing behind me with a shovel, he wasn't bothered. "Oh, poor Claude. So many fell on difficult times. Most likely, I suspect he is in the charity section. But at least it's there for actors in need. It's in the far back over there." He pointed to a particularly dark area that didn't have fountains or sobbing statues.

Then the actor was back to chatting with the headstones. "I was remembering the parties we used to go to. Do you remember how we'd be out all night and we'd toast the dawn and still be ready for more? I miss those days, don't you?"

I left him to it.

"You know everybody," Cornelius said to me as we stumbled our way to the dark corner of the cemetery.

"Hardly! Do you know who that guy is?"

"No, but he looks famous."

It was so dark in the poor actor's section, Cornelius had to use his lighter a lot. There were no headstones, only metal sticks holding up thin metal squares with names that looked like they had been scratched into the metal with the end of a nail.

Cornelius held his lighter up to each square. "Nope, nope, nope." None of the graves looked fresh either.

"I don't think he's here," I said. "Maybe we should backtrack or. . . ." Suddenly, I was tipping, then flying through the air. I was too surprised to scream. The flying lasted about a second, until I landed on dirt.

Out of the blackness above me appeared Cornelius's face glowing from his lighter's flame. "Wow, Sparky, you fell into an open grave." He was grinning from ear to ear. He moved the lighter away. "I can't find the metal square. Wait, here it is. It's been knocked over." He paused, then read, "Claude Cavalerie. It's him!" His face popped back at the top of the grave. "Is Claude down there? Did you break through his coffin?" The kid was giddy. If I wasn't so stunned from falling in a grave, I would have been tempted to jump up and sock him.

I looked around while the kid held up his light. There was

no broken wooden coffin, but there were chunks of what probably used to be a cheap cardboard coffin. "Claude is gone, but Straw Boater isn't here either."

Somebody dug up Claude Cavalerie and took him. But why didn't they make the switch with Straw Boater?

Cornelius held the end of the shovel down so I could grab it. The dirt fell away as I tried climbing up. I ditched both my shoes in the grave so I could grip better with my toes. Once on top again, Cornelius moved his lighter over me and poked me here and there. "Nothing broken. That's good."

Now I could see the scene better. The dirt from the grave was heaped in messy piles that spilled on top of other graves and bent their spindly metal markers. "Somebody got to this grave before us," Cornelius said. "But it's still been fun."

Fun for him.

Suddenly, shouting erupted from the other side of the cemetery. "Hey! Hey! Who's there!"

I saw two hulking forms rushing toward us through the shadows. They must have seen Cornelius's lighter or heard the commotion when I tumbled into Claude Cavalerie's empty grave.

I yanked Cornelius's arm. "Run!"

He ditched the shovel, his canvas sacks, his lighter, and ran with me. The cemetery bulls were gaining. They flicked on flashlights and swung them around the statues and fountains. We ran to the section where the actor still chatted with the headstones. "Remember when your wealthy admirer filled your pool with champagne, and we all jumped in? Who knew the bubbly stung so much."

We ducked behind the stone house as the bulls reached the

actor. We peered around the corner to spy on what was happening.

The bulls suddenly became polite. "Sir, we did not see you there. We're sorry but there have been prowlers lately."

"Prowlers? No, I think it is fans seeking my autograph. Why just this morning, a fan followed me to the beach. They are so persistent. But she was happy when I autographed a bag of cookies."

My heart skipped a beat. Would he tell them I was lurking around the cemetery right now looking for Claude Cavalerie? Luckily, his attention wandered. He turned away from the bulls and said to the headstones, "Remember when that woman asked you to sign her poodle?"

"Of course, we will make sure to send fans directly to you, sir," one of the bulls said. "Sorry to disturb. You have a good evening." They must have been used to this guy visiting the headstones.

The bulls swept their flashlights back toward Claude Cavalerie's grave and trotted in that direction.

We trotted the opposite way until we found the wall again. The brick on the inside of the wall was covered with white stucco, so there were no toeholds for me. I had to clamber up Cornelius's back to reach the top of the wall. Then he jumped and grabbed my hands. His weight nearly pulled me back down into the cemetery, face first. Eventually, he got to the top of the wall. We both fell off the wall and landed outside the cemetery.

Back on the Red Car, we were a bedraggled mess, especially me. I was barefoot and covered head to toe in grave dirt.

A broad sat near us. Her dyed hair was carrot-red. She wore

a snug purple dress patterned with orange stars. Her orange t-strap pumps were dotted with star-shaped cutouts that showed purple underneath. She stared at us while chewing gum. She blew a big pink bubble with her carrot-colored lips, then said to me, "Girl, you need yourself a new man."

This startled Cornelius. He blinked. But it was time to get off at our downtown stop.

He wanted me to come back with him to the pet shop so we could talk about what had happened.

"Nah, I gotta get back to my house." I was sore and beat. I needed to crawl into my bed. "But we do need to talk. If Straw Boater wasn't in that grave, then we gotta look for him in the tunnels."

This intrigued Cornelius. "Tunnels! I'm working the shop all day tomorrow because it's Saturday. Stop by and tell me all about it."

I was glad he was happy about the tunnels because I sure wasn't. There wouldn't just be Straw Boater and Claude Cavalerie in the tunnels, but a whole bunch of dead people. Who knew what shape they'd be in.

I'd think about that tomorrow. Now I had to get to bed.

Before I slipped inside Creepy House's back French doors, I shook as much grave dirt off me as I could. I should have taken a bath, but I worried the pipe noises might wake people. What if Doctor discovered me and demanded to know what I'd been up to? No, thanks.

I crept toward my room as quietly as I could. I was startled when I heard Mr. Exercise and the dance teacher arguing in a room nearby.

"You are a fraud!"

"No, *you* are a fraud!"

"How dare you!"

"No, how dare *you*!"

Good. They were too busy spatting to notice me.

Safely in my room, I pulled Clara Bell close to my bed. I dragged her boyfriend on top so I could snuggle next to him. "I'm scared for Bookie," I told them.

They stared at me with their glass eyes. I knew they cared. That's all that mattered right now.

SATURDAY

I cracked my eyelids open to the sun warming the clear glass transoms above the colored glass panes of my bedroom windows. I felt so stiff, so sore, I wanted to stay in bed and hide from the world.

I knew I had to get moving, get to the bathtub, and wash off the cemetery dirt before anyone saw me. Oh, but it was hard.

Even though it was early, Creepy House was in chaos. On my way to my bathroom, I had to duck behind a pair of vases that were as tall as me and painted with long-tailed, flapping birds. The hand lady was in tears. "Her audition is Monday, and the ancient crystal hand soak won't nearly be ready!"

"Snap out of it." That was one of the face broads. She snapped her fingers in front of hand lady's face for good measure.

"In this business," the other face broad growled, "if you don't toughen up, another hand lady will come up behind you and eat you alive."

This only made the hand lady wail.

While they were busy with the hand-soaking crisis, I slipped from behind the vases and darted to the bathroom. The goblin had already been there. I shouldn't have been surprised. He'd laid out a fresh sailor suit for me. Because it was the weekend, with no school today, this wasn't a dress. It was a white sailor shirt with blue trim and a roomy front pocket and pair of matching short pants. This was the outfit I got used to wearing this summer after I landed in Creepy House.

He'd also laid out a pair of shoes for me, but I left them in the bathroom. No school meant no rules forcing me to wear shoes.

I stood on the stool by the sink to look in the mirror. Shrimpy's bruise had faded. I still had tons of scratches and scabs on my legs from rolling down Onion Girl's drive. There wasn't anything I could do about those. I hoped no one would notice because I usually had a lot of scabs. When I was as presentable as I could make myself, I finally headed to the kitchen. I hadn't eaten last night, and now my growling stomach was making me pay for it.

Goblin was sweating as he ground stacks of green leaves into a paste. He saw me. "Sparky! I have something special for you today. I am so sad that you have been starving all week. I must make this up to you."

With all the pastries he'd been feeding me, I was hardly starving. He didn't say a peep about me not being home for dinner last night. Was he so busy with Tootsie's audition he hadn't noticed?

Doctor was in the kitchen. He stared darkly at me. He'd noticed. He'd probably covered for me, again.

After wiping his stained green hands, goblin brought me a plate covered with a black-and-gold dish towel printed with jazzy rectangles. With a big smile, he whisked the towel away to reveal a matching plate piled with pancakes—pancakes!—steaming with melting syrup and mounded with baked banana and apple slices.

I was overcome. I dove in, grabbing the first pancake with my hands and shoving it in my mouth. It was chewy and soft and melty and so warm all at the same time. It glided down my throat to my waiting tummy.

"Doctor was so kind to drive to a special restaurant downtown for these pancakes just for you because I cannot cook anything until after Mademoiselle's audition on Monday. Doctor is so proud that you volunteered for extra time to help the police yesterday. I told Doctor that you must have a special treat today."

Yep, Doctor had covered for me.

The pancakes turned into cement in my mouth. I had to keep eating like I was happy because Gilbert watched me, smiling and so proud of what a good little police girl I was. He trotted over with a fork, knife, and spoon. "She is so hungry she cannot wait for me to serve her properly." He beamed.

As if this morning couldn't get worse, my eyes strayed to the newspapers on the table. I quickly shuffled through them. There was more about the Mayor "crushing crime," but nothing about Bookie or grave robbers in the Hollywood cemetery. This was not good news.

I shoved the pancakes down as best I could. "These are great," I mumbled, trying to sound happy. "I gotta get going."

As I stood from the table, Doctor said in his quiet voice,

"Your Bobby is coming today to help with your studies. Because you were so busy with the . . . police . . . yesterday evening, he missed seeing you." Doctor's lip curled as he glowered at me.

Right, Bobby. I suddenly realized I'd left my school bag with my books at the pet shop. I'd better hurry to the pet shop to fetch it. Cornelius and I also had to start our planning, because I had dead bodies to deal with. "Yeah, sure. I'll be back. I'll just be out for a second." I took off.

As I hurried through the sunroom to the back French doors, I came upon Tootsie sprawled on the floor, with Mr. Exercise pulling her arms and dance teacher pulling her legs. "Stretch!" Mr. Exercise commanded. "You will become taller!" dance teacher encouraged. Mr. Beele prowled about, watching. Tootsie was wrapped in denim bands again. Different colors of goo oozed from everywhere onto sheets spread beneath her.

"Ahhhhhh," came from Tootsie. They were tearing her apart! No, it was Mr. Beele's voice coaching. "You must warm your vocal cords. Give me a longer ahhhhhh." Tootsie complied.

As she was doing her ahhs, she spotted me. "There you are, protecting us from crime and things," she said cheerfully. This got Beele's attention. He peered at me. "It seems to be up to no good."

Then, with a stronger pull from Mr. Exercise and dance teacher, and a "Ooooow!" from Tootsie, I was forgotten. I noticed those two were mouthing at each other across Tootsie's stretched form: "You're a fraud," "No, *you're* a fraud," "How dare you," "No, how dare *you*."

I was the fraud. How dare I pretend to Gilbert and Tootsie otherwise.

But I had to help Bookie.

When I got to the pet shop, Cornelius was eagerly waiting for me. He showed me another shovel he found. "If we need to drag the bodies out of tunnels, we need more than a shovel. We need a horse," he pointed out.

He was right about that. If we had found Straw Boater's body in Claude Cavalerie's grave last night, we would have been in a bind because I hadn't planned on how to do any body moving.

Bookie said that not making careful plans was the same as dancing up to the cops and turning yourself in because the result would be the same.

If Bookie had planned this body-searching operation, it would sure have been going more smoothly than it was now.

"Yeah, a horse would help." The problem was, I didn't have a horse. The only horse I knew about on Bunker Hill was Dodger, the ex-movie-star horse owned by Marigold's great-uncle Old Bob, who trained stunt horses for movies and sometimes worked as a movie cowboy. Dodger hated me. Old Bob, with his dangerous cowboy six-shooter, hated me even more.

"We can borrow Dodger!" Cornelius said.

My eyes popped. I couldn't believe this. But I should have. All the kids on Bunker Hill knew about Dodger. One of Old Bob's side businesses was having Dodger drag kids around on a cart for birthday parties.

"Maybe we can find another horse," I said, hoping he'd go for it.

"Dodger will be perfect. We can ask Marigold."

This was getting worse and worse. "You know Marigold?" I shouldn't have to ask. Everybody knew Marigold and his charming smile.

"Of course I know Marigold. His uncle Old Bob comes in here all the time to rent animals for the movies he works on. He does more than train horses to do stunts." Cornelius pointed to the puppy-sized lizard on the floor that tugged at the end of its leash while flicking its tongue. "He's trained Damocles to stand on his hind legs and open his mouth like he's about to breathe fire. Damocles played a dragon in a couple of movies already."

I stared at the lizard. He was bigger than any of the other lizards in the shop, but, "He's kind of small for a dragon."

"What the movie people do is build a model castle. When Damocles stands next to it, he's towering over the castle towers. Then Old Bob takes Damocles away and the movie people set fire to the toy castle. But when you watch the movie in the theater, you see Damocles opening his mouth, and in the next second the castle is on fire. It looks like Damocles set the castle on fire. It looks really neat. That was in *Baron Horror and the Castle of Doom* and *Barron Horror's Revenge*."

I looked at the lizard flicking its tongue. "I guess."

"Marigold comes here with his uncle. He also comes by himself so we can study together. He's in a different school and is a grade before me, but he's also in an advanced academic class so it works out."

Figures Marigold was in a smarty-pants class.

"When Marigold's here, that's the only time Cornelius," and the kid pointed to the bald monkey in the sailor suit perched by its spy hole, "comes to the front counter. Him and Marigold are great friends. Cornelius is a star too. He's been in a whole bunch of movies since way back in the silent days."

The monkey eyed both of us. It curled its lip at me. Everybody adored Marigold, didn't they?

Wait a minute, what did he call the monkey? "I thought your name was Cornelius?"

The kid's happy face turned into a frown. "I go by Dr. Arcanum," he cooly informed me.

Okay then. He must not like Cornelius like I didn't like Ambrosia. I wondered if old Dr. Arcanum named his grandson after the monkey. Could be. Marigold was rumored to be named after one of Old Bob's stunt horses.

"I'm sure Marigold will help us out," he said without looking at me. "His uncle does a lot of business with us. In fact, most of the shop's earnings come from movies." He pushed things about on the front counter like he was busy. He wasn't. He was ignoring me.

How was I supposed to know he was sensitive about his name? I should have suspected as much after Bobby told me some of the kids in school called him Corny.

"Though we have to be careful not to take up too much of Marigold's time. He is extra busy lately since his uncle started helping him get into the movies. He has an important audition coming up."

"Marigold wants to be an actor?" I should have known. He thought he was full of pizzazz.

Cornelius sighed like I'd used up his last drop of patience. "You would know that if you spent more time with him. But I suppose you're busy studying with. . .the dead boy." That's what he called Bobby.

"I didn't want to go back to school in the first place. I was forced! Come on, get the bee outta your bonnet. We gotta locate some bodies."

The kid eyed me. At least I think he did. Hard to tell with his fringe of hair hanging in his eyes.

"The thing is," I told him, "Dodger kind of hates me. Maybe we can figure out another way to haul bodies."

"I heard about you throwing rocks at Dodger."

Marigold had a big mouth. "I didn't! Well, I didn't mean to. I was aiming at the birthday party parents. They wouldn't let me ride in the cart with the other kids. Okay, maybe I was crashing the party. But still."

"If you can figure out another body transportation system besides a horse, let me know."

This was the pickle I was in. Cornelius was right. We needed a horse, especially since the actor at the cemetery last night said Claude Cavalerie was hefty. I was slap outta any other ideas. I gave in. "Fine, let's talk to Marigold about Dodger. We'll also need that birthday party cart Dodger pulls. We can put the bodies in the cart."

"You have to go to Marigold by yourself, Sparky, because I have to mind the store all day. It is Saturday."

I would have told him what he could do with himself and his movie star lizard. But I needed his help. And I needed Dodger's help.

I sure was in a bind.

Marigold was in the little horse house off the alley. I heard him before I saw him. "That's a good boy, Dodger. Have another carrot."

I poked my head in the open top half of the horse door. "Hi Marigold." Everything I planned to say next about needing a horse for body hauling flew out of my head when I saw Marigold. His mom always dressed him in neatly ironed shirts that went with his bow tie, suspenders, and kid-sized suit and fedora. When Marigold was home messing around with Dodger, his golden-orange hair that matched his golden face, was neatly hidden beneath a kerchief. His mom only allowed her son's precious, pretty hair out in the world on Sunday for the other jealous church ladies to admire.

Today, a bigger kerchief wrapped around the top of Marigold's head and continued wrapping around his face so that only his eyes and mouth showed. Pink and green goo oozed out from behind the kerchief. Instead of his usual crisp shirt, he wore a rougher denim shirt with long sleeves. Goo dripped from his kerchief onto the denim shirt. I'd never seen Marigold like this. I was shocked.

Marigold gave me his sly, charming smile. "Well, hello, Sparky. How's school? Oh, don't mind me. My face and hair have to be just so for my very important audition coming up."

He'd turned into Tootsie.

"How's Bobby?" Marigold gave me his extra-wicked smile. Awhile back, Marigold dared steal a kiss from me, but I didn't break his nose like I broke Bobby's nose when he stole a kiss. Bobby didn't know this, and I wanted to keep it top secret from Bobby forever. So far, Marigold had never tattled to Bobby. But he gave me those knowing smiles.

"Bobby's fine. He's in the smart-kid class."

"Aren't we all." He left unsaid that the *we* didn't include *me*. I'm sure Marigold could guess I ended up in the dummy class.

"Are you here for study help?" he asked in a way that told me he knew full well I wasn't here about homework. His golden eyes danced. Marigold's mean great-uncle, Old Bob, had the same eye color, but on Old Bob's midnight-chocolate face, those golden eyes were like glittering snake eyes out to get me. I was nothing but a varmint to Old Bob. He threatened to string me up by my ankles a few times. Old Bob took this cowboy stuff seriously.

I launched into a long, rambling tale, steering clear of Knucklehead and Chum-Chum, and being extra vague about Bookie, but touching on a dead guy in Monkey Island who for sure wasn't the dead actor Claude Cavalerie, who was absent from his grave when I went looking for him last night with Cornelius. "So the long and the short of it is that Cornelius and me need to borrow you and Dodger and the birthday-kid cart to help us haul a couple of bodies."

Marigold, the smile never leaving his face, cocked his head at me. "He doesn't like being called that. It makes him mad."

"Cornelius? I'm not calling him Dr. Arcanum." I already knew one Doctor, and that was the one slithering around Creepy House. "What do you call him?"

"Archie."

"Archie?"

"Sure. It's short for Arcanum, as in Dr. Arcanum."

I rubbed my face. "Okay, I'll call him Archie."

"Ah, not so fast, Sparky. You have to ask his permission first."

"Come on! Okay, I'll ask. But will you help with the body problem?"

"You and your gangsters, Sparky. If my mom and my great-uncle found out you were talking with me, they'd string you up by your ankles." But Marigold kept smiling and didn't stop talking with me. "Let's see. When am I free? Not tomorrow. Church with my mom is an all-day thing, so Sunday is out. Tonight my great-uncle is having dinner with some movie people and he's bringing my mom along. They're going to discuss me and my career."

Marigold stood on my last nerve, once again. "So, tonight?"

"My other uncles will be babysitting me, but they're more flexible if they have a bribe. I'm sure you can get some nice booze from all your bootlegger friends."

That's not how it worked! Even if Bookie wasn't in the slammer, I couldn't ask him for hooch. Bootleg booze was valuable. Besides, he'd never give it to a kid like me and would get mad at me for asking. "How about some really nice pastries? Would your uncles like that?"

"Yes!"

I'd have to smuggle the pastries out of Creepy House, but that was doable.

Marigold said knew about the tunnels at the edge of downtown. He agreed to meet Cornelius, aka Archie, and me after dark whenever he could safely escape his house. He'd bring Dodger and the birthday-party cart. "We might be late," he smiled, "but we'll be there."

Time was ticking and I had to get back to Creepy House. Bobby and Doctor were likely looking for me.

I stopped by the pet shop to update Cornelius. He was back in his good mood. He was excited about the possibility of finding piles of bodies in the tunnels. I thought about asking if it was okay if I called him Archie, but then decided not to risk it in case he got mad all over again.

"Before I forget, where's my school bag? I left it here last night."

Cornelius's eyes darted away. "I'll get it," he said without looking at me. He retrieved it from behind the pet shop's counter and slid it across to me. His eyes still avoided me.

My fancy new school bag was ripped and covered with small, dirty handprints. The handprints continued to the inside and onto my books. I stared at Cornelius.

"The monkey got in it while we were out last night," he mumbled.

I looked up toward the monkey. It was watching me, grinning. Suddenly, it screamed with monkey laughter.

I ran out of the shop.

The rest of the day had better go more smoothly because tonight was going to be a long one.

Bobby didn't smile at me when I sat next to him at the kitchen table. He didn't say anything, but I could tell he was waiting for Tootsie's dance teacher to leave. The dance teacher was leaning against the kitchen counter and munching a sandwich while complaining to Bobby about Broadway. "So many cannot stand sheer, raw talent. It's a mediocre world we live in."

When dance teacher finished his sandwich, three cookies,

and his complaints, and wandered out of the kitchen, we were alone. I heard voices and commotion echoing from other parts of Creepy House, so everyone must still be busy preparing Tootsie for her audition.

"Were you out all night last night?" Bobby asked, still not smiling.

I wasn't in the mood for the third degree. "No, not all night."

Bobby leaned back in his chair and sighed.

The morning papers were still on the kitchen table, and they still didn't have good news about Bookie. A pile of school books that Bobby hoped would help me learn something were also on the table. It was a good thing he brought books, because I had to hide my school bag and books in my room before I went to the kitchen. I didn't want Bobby to see them and start asking why they were covered with monkey handprints.

What I was most interested in was in the middle of the table. On a large, black-and-white checked plate was a round ring of glistening, golden bread dotted with raisins and twisted together in a braid. In the middle of the ring, the goblin had stacked more of those delightful donuts. Goblin, you were my dream come true. I decided I'd only eat donuts and squirrel away the round raisin bread ring for bribing Marigold's uncles.

In front of me was another plate covered by a matching black-and-white checked dishcloth. I pulled it off. My sandwich. Come to think of it, I was hungry. While I ate it, Bobby continued to say nothing. I noticed he had a matching black-and-white plate with only crumbs left, plus a smear of chocolate that must have come from a donut. He'd been waiting a while for me.

"I can't sneak out of my house to follow you anymore," he finally said. "I got in a lot of trouble this summer when my parents found out I was disappearing at night. I was under house arrest. They're only now barely starting to trust me again. I worry about you, Sparky."

"I'm fine," I mumbled with a mouthful of sandwich.

"No, you're not. I know you, Sparky. You look tired, distracted. It's only been one week of school, and you've hardly been in class because you've either been in trouble or not even in school."

"The kids make weird drawings of me. No one likes me."

"I know. I'm sorry. I want you to be in the advanced academic class. The kids act better there."

"I'm too dumb for even the dummy class, so I'm not going to the smarty class any time soon."

"You shouldn't call it dummy class. It's remedial class. Sparky, you're lots smarter than you give yourself credit for. I know you. You've just been out of school for too long. Give yourself a chance. Let me help you."

To stop him from going on like this for hours, I said, "Sure. Let's study."

So, that's what we did the rest of the afternoon.

Doctor briefly slithered by and saw that I was there and being supervised by Bobby. Satisfied, he slithered away. At one point Bobby was about to cut pieces from the raisin bread ring for me and him. Thinking fast, I convinced him it wasn't very good, kind of yucky even, and he'd best stick with the donuts. Bobby bought it and took another donut instead, after first selecting a donut for me. Close call.

As the afternoon waned, Bobby had to go back home for

dinner with his parents. "We got a lot done today, Sparky. You see? You did it."

I didn't think reading about how Rover and Betsy found a ball was anything to shout about. But as long as Bobby was happy and out of my hair, that was a good thing.

As soon as Bobby was gone, I wrapped the braided raisin bread ring in the dishcloths that had covered our sandwiches. I tiptoed with it to the sunroom and hid it behind a poofy floor cushion next to the French doors. The bread would be easy for me to grab when I was able to sneak out.

When I returned to the kitchen, Gilbert was there. He was searching for limes. He was happy that Bobby and I had made short work of the raisin bread ring. "I will be sure to order another one."

He disappeared again, but not before placing the evening papers on the table. "I know you like to look for stories about our Mademoiselle," he smiled.

There was a small story about Tootsie, Onion Girl, and some other stars auditioning for some new movie. I was too distracted to pay it much mind. I was looking for something, anything about Bookie, Straw Boater, and grave robbers. Nothing.

This wasn't good.

Soon the goblin was back. Instead of making me a sandwich, he presented me with something else from the bakery. It was a pie, but not a fruit pie. It had a lot of tomatoes and onions in it. It wasn't bad.

"I am so glad you enjoyed it! I know you must be so tired of the same sandwiches every day."

After I polished off the pie and another donut, I said, "I

think I'll take these books Bobby left and go to my room to read them."

"Excellent! I am so happy you've taken to your studies." He beamed.

I couldn't help but feel like a heel. I was lying to everybody: Bobby, Tootsie, Gilbert. I sure hoped this would be the last time I'd have to sneak out to do bad things. Once Bookie was free, I could focus on being a good, normal kid like everyone wanted. Who knew, maybe I could really get in the smart class? Though I'd be happy if I could just get out of the dummy class.

In my room, the leopards helped me look through Bobby's books. There was more about what Betsy and Rover did with the ball. There was throwing and bouncing and a scary moment when everyone thought the ball was lost. But it turned up.

This summer, when Tootsie and Gilbert gave me this room, they also gave me a book about a boy and a girl and their happy family. That was still my favorite. I could get lost in the pictures.

But tonight, I reached in my ripped school bag for *Wild West Carla and the Mystery of the Lost Treasure Map.* I flipped through the pages. I could tell the monkey had also flipped through the book from the messy monkey prints it left. I couldn't make heads or tails of some words in the book. Mrs. Bean told me those words were Spanish. Carla clearly was a pro with the Spanish. Maybe Bobby was right about me learning Spanish.

In Carla's world, she didn't have a Bookie she had to work for. That meant she didn't have to worry about going through all kinds of crazy stunts to get him out of prison. Sure, she got into plenty of scrapes. But they were her scrapes, not Bookie scrapes. That was a big difference.

It would take me a while to puzzle through Carla's book. I got the idea that Carla and Midnight the Wonder Pony were lost in the treasure map cave, and they worried they might end up like the cowboy skeleton. I sure hoped they found their way out. "They should just ditch that stupid treasure and find the exit," I told the leopards. I could tell they agreed with me.

By the fading light outside my room's clear glass transom windows, I knew it was time for me to take off. I slipped through the hallways and successfully dodged Mr. Beele. He was heading in the direction of the kitchen. I'd bet he was looking for that bread ring. Too late, buster.

The sunroom was clear, so I grabbed the raisin bread ring from its hiding spot and hurried out the French doors.

I made a quick stop by the horse house, but Marigold wasn't there. Dodger's huge head suddenly shot out of the open top half of his horse house door and nearly knocked me over. He grabbed at the raisin bread ring with his big teeth. "Hey! Watch it!" When I held the bread out of his reach, Dodger tried to bite me.

Marigold appeared. He had changed out of his oozing-goo outfit and was back in his usual pressed shirt and neat kerchief. I did have to admit that there was more than the usual glow to his golden-orange face. Maybe there was something to this movie star goo.

"Keep it quiet," Marigold shushed me. But he still smiled. "My great-uncle and mom haven't left yet." He noticed the dishcloth-wrapped bundle I was holding. "Is that it?"

I nodded and handed it to him. Dodger tried grabbing it. "Take it easy, Dodger," Marigold said. "I'll trade you a carrot for this. How about that?"

I left Marigold and the horse to work it out. I hurried to the pet shop.

At the shop, Cornelius was in an excited mood. He had the other shovel he found, along with more canvas sacks and an old lantern with a candle inside. The lantern's metal frame was dented and only one of its four glass panes was left. Cornelius stashed a book of matches in his pocket. "Ready when you are," he grinned.

We were able to take a tram most of the way to the tunnels, but then we had to walk. Cornelius got tired of carrying the shovel and started dragging it. The shovel clanged on the sidewalk.

When we got close to the tunnels, we spotted a group of older boys smoking and horsing around. They were the same characters that made my life miserable in dummy class. "Let's sneak around these guys," Cornelius whispered. I wondered if they were the ones who called him Corny.

It turned out there wasn't a good path to sneak around the boys. So we had to hide behind a large *Do Not Enter Danger-ous Tunnels* sign and wait. What was left of the sun disappeared. The shadows deepened. Before long, the boys started arguing and scuffling. Then they took off in two different groups while shouting insults at each other.

Coast was clear.

It was dark now. The weedy area around the tunnels had no lights and was far from any houses with glowing windows. We could hardly see. Cornelius lit the lantern's candle with one of the matches from his pocket. Air drifted through the lantern's missing panes, making the flame flicker, but it held.

Right off the bat we ran into a problem. In front of us were three of these unused extra tunnels. Which do we pick? After some back and forth, we decided to go from smallest to largest. Even the smallest tunnel's entrance still arched several feet above our heads. We quickly saw that it also ended after several feet.

The next smallest tunnel was also a no-go. Blocking our path just inside was a yawning pit stretched across the entire width of the tunnel. A few long, rotting boards loosely crisscrossed it. None looked sturdy enough to even hold the pet shop monkey's weight. Cornelius held up the lantern. After the boards and pit ended, the tunnel kept going. In the flickering candlelight, we couldn't see how far it went. There was no way to get around the pit to explore. I pushed a crumbling board aside and Cornelius shone his lantern down into the pit. "No, I don't see anything that looks like bodies," he said. "But I don't see the bottom either." I dropped a small rock into the pit. It made a splash that echoed from far, far below.

Cross that one off. That left the third and tallest tunnel.

Standing outside the third tunnel's gaping mouth, I could feel air coming from it, like it was breathing. Air in, stop, then air out, stop. The night was still warm, but standing here, feeling the breathing, I was chilled.

The tunnel had bad breath. I didn't like it. It wasn't a garbage smell. No. Not an alley full of hobos' smell. Something different. I wrinkled my nose, breathed through my mouth, then pulled my sailor suit shirt up over my mouth, my nose. Didn't help.

Where was Marigold? He said he'd be here. What would we do if we found the bodies but he didn't show?

A sound. I jumped. There it was again. Oh, it was only dried leaves moving on the ground with the gaping mouth breathing in, out.

Were there ghosts here? The dead people pulled out of cemeteries couldn't be thrilled. Being swells, they probably had roomy plots with views and gardeners tending flowers. And then, what? Some crooks dug them up, stole their rings and watches, and dumped them in a dark, stinky tunnel no one ever visited. Except me and the pet shop kid. We were no better than the crooks because we were only there to dig around the dead people.

What if the hand of an angry ghost snatched me? What if I never came out?

I trembled. I didn't want to go in that black mouth with the bad smell and the rustling sounds. No!

But Bookie needed me. If I didn't go, then Bookie was doomed.

"The mystic warrior prince fears nothing."

I jumped at Cornelius's voice behind me. "You scared me."

"The way of the mystic warrior prince is not to be scared of anything. This is our path, our challenge." He held the lantern up before the black tunnel entrance. Its breathing air made the candle flicker wildly. "Even if we die, we die willingly, happily."

He was not making things better. "I'm not doing any dying. Let's just look for the bodies."

I tried to sound brave, but I didn't feel it. What if there was an army of dead ghosts?

But I had to keep going, for Bookie.

We stepped into the mouth. The stinky breathing decided to give an extra blast. It snuffed out the candle. The tunnel went black. The nighttime darkness outside the entrance gave no light either. We couldn't see.

I yelped, tripped, and fell forward. The kid yelped and fell on top of me.

At first Cornelius didn't make a sound. Finally he said, "We'll try again." He struck another match, lit the candle. The flame waved, leaned, but held. "See, we're fine."

The big mouth didn't think so. It breathed and blew the candle out.

"This isn't funny! There's ghosts here!" Tears popped from my eyes. What a baby I was, but I couldn't stop. "Don't tell anyone I'm crying, or I'll sock you something good!"

"I won't say anything!" I could tell he was nervous now. He pushed the lantern at me. "Hold the lantern and hold your hand in front of the flame after I light it. It's just a draft. Really."

I snuffled away the tears. I held the lantern tight with one hand and held up my other hand, ready to protect the candle. "Okay," I said in a sobby voice like a baby.

"If there's ghosts, don't worry. I'm here. I told you, I'm a prince."

Not that again.

Cornelius struck another match. I held my hand at the ready. The candle flamed and stayed flaming. I could tell the breath was trying to snatch it away. I turned the lantern so that its one glass pane faced forward, toward the breath. That did the job. Ha! I outsmarted the gaping mouth and its tricks.

"See? No ghost will bother us," Cornelius said. But his voice didn't sound so sure anymore.

Still, he marched forward into the darkness. I followed, holding the lantern high.

"Is that it?" He suddenly stopped. I almost ran into his back. The moving shadows from the candle flame wove about the walls and curved ceiling of the tunnel and danced on a pile, no, three, no, a whole crowd of piles covered in dirty canvas sacking.

"I think we found our treasure!" he said, excited.

Just then, the breath caught me unawares and slipped around the glass and through the sides of the lantern. It blew out the candle.

This time we both screamed.

"Where's the lantern?" He sounded panicked.

"I dropped it, somewhere!" I for sure sounded panicked.

In the darkness, we felt around the dusty ground. We bumped heads. "Ow!" I hollered.

"Sorry," he mumbled, then, "Here it is!" I heard the snap of a match. In an instant, he had lit the candle. He grabbed the lantern. "Sparky, my hand is bigger than yours. I can keep the flame safer. You can dig in the piles." He handed me the shovel.

He wanted me to dig through the dead bodies all by myself? What happened to his *I'm a brave mystic warrior prince* talk? Scaredy cat.

The first pile wasn't too large. I could handle that, right? I leaned forward. The candlelight sputtered—please don't blow out! With the tip of the shovel, I flipped the canvas aside. The horrible tunnel smell hit me ten times harder. I slammed my eyes shut. I started shaking. I really didn't want to see a pile of dead people.

"It's not a body, Sparky. Relax," Cornelius said.

Carefully, I opened my eyes. It was stack of mismatched department store mannequin parts: legs, hands, the middles. They were different sizes, like some were for kids and others for big people. They were damp and splotchy with mold. Okay, that was the smell.

I felt a little braver going to the second pile. It didn't smell, but I still shut my eyes before I tore off the canvas with the shovel.

"Still not a body, Sparky. You're taking too long. The ancient mystic princes moved like silent waves of lightning."

Where was he getting that nonsense? I was tempted to tell him what those lightning bolts could do with him and his mystic princes, but I opened my eyes. Car fenders and a lot of car license plates from a lot of different states. No ghost here.

Under a tiny pile was the door to a small safe. Under a big pile that made me nervous because it also stank were nothing but tires and hubcaps filled with puddles of black, smelly water. Under another were wooden boxes packed with uncut keys of all sizes and types.

I admit I was feeling cocky by the time I got to the last pile. It wasn't the biggest, so must be safe. No ghosts, no problem. Though the back of my mind pointed out that if we didn't find any switcheroo bodies, that spelled trouble with about ten capital Ts for Bookie. Okay, that's not how trouble was spelled, but you got my drift.

"Hurry, the candle is burning down. Be a mystic of air and fire!"

I turned around and saw he was right. The candle was drowning in its own melted wax puddle. The flame was small and getting smaller. Its light was sputtering and thinking about snuffing. The tunnel shadows were closing in.

We were almost done. I was done with his mystic prince talk. "Those princes can't measure up to me. Just watch."

Without even turning back to the canvas to see what I was doing, I snagged it with the shovel and ripped it off. "See."

"Sparky. . . ."

"Put a plug in it. I don't need any mystic princes."

I turned back to the now uncovered pile. I screamed.

The gaping tunnel breath blew out what was left of the candle, plunging us into pitch-black darkness.

But not before I'd found a body.

Cornelius wasn't talking about mystic princes anymore. Neither was I.

"Sparky? Where are you?"

I followed his voice. "I'm here!" I was crying again.

"Don't worry. I know what to do." But he didn't do anything. I kept crying.

I know what you're thinking: what a baby. But, guaranteed, you'd cry too if you'd been me.

I only got a quick glimpse before the candle went out. It wasn't Straw Boater. It was Claude Cavalerie. He wasn't hefty anymore, his hair and moustache were more white than black, but it was him. I recognized that face from the papers, even though it was gray beneath the sprinkling of grave dirt.

Suddenly, a spot of light appeared from the tunnel entrance. A sound came with it, a steady thump, thump. What was it?

"The ghosts are coming for us!" I was full-on panicking.

The light bobbed and grew closer.

"I know what to do." His voice shook. Then he shouted, "Ancient creature of darkness, I defy you! Begone!"

Laughing came from the light.

"Not working. Not working," he mumbled. No kidding.

Another laugh. Then, "It's me, Marigold. I said I'd be here, didn't I?"

The light moved up to shine on Marigold's face. He had a hefty flashlight. The tunnel wouldn't be able to snuff that out. "Didn't think I'd show, huh?" he grinned.

Next to him was the brown-and-white splotched Dodger. The thump, thump noise came from his big feet stepping on the dirt ground. He wore his fancy birthday-party harness with the brass fittings. The brass glimmered in the flashlight's glow. Behind Dodger, I could see he was pulling the birthday-party cart.

Dodger did not look pleased to be in the spooky tunnel. He widened his nostrils to whiff the tunnel's stinky breathing. Suddenly, his ears flattened. His angry brown eyes moved in my direction. He'd whiffed me.

Ghosts barreling down, a dead body, and now this. An angry horse.

"Marigold, we found a body," Cornelius said. "I need your help moving it on the cart."

I saw by his flashlight that Marigold's eyebrows went up and down. "I can't dirty my wardrobe. My mom would throw a fit and ask questions." His eyes looked down over his crisp gold shirt collar and brown bowtie resting atop his summer-weight tan sweater that matched his knife-pleated and cuffed trousers that were tan with darker brown flecks. Instead of a kid-sized fedora, he wore a slouchy, casual cap that matched his trousers. A gold kerchief peeked from beneath his cap. As always, Marigold was a fashion plate. He smiled. "Sparky can help you."

Gee, thanks.

"Sparky, stop crying." That was Cornelius who was about to wet his pants two seconds ago. "If we each grab one arm, we can haul him onto the cart."

"I'm not crying!"

I shouldn't have been mad. Both of them were doing me a favor. I should have been happy that the tunnel wasn't a train station for dead bodies, either, like Knucklehead made out. Still, talking about moving bodies and actually doing it were two different things, as I realized.

And it was only one body, Claude Cavalerie. Straw Boater wasn't here. Was he finally being planted in Claude's open grave at this very moment, and was Claude here waiting to fill Straw Boater's empty spot in the morgue?

It dawned on me that I didn't understand why the body switching was happening in the first place. This body switching was a lot of work, and for what? Why hide Straw Boater? Did Chicago want to keep Straw Boater's visit to LA under wraps, and, more importantly, what Chicago was doing in town? That had to be it.

Still, I felt like I was missing something about this whole caper.

"Okay, Dodger," Marigold said. "Let's turn you around."

Dodger wasn't having it. He didn't want to take his eyes off me. He snorted and waved his head from side to side to say, "No!"

Marigold looked at him, then said, "Action!"

Instantly, Dodger stood tall, head up like a gallant steed. Marigold smoothly steered Dodger around so that the horse faced out toward the tunnel entrance and the empty birthday cart faced toward me, Cornelius, and the dead actor. Dodger strutted like the cameras were on him and him alone.

When Marigold called, "Cut!" Dodger turned his head back around and snorted at me.

We had another problem. "There's no way we'll be able to lift him and push him up and over the back of the cart," I worried.

"Have some faith," Marigold smiled. At the back of the cart, he undid latches and released the back panel. It fell forward to make a ramp. "See?"

"Great. Sparky, you grab one arm, I'll grab the other, and together we can drag him up onto the cart."

Easier said than done. I didn't even want to look at Claude's gray face, but I had to get this done. For Bookie.

Claude Cavalerie turned out to be a lot heavier than he looked, even if he was thinner than in his silent picture days. I ended up in the cart, pulling one arm, while Cornelius crouched on the ramp and heaved him forward by his belt loops. Someone had dressed Claude in the world's cheapest suit before planting him in the cemetery. The belt loops ripped as Cornelius pulled.

Dodger grew restless again, not approving of this dead body on his cart. Marigold had to call "Action!" a few more times. Whenever he did, Dodger froze into his gallant steed pose.

The tunnel breathed again. Cornelius and I jumped. Marigold laughed. "That's just from trains moving in other tunnels. They're all connected." Finally, Claude, clothes ripped, was in the cart. He was barefoot, but we found him that way.

I couldn't scramble out of the cart fast enough. Cornelius lifted the ramp back up and Marigold latched it into place.

When I lived on the streets, I longed to ride in that birthday-party cart and have a good time with the other, normal kids. I suddenly felt sick realizing that I'd finally gotten in the cart, not with birthday kids, but a dead guy.

It wouldn't be long before birthday kids were in the cart again. They would have no idea the last passenger was a dead actor. For all the times those kids didn't invite me, didn't want me within a mile of their birthday parties, that should have made me laugh. But I was all out of laughs.

"So, who left his guy in the tunnel, Sparky?" Marigold asked. Cornelius looked at me, interested in my answer.

"That's what I'd like to know," I mumbled.

It could be Chicago. That was the obvious choice, though I still wasn't clear why they'd kill Straw Boater, one of their own. It could be Chum-Chum, but why would he frame Bookie, one of his own? Though, after Chum-Chum's double-cross over the silver dog and the autograph, anything was possible. I couldn't discount Whisper-Whisper. He usually had a hand in any weird happenings in the city. He could have ordered his pair of kid cops to dig up Claude Cavalerie and haul him from Hollywood to this tunnel in a cop car.

I'd love to ask Bobby for his ideas. But I couldn't tell him I was creeping around at night with a dead actor and Cornelius, a kid he didn't like.

After Dodger stomped out of the tunnel, Cornelius asked the obvious question: "Where are we taking him?"

Right. Where were we parking Claude? I hadn't thought about the answer. We had to leave him where people would find him. City Hall was out. Whisper-Whisper lurked there and could not be trusted. No to Bunker Hill with Chicago prowling around.

When I didn't say anything, Marigold pointed out, "I can't take the body home with me. My mom won't like it."

"I can't take him to the store because there's other things taking up space," Cornelius said mysteriously.

Where? Where? Then it hit me: "The old police station!"

With LT running that shop, there would be no more monkey business with this body.

We reached an alley a few buildings uphill from the police station.

"This is close enough. Cut your flashlight, Marigold," I whispered. "Let's dump the body in the alley, but with his feet sticking out so the cops won't miss him. But we have to hurry."

Marigold led Dodger into the alley in case any cops came out of the station and wanted to know what the heck a retired movie horse was doing stomping around at this hour with a bunch of kids and a dead guy.

After whispering, "Action" to Dodger, who was getting restless again, Marigold undid the latches on the cart. Cornelius lowered the ramp. Cornelius grabbed one foot and I grabbed the other. We pulled, pulled, yanked. His pants nearly ripped off. Without warning, Claude Cavalerie suddenly rolled out and landed in a sprawl half out of the alley and into a hazy ring of light from a streetlamp.

"Time for me to go," Marigold said. After Cornelius helped him lift the cart's ramp back up and latch it shut, Marigold started leading Dodger toward the other end of the alley, which opened a couple of blocks over to another street.

"Wait a minute, Marigold. Could you ask your great-uncle if he's heard any talk about Claude Cavalerie? Rumors about who might have dug him up and why? Anything will help."

Dodger turned his head back and gave me an annoyed snort. Marigold smiled. "You and your gangsters. Sure, I'll ask. I make no guarantees."

Then Marigold, the cart, and Dodger clomp-clomped off into the night.

"So you do know a lot of gangsters," Cornelius asked with an interested smile.

"Don't listen to Marigold. He doesn't know what he's talking about." I could tell Cornelius didn't believe me.

Before he could quiz me about gangsters, we heard footsteps on the sidewalk. They were headed toward the police station. They would pass by the alley and the dead guy.

"Hide here," I whispered and pulled Cornelius with me behind a stack of crates against the alley wall. We peeked out to see who it was.

The person stopped under the streetlamp. It was cop. Spooky. He looked down at Claude Cavalerie, then straightened up. He was silent until suddenly, he shrieked, "Gas Attack!" followed by a long wail.

His voice was so loud, so filled with deathly horror, I

slammed my hands over my ears. A shudder ran through me. The only time I'd heard him speak, it was a ghostly whisper. Now he'd turned into a howling ghost.

I'd never meant to upset Spooky.

He ran and wailed about gas all the way back to the station. In a moment, the sound of cop feet thundered from the station toward the alley. The cops reached Claude. In the group, I saw the young cop who lectured me about Officer Bun-Bun's standards. Behind them, I heard Mug's voice. "There, there, Spooky. The medic's been called. Don't worry. Let's get you back inside the barracks."

LT pushed her way forward through the cluster of cops. The antique pistol shone in her belt. Officer Bun-Bun hopped next to her.

"It's the Monkey Island dead man from the papers," the young cop said to LT.

"So it is, Officer," LT responded. "So it is."

At her feet, Officer Bun-Bun sniffed, then pulled back. Nothing to eat here.

Cornelius and I snuck out the other end of the alley before the scene got more packed with cops.

"Tomorrow, come by the pet shop and we'll talk about what happened," he whispered.

"Okay," I lied. I didn't want to talk about this night for the rest of my life. I just hoped this body hauling got Bookie out of the slammer. I felt like crying. Again.

Would Spooky ever recover? He'd always been a pal to me, never ratted me out. Sure, he mostly stared at his Bunker Hill lamppost, lost in the Great War. But when the chips were down, Spooky came through.

Now he thought he was under a gas attack in the War. It was my fault.

"We'll go over the South Seas stowaway plan. Sparky, there's so much detailed preparation we must take care of before we're ready. We'll have to make practice runs for sure. I'll help you learn Korean."

It was bad enough with Bobby trying to teach me English, and now Cornelius wanted to load Korean on top of me.

Escaping on a ship was more and more appealing to me. Especially after tonight. But not if it came with homework.

Back at Creepy House, I stared wide-eyed at the night sky outside my room's clear transom windows. Clara Bell was close by and the flat leopard rested on my bed. I was sure I wouldn't be able to sleep. But I was so exhausted I dropped off to dreamland before I knew it.

I dreamed of Claude Cavalerie. He looked like his actor photos in the papers, except he was sad. He turned to me and said, "Everyone is going for the auditions except me."

I shot awake. My eyes were wide and I was shaking. I had a death grip on the flat leopard's paw.

This time for sure, I wouldn't go back to sleep. But I did.

I dreamed of Claude Cavalerie again. He sat at the kitchen table in Creepy House. On the table was the same braided raisin bread ring I gave Marigold to bribe his uncles. Claude looked like he did tonight, shrunken with a gray face. But he was cheerier than in my first dream. He asked me to help him get the audition. I got on the kitchen phone and called the studio. "Tell them," he said, smiling, "that I've lost so much weight. I'm a great dancer, and I've still got it. Did I mention my speaking voice is perfect for the talkies? Please tell them that being dead hasn't lessened my talent by one drop." As he chatted, he pulled pieces off the raisin bread ring on the table with his gray fingers and nibbled. "Mmm. This is most delicious."

In another dream, Spooky stared at me with his lost, faraway eyes. "You frightened me, Sparky," he whispered in his ghostly voice. "I thought you were my friend."

Over and over, my dreams shocked me awake.

Sunday

When I finally woke to morning sun warming the transoms, I was groggy and felt half-asleep. I was still nervous from my bad dreams. But I needed to see the morning papers.

I dragged myself into the kitchen only to be horrified by a braided raisin bread ring on the table.

The goblin's cheeks were red with a huge smile. He paused from grating and smashing carrots to tell me, "Because you enjoyed the last one so much, I specially ordered this one so you would have it first thing this morning. Doctor drove to pick it up. Just for you."

I sat down and stared at the bread ring. All I could see was Claude Cavalerie's gray, dead fingers picking at it. I was about to tell Gilbert that we should save it for Bobby, when I remembered I told him yesterday that the bread was yucky. Drats.

So I came up with: "Since I gobbled the whole thing up yesterday, I want to share it today with everybody here because they're working so hard to help Tootsie with the audition."

The dance teacher, who happened to be passing by the kitchen doorway, overheard this and zipped inside. "How very kind," he said as he pulled a sizeable chunk off the ring. "Mmm. This is most delicious."

That was the same thing Claude Cavalerie had said in my dream. I shivered.

Word spread and others trickled in. Gilbert held his hands to his heart and declared, "Sparky, you are so thoughtful of others."

Mr. Beele was soon at the table. When treats were involved, Mr. Beele was never far behind. "You certainly took a large portion for yourself," Beele said, squinting at me suspiciously.

"It wasn't me!"

He eyed me like I was clearly lying while he pulled off the largest chunk yet. "Mmm. This is most delicious," he murmured, mouth full, as he made his way out of the kitchen.

Was I in a waking nightmare?

In stomped Mr. Exercise, angry. "He got a piece, but no one told me." I was pretty sure the *he* was the dance teacher. About a third of the bread ring was left. He grabbed the whole thing and stormed away. From the hall outside the kitchen I heard, "Mmm. This is most delicious."

At least the bread ring was gone.

"Look at how happy you've made everyone," Gilbert smiled. "Don't worry. I have more wonderful pastries for you."

And he did. They were buns rolled into a tight pattern and stuffed with cinnamon, apples, and lots of nuts. Oh, yes.

I couldn't put off searching the newspapers for another second. Was Bookie out? What did the rags say about the body found by the police station?

Nothing on the front pages. It should have been there. I flipped through. There was another little mention about the auditions. Hey, was that the actor who autographed my cookie bag? I could tell the photo was from the last decade, but he still looked mostly the same.

In another paper, I spotted a photo of Claude Cavalerie. It was a head-to-toe shot. From this photo I could see he used to be a hefty guy. He wore a preacher outfit of some kind. The story said he would have been cast to play Reverend Dullness again—if he hadn't been too dead for the auditions.

Tough break, Claude.

Tootsie drifted in and settled next to me at the kitchen table. "I'm so nervous, Sparky. My audition is Monday."

Other than what looked like cracked mud dried on her face, her getup this morning was mostly normal, for her. She was draped in a long, fringed dressing gown decorated with golden flying dragons with red eyes under a full moon against a deep purple sky. Her purple turban, which was adorned with a pair of staring red dragon eyes, covered most of her hair.

The hair peeking out was her lighter beach-look hair she'd been sporting since her tea with Onion Girl this summer. I liked her original, black, vamp color better. I kept hoping she'd go back to that color, but all her people insisted the beach hair was the new fashion.

"You'll knock 'em out, Toosie!" I told her.

"Oh, yes," the goblin agreed. "You are more prepared for this audition than for any other."

"Thanks," she murmured. She tweaked my nose and gave a smile to the goblin.

Her eyes drifted to the page with Claude Cavalerie's photo.

"He's been cast? It would be nice to have him play Reverend Dullness again. I haven't been in a picture with Reverend Dullness, have I?"

"No. He was almost cast in *Baby Vamp Dancing Crazy*, but his studio wouldn't release him."

"Yes, I remember. He is so much fun and such a great dancer."

They didn't know Claude Cavalerie was a dead guy. They'd been so busy with audition preparations, they hadn't noticed the newspaper stories about him being murdered in Monkey Island.

Quickly, before they realized, I slid the other paper on top with the photo of the actor who talked to headstones.

"Gilbert! Look!" Tootsie shrieked. "Dante was cast! His audition must have been last week. This is so exciting."

"It is!" Gilbert abandoned his carrots to sit at the table for a closer look. "Not a current photo, but I'm sure he looks the same. A face like his will hold up well."

"So, Tootsie, you were in movies with that guy, right?" I had to pretend like I knew. Otherwise, Tootsie might figure out I'd never seen any of her pictures. That would make her crawl into her peacock bed and be useless for the audition. Then Doctor would really have it in for me. Not that he didn't already.

Her mud-caked eyes were bright. "Oh, yes! *Baby Vamp Walks Down the Aisle*, *Baby Vamp Walks Down the Aisle Again*, and *Baby Vamp Third Time's a Charm*. I married Dante Amadeo in each picture. Of course, in real life, he only had eyes for that cow."

"That cow!" Gilbert huffed.

That cow was their special nickname for Onion Girl. At the beach, when Dante spotted the silver dog I'd swiped from Onion Girl, he told me he'd given someone a dog like that once. That someone must have been Onion Girl, which meant he must have had the serious hots for her back in the day. Wonder what happened.

This was all very interesting, but the problem was that the rags didn't have a peep about dead Claude Cavalerie being dug out of his Hollywood grave and dumped in an alley by the downtown police station.

If that wasn't news, I didn't know what was. Everyone saw him: LT, Officer Bun-Bun, everyone.

This was a bad sign. Really bad.

I had to find Marigold and ask if his great-uncle Old Bob heard any talk about Claude Cavalerie and his wandering corpse situation.

I was too late.

I saw Marigold in the back of a large, burgundy sedan. He was sitting next to his mom. She wore a dusky blue hat with a crown that slanted forward, no brim, and a matching blue veil dotted with rhinestones. With dusky blue-gloved hands, she plucked off Marigold's beige, kid-sized fedora to smooth his shining hair. Usually he wore a kerchief under his hat. But today was church day, when his mom showed him off.

Old Bob stood at the driver's door. He surveyed the street, like he was watching for bad cowboys. He wore his full cowboy gear with fringed gloves, fancy boots with scrolling designs, chaps, white shirt with gold-colored embroidery, and a white cowboy hat that set off his deep chocolate face. On one hip was his silver cowboy shooter, and on the other was his snake-like whip that I'd almost got a taste of this summer for talking with Marigold.

I crouched low in the gutter so Old Bob wouldn't spot me. After he got into his car, I dared to stand and wave toward Marigold. At first he didn't see me. Then he spotted me. He shook his head "No."

I knew it was a long shot, but I had hoped Old Bob knew something. Now that the body snatching hadn't worked to help Bookie, I didn't know what else to do.

Feeling glum, I walked back to Creepy House. When I stepped through the back French doors, I noticed the familiar rainbow patterns that the sun made by shining through the cut glass transoms. The rainbows danced around the sunroom as a slight breeze rustled the tall jungle plants nearest the windows. I stood there and stared at the rainbows until clouds moved in and made them disappear.

I wandered to the kitchen, changed my mind, and told the goblin, "I think I'll go in my room and read some books."

"Your Bobby is having an excellent influence on you," he said cheerily.

Doctor was also lurking around the kitchen. He gave me a skeptical look. Doctor was wise to me.

Hidden in my room, I picked up one of the Betsy and Rover books Bobby had left me. In this one, Betsy and Rover suspected the family down the road had taken their ball. That's more like it. Now these books were talking about how life really worked. I was soon disappointed because it turned out the family had found the ball and were trying to figure out who'd lost it. I didn't buy that malarky for a minute.

Enough with Rover and Betsy. I went back to Carla and

Midnight. If they could figure out the map, find the treasure, and escape the cave, how would that help them? Would they really be happier with this treasure that the cowboy skeleton died trying to find?

Maybe I was looking at things wrong. Maybe it wasn't about finding the treasure. Maybe it was about Carla and Midnight going off on their own adventure and doing what they wanted to do, for better or worse.

I wished I could be like them.

Whatever the case, Carla had no clues on how to get Bookie off the hook. "I don't know what to do," I told the leopards.

Bobby tapped on my door. "Gilbert told me you were reading in your room." He smiled when he saw I was sprawled on my bed with books. Before he noticed, I slid Carla under one of the Rover and Betsy books. I told him I disagreed that the family had found Rover and Betsy's ball by accident. "Life doesn't work like that," I mumbled.

"But you were able to read the story, Sparky. That means I should find you more advanced books. I'll bring by one of Reginald's books."

He prattled about how we'd be studying during lunch all next week, then studying more in the library for recess, and then topping it off with a heap of even more studying at Creepy House on weekends.

I barely heard him. I felt like I was far away. I felt hopeless.

Suddenly, I realized Bobby had stopped talking. I looked up at him. He was staring at me like he was worried. "Sparky, you will come to school next week, won't you?"

"Sure," I said. I had no idea if I'd be in school or not. I didn't want to think about school.

He gave me a pointed look. "This is about the body snatching business, isn't it?

I didn't say anything.

Bobby didn't say anything for the longest time either. Finally, he said, "Sparky, if there's anything you need to tell me, you need to tell me."

There were about a million tons of things that I needed to tell Bobby, that I wanted to tell Bobby. But I couldn't. I felt myself falling deeper and deeper into a pit of secrets, like I'd fallen into Claude Cavalerie's grave. Could I ever climb out?

When I didn't answer, he said, "You look really tired, Sparky. Let's cut studying short for today. I think it's best for you to rest up so you're ready for a full week of school."

A full week of kids oinking at me and drawing weird pictures of me. And Bookie was still in the slammer.

Before Bobby could leave, Gilbert was at my door. "Come quick! Tootsie is modeling her new costume for tomorrow's audition!"

We followed Gilbert to the base of Tootsie's stairs with squares. With us were most of Tootsie's people except for the dress lady, her assistant, the jewelry man, and Doctor. They must still be upstairs making last-minute adjustments to their newest creation. Doctor would be there to keep her spirits up and her nerves calm.

First the dress lady and her assistant stepped out from Tootsie's closet maze. They had measuring tapes hanging around their necks and pincushions strapped to their wrists. The jewelry man was not far behind. He looked happy with whatever getup they had put together for her today.

Doctor emerged next. He looked behind and held out his hand. I couldn't hear what he said, but it probably was along the lines of, "You look wonderful." He wore his little smile he saved only for her.

Even though I'd gone through this routine several times since I started living in Creepy House, I couldn't help but become excited by the buildup to the main show. What would she wear? How did the dress ladies mix her old vamp look with her new beach look?

Then, Tootsie stepped to the top of the stairs. Everyone upstairs and down below clapped and called out "Bravo!" and "Beautiful!" I let loose my specialty, a two-fingered whistle. Doctor clapped hard and kept saying his reassuring words to her. Tootsie turned this way and that to give everyone a good view.

She wore pale green and white. First, the dress. It had a nubby texture, and I realized it must be raw silk like what Dante Amadeo wore to the beach. The dress was white with random pale-green squares of different sizes. The squares were not sharp, crisp squares. I wondered if the dress ladies had hand-painted the green squares on the silk dress. I liked how they looked.

Thin spaghetti straps held up the dress, which was short, hanging well above her knees. It reminded me of Tootsie's old flapper dresses, except a wide white belt cinched it at the waist. Peeking beneath the hem of the dress was a pair of short, short pants in pale green, like a swimming costume. But no one would go swimming in raw silk. In each hand she held the ends of her wrap. No, she wasn't holding the ends, they were attached to wide, silver rings, one on each hand. The wrap's gauzy pale-green fabric draped loosely behind her. Long white fringe hung from her wrap, similar to the old flapper style. But here, the strands of fringe were gathered into bunches every few inches, and those bunches were knotted together at the ends. Must be part of the casual beach look.

Tootsie spread her fingers, palms out, and moved her hands as she smiled, causing the fringed wrap to sway. She moved carefully, though, because her tan was painted on her arms, her neck, her face. Even her bare legs were painted. Tootsie turned. The back of her dress dipped down low to her waist, like a long, backwards shawl collar, and disappeared behind the belt, about where her wrap draped. Her bare back was also painted tan. She'd have a heck of a time not smudging that paint on the ride to her audition. Though I was sure Gilbert and Doctor would figure out a way to keep her in one piece until the audition show was over.

Tootsie spun back. She had plenty of paint around her eyes, but not black, like her vamp look. It was the same brown as her tan, but darker. Her lips were brown with a hint of coral and brush of shimmer.

My hopes that her hair would go black again were dashed. Her lighter hair was cut shorter and slicked down and back, like a 1920s style. Besides the silver rings attached to her wrap, her only jewelry was a clip that held back her slick hair above one ear. The clip was made of multiple silver strands that swept up and curled like an ocean wave. In each silver strand I saw white stones, maybe opals, and pale-green gems that could be a type of garnet. From where I stood, I couldn't tell for sure, but

I suspected they weren't the most valuable of rocks. Maybe that was the point for her going-to-the-beach look.

The biggest surprise was her shoes. Sneakers. She wore sneakers with no socks. The sneakers were the same pale green as her dress squares. The dress ladies must have also painted them green. Her laces were fat and bright white.

Tootsie beamed. Suddenly, she shook the rings from her fingers and tossed her pale green wrap aside. She started doing a dance where she bent her knees and jumped to face this way, then that way. All at once, everyone began clapping time. Beele belted out sounds to a tune: "Dut da, dut da, dut-dut-dut da!" He could sing better than Tootsie, that's for sure.

She made a big kick. Her knee almost touched her nose. Then, with everyone clapping the beat and Beele bopping out his tune, she did a bent-knee hop all the way down the stairs, hop to the left, hop to the right. In between the hops, she did fancy foot shuffling and more high kicks. When she reached the last step, she hopped high and landed on the rug below in a full-on split.

Tootsie laughed and threw up her arms.

I couldn't believe it. I was clapping like a crazy person. Bobby kept saying, "Did you see that? Did you?" Gilbert was crying a stream of tears. His old scar was so red it looked like it was glowing.

Tootsie sure had a fighting chance with this audition.

Bobby finally had to head home. Tootsie vanished once again into her closets upstairs. Trailing her were Doctor, the dress lady, her assistant, and the jewelry man. "I spotted some errors," I overheard the dress lady say. "We'll need to get those fixed before tomorrow." The jewelry man added, "The hair ornament demands adjustment. It is not quite perfect."

Looked perfect to me, but what did I know? Though she did smudge off most of the painted-on tan covering her legs when she did that split.

The rest of Tootsie's crew milled about, excited by Tootsie's show. Even Mr. Exercise and the dance teacher stopped sniping at each other. Soon her crew left. They had to be back extra early tomorrow, the big audition day.

The tears continued to pour from the goblin's eyes as he served me what he called a "savory pie." He scooped out a hefty piece with a silver server that wasn't a spoon or a knife but a pointed, pie-piece-shaped server. Whatever it was, it worked for me.

My pie slice was similar to the tomato pie from yesterday, but this one was heavy on the mushrooms. Dotted on top were little green nuts. Or, no, they must be olives, which Spots told me weren't nuts. These must have been particularly little olives. "Yeah, this is good. I like the little green things," I told the goblin.

He clapped his hands. "You, my Sparky, have gourmet taste! Those little green things, as you say, are capers. They are the unopened buds of beautiful flowers that have been preserved forever in delicious brine. Beautiful flowers, like our Mademoiselle, who will forever be the most beautiful girl in Hollywood!"

He was so full of tears, he had to run from the kitchen.

Fortunately, before he ran off, he left dessert on a plate with a swirling pale blue-and-green design. The dessert? Cookies so soft, they melted in my mouth. The goblin was so nice to me, caring that I had such tasty treats. I certainly hadn't done anything to deserve him or them.

I was in a better mood when I returned to my room. I could see why people went to the theaters to watch Tootsie's picture shows back in the day. When she turned into her movie star self, she was so fun and full of life she could make everyday cares vanish. My current cares weren't everyday, but even so, she'd made me put them in the back of my mind.

"I can't do anything about anything right now," I told the leopards. "Tomorrow, I'll worry."

My dreams did not forget my troubles.

I dreamt that I saw Bobby. But only his back. He was turned away from me. I called to him, asking him what I should do, who he thought dug up Claude Cavalerie. Bobby did not turn around, did not say anything to me. I kept calling, but he ignored me. In my dream, I knew he was angry with me.

The Following Monday

I woke with a start. I saw a breath of light in the sky outside my clear glass transom windows. It was early, but I might as well get up. I felt rattled. In real life, Bobby never turned his back on me. Maybe I was dreaming of the future.

In the kitchen, I noticed the goblin's face was red and blotchy. I wondered if he'd been up all night crying his happy tears.

He'd laid out my breakfast on the table. The fresh-squeezed orange juice was there, looking cool and sweet. I pulled off a pink-and-red-flowered dishcloth to find several pastries resting on a matching plate. They were shaped like fat pickles, but they sure didn't look or smell like pickles. I picked up one of the golden pastries and bit down. It felt like it was made of a million delicate flakes held together with melting sugar and stuffed with jam. I had another bite, and another.

All the while, Gilbert kept saying, "I am so excited for today. So excited."

Doctor was there, like a dark cloud. "Yes, so excited," he repeated in his whispering voice.

I started on my second pastry. I knew I was avoiding the morning papers sitting on the table. I couldn't handle more bad news.

Finally, I forced myself to look. Maybe I'd just check the headlines real quick.

When I did, I was surprised to see, "Mayor Quits!" and "Crooked Cops!" They printed a new close-up photo of the Mayor. His eyes were nervous, and his face was turning away, like he was about to flee reporters. The papers said something about the Mayor really living in Pasadena, not Los Angeles, and being a spy for the Mayor of Pasadena, who did not return the reporter's calls for comment.

There was a photo of the new Mayor—"a fresh face for Los Angeles." This Mayor looked like a tanned high school kid with a mess of curly hair. He posed in a swimming outfit by the beach. He held some kind of board that was propped up next to him. It was taller than he was. "Our new mayor will boost our beaches and bring money to the city!" This must be the replacement Mayor Whisper-Whisper dug up. I could care less.

On the front page of another rag was a strange photo of a mannequin with a much smaller hairless, one-eyed doll's head on top, and a mismatched doll's arm and doll's leg stuck in the mannequin's arm sockets. The contraption was messily held together with wires and shoelaces. The headline blared, "This Is The Body In The Morgue!" Then there was more about "Nest of Cop Crooks!" What did that mean?

I looked through all the pages but saw nothing about Straw

Boater or Claude Cavalerie showing up in the alley by the police station.

This was strange. Though, if the papers said there was only a fake body in the morgue, that must mean Bookie can't be a murderer, right? That must mean he was out.

The goblin busily puttered about making "our most special formula from rose water." It smelled lots better than Tootsie's usual youth potions. Doctor did not look at Gilbert or the rose water, but at me. His black eyes drifted to the papers, then back to me.

Did he realize I was interested in what happened at Monkey Island and if Bookie was free? I found out this summer that Doctor knew Knucklehead. He probably knew Bookie and the rest of the crew. Did he know Chum-Chum, the Chicago people? It dawned on me that Doctor might know what happened with Straw Boater and Claude Cavalerie.

None of that mattered, though, if Bookie was out. Today I had to ditch school. I needed to search for Bookie.

I pretended to get ready for school. In my room, I left my school bag and, though it broke my heart, I also left the goblin's lunch tin. I couldn't have anything weighing me down while I searched for Bookie. There was more chaos than usual this morning with Tootsie's full crew of wackos getting her ready for her audition. While everyone was preoccupied, I'd slip out. Doctor would be none the wiser.

I almost reached the back French doors when Doctor stepped in my path. He held up my school bag and lunch tin. "Forget something?"

On the drive to school, Doctor criticized the state of my ripped, monkey-printed school bag: "You ruin everything you touch." Mostly, he snarled at me to behave myself at school and not "destroy Mademoiselle's most important day."

By basically kidnapping me, I felt that Doctor forced my hand. I decided to ask. "So what do you know about that actor Claude Cavalerie and why the papers say he was murdered in Monkey Island when it was that other guy from Chicago?"

Doctor jerked the wheel hard to the curb and slammed on the brakes. He bent down so his broiling face was close to mine. "Don't you ever ask me anything like that again," he hissed. His black eyes burned into me and he bared his teeth.

Wow. What kind of crime history did Doctor have? Maybe I'd ask Bookie about Doctor once I found him. Or maybe Bookie would have the same angry reaction.

Doctor laid on the gas and tore away from the curb. At school, he marched me to the door to make sure I didn't "sneak off."

Two girls and a boy from the smart class were near the door when Doctor left me there. The three of them tittered. "That girl is so weird," one of them snickered to the others.

So much for Bobby's claim that the smart class kids were better behaved. These characters were no different than the dummies in dummy class.

Morning in dummy class went how it usually went. It didn't take long for me to be sent to Miss S (you don't want to know). I was surprised I wasn't ordered to the library with Mrs. Bean. When I came to Miss S, I found out why. She pointed to the Principal's door. "In there," she said as she stood and opened the door to shoo me inside. I was condemned not to Miss S's punishment chair, but to the Principal's bad-kid chair.

Principal's few strands of hair were in disarray. He shook his head and gasped in frustration. "I have had enough! Miss S! Call this girl's aunt Miss LaFemme and tell her to come and take this child away. I am expelling her now!"

"Perhaps more time in the library will improve her," Miss S drawled.

"No! My last nerve has been stepped upon!"

"Okay then," Miss S said and went to her desk to call Tootsie.

Principal's harassed eyes wandered to the small photo of Tootsie that she gave him when she and Doctor registered me for school. She pretended to be my aunt and Doctor pretended to be her ex-husband who hated her. They put on quite a show, but it got me in school, despite Tootsie not being my family. Principal was such a moon-eyed Tootsie fan, he bought their story.

I wondered if he was expelling me so he could catch a glimpse of Tootsie again. I'd find out soon enough.

Hold on. Today was Tootsie's most important audition in the world. If she had to come here because of me, she'd miss her audition, miss her chance at actually landing a part in the movies again, miss her chance at her dream.

It was all my fault.

Principal's office clock seemed to bang in my ears as it ticked the minutes away before Tootsie showed up. What a bad kid I was. After everything Tootsie and Gilbert did for me, I had to go and ruin her life.

Principal glowered and grumbled about his last nerves. He tried to write something on a paper, angrily crunched the paper into a ball, threw it at his wire trash can, missed, and pointed a finger at me. "My last nerve!"

Suddenly, I heard footsteps coming through Miss S's room. It was Tootsie, missing her audition.

Into Principal's office flew not Tootsie, but Doctor. He pounded on Principal's desk, alarming the little man. "Yes! Expel that creature!" Gone was Doctor's whispery voice. He flung his accusing finger at me. "Miss LaFemme begged me to save the girl from expulsion. She fell to her knees and clung to me. I walked away, dragging her, sobbing, until she could not hold on to me any longer. 'Please!' she cried, and I laughed. I promised her that I would ensure Sparky is expelled, ensure that Miss LaFemme is in tears forever!"

Principal's face went white. He shot up from his desk, "You blasphemous monster! I will never expel Sparky. Miss S!"

"Yes," drily from the front.

"You miscommunicated my intention!"

"Did I?" archly.

Principal didn't answer. He turned his wrath back to Doctor. "You tell Miss LaFemme that I am her knight. I shall protect this girl, save her from expulsion, save her from you!"

Doctor sneered at Principal. "Well, look at you. Maybe you've won this round, but we may yet do battle again."

Principal puffed his chest at being told he'd won the round. "Begone, sir!"

Before Doctor left, he bent down and hissed in my ear, "Don't ever make me do this again."

Doctor put on a show. It was almost better than the show he and Tootsie put on to register me for school. Doctor sure wasn't happy about it.

The good news was Tootsie didn't have to miss her audition to bail me out.

Principal sat down, befuddled. He seemed to suddenly realize he'd done exactly what he didn't want to do: promise never to expel me. He crumpled another paper into a ball. "Miss S!"

"Yes." I could almost hear the roll of her eyes.

"Deal with this girl."

"Okie dokie." I'd bet anything she raised her eyebrows just so, like she did with me.

Then I was back in the punishment chair.

The little room grew hot as the minutes ticked by. She gave me a stack of old rulers to check to see if any were shorter than the others. They were all the same. She noticed the monkey prints on my school bag. "Don't tell me; I don't want to know." The lunch bell rang. "You can eat, but only in that chair."

In addition to my sandwich, goblin packed two fat cupcakes. One was chocolate with thick, thick chocolate frosting. The other was pink with thick, thick strawberry jam-dotted icing. I barely tasted them. I needed to get out of this punishment chair and start looking for Bookie. I was trapped.

The bell for recess rang. "No library for you today," Miss S informed me.

That meant not only had I missed lunchtime studying with Bobby, but I'd also miss recess library studying. Before Doctor kidnapped me this morning, I'd already planned to ditch school, ditch studying with Bobby. I wasn't much of a friend, was I? He'd be mad at me, like in my dream.

I started nodding off, so Miss S gave me a box of papers that had been crumpled into balls. I wondered if Principal had done that. "Straighten them out," Miss S told me.

By the time the end bell rang, I felt groggy. I rushed out of school as fast as I could so I wouldn't run into Bobby and hear his questions about what bad thing I'd done this time. I saw him in the school yard. His back was to me, but I could tell he was looking for someone. That someone must be me.

I was so tempted to run up to him, talk to him. But I couldn't.

I needed to get out on Bunker Hill to find Bookie, make sure he was okay.

I couldn't ditch the cops, though. LT would have my hide.

The first thing I noticed was LT's office. Sure, she kept it on the empty side. But today there was an extra feeling of being vacant about it, except for Mug sitting in her chair. In one of his cast-bound arms, he held a wilting red rose. He looked near tears.

None of my business.

I was about to head to Detective Bernie when I heard, "Right this way."

Whisper-Whisper.

I slipped into the shadow of an overloaded coatrack. I watched.

Whisper-Whisper strode to LT's office. He was trailed by his two kid cops. The kids wore huge smiles. They spotted Mug.

Mug spotted them. His sorrowful face vanished. He stood so quickly, LT's metal chair toppled over.

"Meet your two new co-lieutenants," Whisper-Whisper informed Mug with a sly smile. "The former Mayor's last act before he resigned was to promote these two fine young gentlemen." He looked Mug slowly up and down. "I think you are in their office."

The kid cops snickered. The rifle kid cop said, "Nice flower."

Layers of enraged red rolled over Mug's face. A growl rumbled from his big gut. But he was in a bind. I could sense it. There was nothing he could do, at least not now.

Mug stormed from the office, roughly brushing past the kid cops and Whisper-Whisper. I heard him stomp down the stairs.

Before Whisper-Whisper spotted me, I darted toward Detective Bernie. On my way, I noticed the young cop was reinforcing Officer Bun-Bun's barricade with a spittoon, a dented car door that looked like it came from a wreck, and a cracked chalkboard on wheels. I overheard other cops whispering, "We gotta hide Spooky."

The air was tense.

"What's going on?" I asked the Detective.

He rolled the end of his cigar slowly into the tin of paper clips on his desk. "There are some, Sparky, who will do the right thing even if it means losing it all. Then there are others who aren't like that." His red-rimmed eyes drifted toward the laughing sounds coming from what used to be LT's office.

"Where is LT?" The open grave in the Hollywood cemetery flashed through my mind. There was room for more than just Straw Boater down there.

"She's been exiled, you could say. Reassigned to the farthest, rattiest corner of Los Angeles."

"Will she come back?" Before the question left my mouth, I knew she wouldn't. That's what the crooked police stories in the papers were all about. LT was blamed for the roaming body problem, along with the now ex-Mayor.

Detective Bernie didn't answer. His eyes fixed on mine. "You'll be seen as LT's girl. You best make yourself scarce. There's a back way out." He nodded his head toward the far end of the room where there was a dingy frosted glass door with a cracked pane. He chomped back down on his cigar. "I'll have to start getting my sandwiches myself," he grumbled.

I didn't waste time and beat it out of that scene.

A bad feeling was sneaking over me.

I had to find Bookie. I had to see him, make sure he was okay. I kept thinking of the open Hollywood grave.

The five-and-dime's front store space was empty. I never saw it like that when Bookie ran the operation. I heard voices drifting from Bookie's office. Carefully, I stepped toward the voices. I should have trod hard on Bookie's rug squeaker to make sure he knew I was coming. Though, something told me not to. I wasn't positive the voices belonged to Bookie or his crew.

Sure enough, it wasn't Bookie lounging in his office chair with feet propped up on his desk. It was the moll I saw in Monkey Island. It hit me. She was no moll. She was the boss lady.

She wore a cranberry dress with large cream buttons, cream collar, and wide cream belt that matched the cream pumps crossed nice and easy on Bookie's desk. A cream cap with cranberry veil topped her look. A cigar hung from her cranberry lips. She stared at me. She said nothing.

By the desk stood a man with his back toward me. He wore one of Bookie's new suits, the green one flecked with dark gold. He didn't wear a hat, so I clearly saw his white-blond hair.

It couldn't be. Could it?

As if answering the question in my mind, the man turned.

It was him. Straw Boater. He wasn't dead. Never was dead. He grinned at me.

The Chicago kid sat on the floor in front of Bookie's desk. What was left of my books were scattered around him. He held one up and shook it. It no longer had pages, only the covers. "Hey, Sparky, I need more toilet paper."

The kid laughed. Straw Boater laughed. Boss lady didn't. She kept staring at me, her cigar turning around in her mouth.

I ran.

I kept running until I reached Chum-Chum's storefront office. Maybe it was hopeless but I had to find out if Chum-Chum would tell me something, anything. Maybe Bookie was inside with him.

The door wasn't cracked open like it usually was in hot weather. I tried the handle. Nothing happened. I jiggled the handle. It was locked. The blinds were cracked open enough for me to peek inside. No light was on. In the shadowy space, I saw no dolls' heads, no collapsing boxes, not even Chum-Chum's desk. It was an empty room.

My mind whirled. I felt lost. Then I remembered the saloon with the high-class speakeasy where Bookie's two gorillas now worked. Yes, I'd go there.

I was out of breath and felt like falling over by the time I ran to the saloon. I flung open the door. Instead of Bookie's two gorillas sitting on either side of the speakeasy's secret entrance, I saw the two Chicago toughs I'd seen in Bookie's office on Tuesday.

The toughs saw me and rose from their chairs. I tore out of that saloon.

Where to go? What to do?

Spots. I had to find Spots. He might be at the flophouse. I had to go there, even if that meant I risked a run-in with Shrimpy.

Shrimpy's older brother was slumped over the check-in counter. The small, rattling fan on the counter blew his hair and blew his strong booze smell toward my nose.

There was no sign of Spots. I stood on my tiptoes and leaned over the counter. The canvas sack wasn't dropped on the other side. Spots hadn't come here yet. At least the coast was clear of Shrimpy. Carefully, I made my way up the staircase. I planned to go to the fifth floor where I'd seen Straw Boater on Tuesday and thought he was a corpse. Now I knew he was probably napping.

As I neared the second floor, I recognized a voice booming from one of the rooms. "Yeah, the thing about poetry is it's a bear to memorize."

Knucklehead. Who was he talking to? I crept down the hall-way's threadbare carpet, looking right and left for signs of Shrimpy. I passed the usual people in the other rooms: man picking a guitar, woman pacing, guys playing dice. Then I reached the room where I heard Knucklehead's voice.

"Bookie!" I shouted.

I ran in, then stopped.

Bookie looked like he did in the slammer: small, defeated, sad. He sat on the room's cot and leaned against the wall. His head was turned away like he was trying to hide in the yellowed wallpaper. He wore the same suit he'd worn when he fell off Monkey Island's roof. It was torn, stained, and shapeless. He wasn't wearing the gold watch, chain, and cuff links that Chum-Chum had given him. He had them on when he went to Monkey Island. Did Whisper-Whisper take them? Did Chicago? Or did Chum-Chum want them back? They must have been payment for something. Bookie didn't turn to look at me.

"Well, hey, hey, hey! Bookie, lookie who's here to visit you. It's Sparky!"

Bookie frowned and said nothing.

"Ah, don't mind him, Spark. Books just is getting his wind back from being inside. As much as you think you know what it's like in the big house, believe me, and I'm talking from experience here, it's much, much worse." He grinned.

No. Something else was going on, but I didn't know what. The world was turned upside down.

Knucklehead still wore his poet outfit and his fake nose bandage. The poodle curled in his lap. He wagged its ears. Its tongue hung out. "Sparky, did you know somebody bleached this dog?" He pulled some of the dog's curly hair apart. Sure enough, it had chocolate roots. "I think this poodle was stolen."

"Didn't you ever give that dog a name?" I asked, not sure

why any of that mattered. The dog wasn't growling or barking at me. It must have forgiven me for sneaking up on Onion Girl's house.

"Sure! Pooch is the pooch's name. Say, Spark, you cost me a sweet deal with Sally. Well, to be honest, I think she was getting suspicious of me. I do only know two words of French. Unlike Hothead here." He looked at Bookie. "He spent time in Canada picking up the French, driving deliveries over the border, across those big frozen lakes in the pitch dark. Not me. I came to Cali to get away from the cold. But this tough guy?" Knucklehead laughed. "Didn't your truck fall through the ice once or something?"

Bookie's eyebrows crunched together, angry. Bookie liked to keep his cards close. I could tell he didn't appreciate Knucklehead yabbering on about things in the past. Though it was interesting to find out Bookie was in Canada. There was a whole lot I didn't know about Bookie, Knucklehead, Chum-Chum, all of them.

Knucklehead shook his head and went back to his story. "Sally didn't call the cops about the missing dog, and you know I'm not talking about this one." He rubbed Pooch's tummy. "She didn't care about that too much. It was your sparkly shoe you threw at Pooch. She found it and was convinced I was having an affair with some other movie star at her house. She threw me out!"

"She should care about that dog statue. It was made out of real silver."

Knucklehead threw back his head and let out a loud guffaw. "Did you hear that, Books?"

Bookie said nothing and kept trying to push his face through the wall.

"Spark, have you lost your marbles? That was white gold. Didn't you notice that thing didn't have any tarnish? Some idiot with more money than brains gave it to her. She's got so much valuable junk, it hardly matters. But that sparkle shoe you left? Yikes. That made her mad. We had it good while it lasted, though, huh, Pooch?" The dog waggled its stubby tail and its whole little self.

"But Chum-Chum came through for Bookie," I pointed out. "He musta' liked that gold dog." I probably said too much here, but I was trying to piece things together. But the puzzle had too many pieces missing.

Knucklehead gave me a steady stare. He grinned but his eyes stayed cool. "Sure."

I looked at Bookie. His frown dipped lower. Knucklehead kept staring. They already knew I gave the dog to Chum-Chum.

"I mean, Bookie's out," I pleaded, wanting answers.

"Sure," Knucklehead said again. Then he chuckled. "Since the body wasn't where it was supposed to be, hard to hold him. Somehow it traveled from a certain tunnel to a certain cop station with a certain hardline, non-flexible cop." He cocked his head at me. I noticed Bookie's eyes darted toward me for a second before darting back to the wall.

They knew I was behind moving Claude Cavalerie and dumping him near the police station. It was an easy guess since I'd pressured Knucklehead into telling me about the body exchange tunnel. I had the horrible feeling they also knew I'd been working for the cops. I was too afraid to ask.

"That guy in the straw boater hat at Monkey Island was never murdered. He's in Bookie's office, alive, right now with this boss lady from Chicago. Chum-Chum is missing. His office is empty. You have to do something!"

Knucklehead moved his eyes up as if to ponder the dusty spider webs clinging to the ceiling. "Aw, come on. You know Chicago is Chum-Chum's boss. Or was." He paused. "There's not a lot of wiggle room in this tight situation. But Chum-Chum is fine. He's got other ideas cooking. Everybody has, with Prohibition on its way out. Look at the operations Chicago has here in California: the orange groves, the orchid growing." He eyed Bookie, who didn't move. "Too bad Chum-Chum likes those little orchid flowers so much. That would've been fun."

None of this made sense. I felt lost. "I don't know what's going on!"

Knucklehead's eyes swiveled back to me. Pooch also eyed me. "You don't need to. And maybe you shouldn't know."

"But why was Bookie even at Monkey Island to begin with?" I looked with pleading eyes toward Bookie. He ignored me.

"Chicago came to town. They didn't say anything to Chum-Chum. There were only rumors. So he needed Bookie to meet with them, see what's up. Didn't I just tell you Chicago is Chum-Chum's boss? Or was." He paused again and looked at the dog. "Listen, we'll be hitting the road soon with Chum-Chum. Heading outta town."

"What?" I looked at Bookie. I almost said, *You're leaving me?*

Knucklehead laughed. "Don't look so sad. Aw, Books. Spark's gonna miss you." Bookie said nothing.

"You should get a move on yourself before Shrimpy sees

you. She was complaining about you and the trouble you caused her. You seem to make enemies wherever you go, Sparky. You gotta stop that. Learn how to be charming, like me." He grinned wide. "Shrimpy's loaded and takes no prisoners. Not smart you got on her bad side."

I just stood there, Shrimpy or no. I couldn't move.

"Aren't you busy going to school and becoming a scholar or something like that? Hanging around other school kids?" He pointed his little finger toward my school bag I clutched hard like it was a lifeline. "What do you want with a bunch of old thugs like us? Isn't that right, Pooch?" The dog made a happy yip.

"Where are you going, Bookie? Take me with you!"

Finally, he turned his head toward me. His big, liquid-brown eyes glared at me. "Why do you want to be like me, Sparky? I'm nothing but a two-bit crook." His voice was so angry. He turned his face away from me to stare at the wall again.

Knucklehead jerked his head toward the room's door. "Maybe it's time to take a hike, Spark. We'll be back in town someday. Don't worry."

I left.

I was in a daze walking down the staircase, walking by the boozed-up brother. I wandered out the set of double doors and was about to land my foot on the first of the front steps, when a powerful shove knocked me forward. I fell on the concrete steps and skidded down to the sidewalk.

I looked behind me. There stood Shrimpy at the top of the steps. "Don't ever come back," she growled.

My knees were scraped raw. My forearms were no better. One strap on my school bag was torn loose. A couple of pencils had slid out of a rip the monkey had made. I stuffed the pencils back and held my bag close to my chest. I wandered to no particular place. I just wandered.

Until my wandering took me by Monkey Island. I was about to turn away because of the bad memories, but then noticed commotion. I walked closer.

Spots and Bookie's gorillas were loading a box truck with crates. They weren't having an easy time of it, probably because the crates were packed with screaming, thrashing monkeys. The monkeys looked crazier than ever. Spots saw me. "Monkeys. Can you believe it?"

The gorillas pushed oranges through the gaps in the crates. "You like these, huh? Yum, yum," from Gorilla #1.

"Be happy! Plenty more where you're going!" from Gorilla #2.

I remembered what Knucklehead told me and put two and two together. "You're hauling these monkeys to Chicago's orange groves?" I asked.

Spots gave me his closed-mouth, cagey look. Gorilla #1 laughed and Gorilla # 2 said, "They're professional pickers!"

So the monkeys were Chum-Chum's goodbye present to Chicago.

Monkey Island's doors were wide open. No ticket taker stood by. I wandered inside. It still stank, but not as bad. The Ice Cream King and his stand were gone. The Monkey Island moat was drained. The bottom was thick with slime, cigarette butts, and a cracked doll's head. No trace of tourists. The city had shut it down like the newspapers said.

More of Bookie's old five-and-dime crew struggled to herd

the last of the monkeys into more crates using brooms and oranges. The big monkey remained defiant at the top of the mountain. He jumped up and down, screaming. The hoods threw oranges at him, hoping to bribe him. But that monkey wound up and fastballed those oranges back at the crew. "Ow!"

I noticed Big Otto's cage wasn't empty anymore. I wandered closer.

Big Otto was huge, almost the size of his huge cage. He was hunched in the back corner like he was trying to push his face into the wall. He didn't look anything like the other monkeys and didn't have a tail either. A thick metal collar was fastened around his neck. From it hung a heavy chain that was attached to the wall behind the cage.

"You gonna pick oranges too, Big Otto?" I asked. He turned his head a little toward me. He looked so sad. He reminded me of Bookie. "You're not the only one having a rotten day," I told him.

There was another weird thing about this weird monkey. Otto was covered with black-and-gray hair, except for his face, neck, and hands. I saw stubble. Did someone shave him? Why? I stepped closer to the bars. He grunted, glared angrily at me, and turned his face back to the wall, but not before I noticed traces of thick pancake makeup.

The Mayor.

No, the ex-Mayor now. The angry glare he gave me matched the rough, hard-case look in his newspaper photos. I couldn't believe it. But I could.

Didn't Whisper-Whisper once say it was tough to find the right trained monkey to be a mayor? He found one in Big Otto. They shaved him, plastered him with face paint, shoved him in a suit, and took photos to send to the papers. When they needed fall guys for the mannequin-in-the-morgue fiasco, he was an easy target. Whisper-Whisper sent him back to his cage.

Spots shuffled up beside me. The gorillas were not far behind, with oranges in their arms. "You're getting underfoot, Sparky. We need to load the gorilla now." He glanced back at Bookie's gorillas. "The real one, not you guys." They all chuckled. Big Otto turned his head toward them. He looked about to cry.

I suddenly realized that Monkey Island was one of Chum-Chum's operations. Chum-Chum must have rented Big Otto to Whisper-Whisper when he needed a new mayor.

That's why Chum-Chum wanted Bookie to meet Straw Boater here. It was Chum-Chum's home territory, but it didn't end up being safe.

The rest of the five-and-dime crew had corralled the remaining monkeys into crates. The boss monkey still held out. The hoods had given up on bribing him with oranges. Instead, they were having better luck using a much smaller monkey they'd tied up and slathered with katsup and mustard as a lure. The little monkey wailed, and the big one regarded it with interest.

I was done here.

All I wanted to do was go back to Creepy House, run in my room, and hold the leopards tight.

I cried on the Angels Fight tram as it clacked up steep Bunker Hill. The man and woman who rode Angels Flight too often for my liking peered at me and frowned, as they always did.

"What on earth does that girl do to make such a mess of

herself," the woman commented to the man who wore his usual cool, crisp beige suit.

"The authorities should be involved," he added sternly.

The second the tram reached the top of Bunker Hill, I ran out before they could make any more comments. Yeah, I knew I was a mess. I didn't need those two reminding me.

As I headed to Creepy House's back French doors, I realized I didn't have the energy to clean myself up and try to hide my new Shrimpy cuts and scrapes before Gilbert saw me. I was a mess of a kid, like the lady on Angels Flight said. I'd come into Creepy House so many times looking like a complete disaster. One more time wouldn't matter.

Bookie said I shouldn't be a two-bit crook like him. Problem was, I already was nothing but a two-bit crook. A messy troublemaker, good-for-nothing kid crook.

When I opened the French doors, I was blasted with gramophone dance music. I heard laughing, happy voices.

Dance teacher passed into the sunroom. He was stuffing cake in his mouth with one hand while holding another piece of cake in his other. "Better get some before it's all gone," he advised me.

"What's going on?" I asked him.

He raised his eyebrows at me. "She got the part. Don't dawdle getting your cake. They'll be taking off soon. Filming on location, you know."

They're leaving me?

I was about to demand answers, but dance teacher spotted Mr. Exercise. "Somebody is getting fat," he said archly. Mr. Exercise whipped sharply around to glare at dance teacher. "No, somebody *else* is getting fat."

I hurried to the kitchen. On my way, I passed Mr. Beele bragging to the dress lady and her assistant. "Of course, I will also travel to the filming location. Mademoiselle needs my ongoing coaching. But my time will be limited because I will have other duties. The production requires so much of my talents."

Travel? Where?

On the kitchen table, I saw two half-eaten cakes, one chocolate, one pink. The remains of something written with frosting was scrawled across them. So much of the cakes were gone, I couldn't read what the frosting said. Not that I was much of a reader.

The goblin loudly sobbed at the table. He clutched Tootsie, who sat next to him, smiling like she was on a cloud. He kept touching her face. "You are the most beautiful girl in Hollywood. I am so happy. I cannot possibly get any happier."

Tootsie still wore her half-beach, half-vamp outfit. Most of her suntan paint had rubbed off. She spotted me. "Sparky! You are my good-luck charm. This has been the most wonderful day in the entire world. Do have as much cake as your heart desires!"

Then the face broads were congratulating her. "Knew you were going to get it," and "Once a star, always a star." Slimming man and raw-food lady joined the crowd around the kitchen table. "We are overjoyed!"

I faded out of the kitchen but bumped into Doctor. He looked down at me with his cool black eyes. "Don't think you're off the hook, Sparky," he said quietly. "You'll stay with Bobby at his house. I've spoken with his parents. I've cautioned them that you need close watching and should be driven to school to make sure you don't wander off." He gave me his smirking smile. "By the way, your Bobby was here, but you weren't. He was disappointed."

I ran to my room and closed the door. I sat on my bed and breathed hard. The leopards watched me. "I don't know what to do," I told them.

Tootsie got her part. That was good news, but not for me. Gilbert and Tootsie were leaving me.

Thanks to Doctor, Bobby's parents knew I was a bad kid. Did they now suspect I was the culprit who'd lured Bobby out at night this summer? Would they even want me in their house? Would Bobby? I ditched him today, like I'd been ditching him for a week. He had to be angry at me. Like in my dream.

Bookie was out of the slammer and safe from the hangman's noose. But nothing was back to normal, nothing was right.

Chicago muscled in and muscled Chum-Chum, Bookie, Knucklehead, and the rest out. The silver or gold dog I gave to Chum-Chum didn't matter. He'd given up on Bookie, abandoned him as a sacrifice to Chicago. Is that why Bookie was so nervous when we went to Monkey Island—he had a bad feeling he was being sacrificed? If I hadn't found Claude Cavalerie, Chicago would have hauled the dead actor from the tunnel to the morgue. And there you have it: a body to charge Bookie with murder. Because Straw Boater sure wasn't dead.

Their plan might have still worked if not for LT. She wouldn't play along with Chicago. No surprise Whisper-Whisper had his fingers in the nonsense. He made sure LT was punished, and at the same time he made sure his two pet kid cops were promoted to primo positions in the downtown central station.

How did Claude Cavalerie figure into Chicago's scheme? The washed-up actor had the bum luck to keel over on a convenient day, and he had no family to question the murder story. That's all. He had the worse luck to keel over before he got a chance to go on the auditions that every other actor in town was trotting off to.

Did Chum-Chum do anything to help Bookie? Anything at all? The morgue mannequin in the papers must have come from Chum-Chum, seeing as he had piles of mannequin and doll parts. Hadn't I seen Chum-Chum with a hairless, one-eyed doll's head before I even gave him the gold dog? Maybe he was already thinking of a way to help Bookie. Did he cut a deal with Whisper-Whisper: Bookie in trade for shocking mannequin photos the papers would gobble up?

Maybe that was the best Chum-Chum could do to save Bookie. Maybe Chum-Chum worried he'd be framed next.

So he decided to just skip town, which is probably what Chicago wanted all along. Though Chum-Chum was getting a little revenge on the way out with those monkeys.

The defeated look on Bookie's face haunted me. Even if Chum-Chum had helped with the morgue mannequin, I knew Bookie still felt abandoned. Despite that, Bookie was following Chum-Chum wherever they were running off to. I supposed that was because Bookie had nowhere else to go.

Did I have anywhere else to go?

Bookie gone, Tootsie and Gilbert gone, Bobby mad at me, school a complete disaster.

I pulled out Carla's book from my school bag. Did she have a home? Or did she just ride the range with Midnight and sleep under the stars?

I decided the only thing I needed to take was Carla's book. Carla and me had a lot in common, except she was smarter than me and could speak Spanish. One of these days, I'd be able to puzzle through the book and figure out if she and Midnight found the treasure. Soon I'd have plenty of time to do that.

"You're too big to take with me across the Pacific," I told the leopards. "I'll miss you." They stared at me with their glass eyes. I could tell they'd miss me too.

I pulled a pencil and paper from my school bag. I should write a long note explaining my thinking. But I wasn't the best speller. I wrote, "By," and let the paper float down to my bed.

I left my shoes behind. I didn't need them anymore.

With the party still loudly going in full swing, I left Creepy House.

For the last time.

Cornelius was bent over his school books at the front counter when I barged into the pet shop.

"I'm ready to go. Now."

He looked up, excited. "There's another body?"

"No! I'm ready to stow away on a boat. I need you to tell me how to get to where the boats are and which boat to catch."

Beneath his fringe of hair, his eyes grew wide. He stared. "We're not prepared. It can take a year, maybe a bunch of years before we're ready. I have to learn more Korean. So do you."

"You can stay. That's fine. But I need to go."

"Now?"

"Yes, now."

"Maybe we can wait for the weekend. There's school tomorrow."

This kid wasn't getting it. "Stay here if you want. I'm going. I'll figure out how to get to the boats myself." I turned to leave.

"Wait!" Cornelius looked toward the monkey, who cocked its head. Cornelius stared down the aisle toward the guinea pig and rooster. They paused in their math figuring and stared back. "Let me go to my room and get stuff."

In a daze, he moved to one of the closed doors in the back of the shop, opened it, and went inside. He must live here. That made sense. He was always at the shop no matter the hour.

Cornelius took forever. Once he was done grabbing stuff in his room, he had to open the old trunk and dig around there for more stuff. That took another forever. When he finally returned to the front, he was weighed down by a bulging knapsack.

He was sweating and trembling.

"Seriously, you really don't have to go. I'll be fine."

"No," he said. His voice sounded distracted. "I wanna go." But he said it like going was the last thing in the world he wanted. He dropped the knapsack on the counter. He picked up a pencil and paper and scribbled a note in cursive. I couldn't read or write in cursive. That was another thing I didn't know. He walked the note over to the monkey and said something to it. The monkey took the note and chattered suspiciously to the kid. The monkey looked toward me and glared.

I heard the guinea pig chirping and the rooster clucking from the back.

When he returned to the front counter, he heaved up his heavy knapsack. He stared at me like he suddenly remembered I was there. "Aren't you bringing anything?"

"Got my book. I don't need anything else."

He let the knapsack drop to the counter again. "Sparky, this is a dumb idea," he said like he was coming back to his senses. "You can't travel the Pacific with only a book. We'll talk more about our plans this weekend, okay?"

I charged out the door. "Wait!" I heard him call behind me. I kept going and marched to the top of the stairs. "I have to turn off the lights and lock up!" his voice pleaded from below.

I waited. It was later than I thought. The sun was rapidly disappearing, replaced by evening shadows. Cornelius kept taking forever inside. Through the glass-paned door, I saw lights flick off one by one. Then he took forever again fumbling with the keys. He dropped them twice before he finally locked the door. He struggled to climb the stairs with his heavy knapsack.

"Really, you don't have to come with me. You have a place to stay with your granddad and you like school, even if you say you don't."

"No, I'll go," he said softly. "I'm a warrior prince and. . . ." He trailed off.

It would take a couple of trains to get to the docks. As we rode, he kept rubbing his chin and staring out the train windows with lost eyes. Outside, city lights popped on as night fell. Cornelius didn't stop trembling.

This kid never wanted to stow away to Korea. That was just something like a hobby to distract him from thinking about what his dad and granddad were really up to. They could be in Pasadena, for all he knew.

All this sword fighting and kidnapped mystic prince business was probably something him or his granddad or both of them pulled from books, like Bobby's Reginald stories. There probably was a whole stack of books about a mystic warrior prince kid who solved crimes.

I planned to jump ship at Hawaii anyhow. Maybe, if he really did come with me, I could convince him to jump ship with me.

Thinking I'd cheer him up, I asked, "Do you mind if I call you Archie?"

He looked at me like he was confused, then seemed to realize what I was talking about. "Ah, that's fine." He went back to nervously watching where the train took us. Now that I'd asked him, I realized I liked his name Cornelius better than Archie. Oh, well.

He didn't say a word as we stepped off our last train stop and walked past dimly lit, looming warehouses toward the smell of the ocean.

We turned the corner of a dark warehouse, and there they were: two towering ships lit up like movie palace marquees. We both stopped and stared. They were beautiful, painted bright white and strung with a million lights. They glowed against the dark-blue night sky.

Dozens of high-end autos were parked on the docks by the ships, and more kept rolling in. These were huge movie star-sized machines, sporty convertibles, and sleek sedans. The people stepping from the vehicles matched them for jazz and pizzazz. Trailing gowns, glitter, white tux, blue tux, top hats, and jewels. From how some of them wove and stumbled, I could tell these partygoers got an early start with the bubbly. They laughed in the night air. A live band played fast, happy music as the swell set climbed the ramps to the ships.

"Which one?" I asked, pointing to the two ships.

He stared, blinking. "I don't know."

The first one had "South Seas" painted in large letters on its side. "It must be that one, don't you think?"

"I guess," he said. Even his voice was shaking now.

I noticed hefty guys wearing dark porter uniforms milling around the rich folks. Their sharp eyes scanned the scene. They were looking for stowaways, like us.

I pointed them out to Cornelius. "Those must be the ship bulls. If they're anything like train bulls, we need to steer clear of them. The trick is to move fast, stay low, and get lost in the middle of the party people until we're at the top of that ramp. Then we scramble to find somewhere to hide on the boat."

He looked away, distracted. He hadn't paid attention to a word I said. It suddenly occurred to me that ships do have a habit of sinking. Just look at the Titanic. Even a dummy-class kid like me knew about that boat. Was Cornelius afraid the ship might sink? Come to think of it, was I?

I couldn't let that thought worm its way too far into my head. I was committed. I was stowing away tonight—end of story. This kid? He didn't want to follow me whether the ship might sink or not. "You really don't have to come. I mean it."

He turned his head back to me, suddenly angry. "I said I would! I said I'm a prince!"

"Okay. Let's go then." I took off running. I heard him call behind me, "Wait! I wasn't ready!" Soon enough, I heard his footsteps following. He wasn't moving very fast with that hundred-ton knapsack of his.

I darted behind a long convertible that pulled to a stop. I stepped between the woman and man who climbed out. "Oh, look, it's one of the dancing girls," the dame said. She wore an evening gown in slinky platinum satin and a wrap of dark-blue velvet. Around her neck was draped a silver necklace heavy with dark-blue stones, probably sapphires. "So charming," the man added. His silver-framed spectacles matched her dress, and his dark-blue evening wear matched her wrap. His silver and dark-blue stone cuff links matched her necklace.

I heard a thump. Did Cornelius fall? I turned. Yep. He'd tumbled forward on top of that huge knapsack. In a second, the ship bulls were all over him. "I shall battle you!" I heard him shout. "You will rue the day you met a warrior like me!"

Just as well. He didn't really want to go. I bet he would have complained about missing school all the way across the Pacific. Anyhow, he was having more fun tangling with the bulls.

I stayed tight with the glitzy couple as they walked up the ramp and onto the ship. Then I ducked low and dashed out of sight. "Bye!" I heard them call after me.

I slipped though the shadows to an empty area of the ship's deck. I heard party music, dancing, and laughter echoing from other parts of the ship. This must be a boat for the swell set. If I was stowing away across the ocean, I might as well stow away on first class.

I froze when I heard whispering. It was coming from beneath the cover of a lifeboat attached to the ship's railing. I stepped closer. Two faces were lifting the cover, scanning the deck. They looked like a high school boy and a girl closer to my age. They both had wild, curly hair like mine. How many stowaways were on this ship?

They spotted me, looked me up and down, pausing at my scraped knees and dirty dress. They put their fingers to their mouths. "Shhhhh."

They must have pegged me for another stowaway. I winked at them to let them know I wasn't tattling. Their faces disappeared into the lifeboat.

I moved further down the deck and leaned against the railing. The air had cooled fast since I left the docks. A strong breeze rustled through my hair. I shivered. The air smelled like a mix of salt, tar, and smoke from the ship's rumbling engines. After a while, I felt a jerk. The ship began pulling away from the docks.

As I watched the lights of Los Angeles grow smaller, I suddenly remembered the Reginald book about the ranchers and the mountain that Bobby showed me. In the book, the missing horses were never eaten by the mountain monster. Reginald, being the smartest boy in the world, figured out they were still alive, only hidden. It was exactly like Straw Boater. He'd been alive all this time, only keeping a low profile.

The key clue to the Monkey Island murder was right in front of me, if I'd only listened to Bobby.

It was too late now. I'd never see Bobby again, or Gilbert or Tootsie or Marigold or Cornelius. Or my Bookie. Tears filled my eyes and made the city lights blur.

Whatever adventures I went on next, I'd be alone.

I couldn't look at the city lights anymore. They made me too sad. I turned away. I needed to find a place to hide from the ship bulls anyway. Maybe the other stowaways had room in their lifeboat for me. As I neared the lifeboat, I tripped and landed with a thunk on the ship's wooden deck. What did I trip on? A foot?

I started to get up, but something shoved me over. It was definitely a foot. Flat on my back now, the foot landed on my chest.

I looked up at who owned the foot. From beneath the ship's swaying strings of lights, I recognized Petunia, the deranged twelve-year-old nightmare who thought pain was fun, the girl I thought was a cannibal this summer. And she might still be a cannibal.

"Well, hello there, Sparky," she said like a cat to a mouse. "Happy to see me?"

Oh, no. What did I get myself into?

ACKNOWLEDGMENTS

Thank you so much to Laurie Buchanan, author of the Sean McPherson crime thriller novels, for taking the time to write a fantastic blurb for *The Monkey Island Murder*. Thank you to Marco Pavia and his team: Matthew Auerbach for proofreading, Tabitha Lahr for cover design, and Brent Wilcox for the interior design. You've done an amazing job on a tight timeline.

And thank you to my readers for your support, your input, and your enthusiasm. You are who make all of this worth it.

1

As the lights of Los Angeles faded in the distance, the latest tunes from 1932 thumped through the wooden deck from the shipboard band, along with laughter and the rumble of the ship's engines.

Beneath the rising moon and the strings of lights, I saw the other two stowaways peek from under the lifeboat's canvas cover. One looked like a high school boy with a tanned face. The other was a girl about my age, eleven. Both had matching blue eyes and the same unruly dishwater-blonde curls. Funny, I had curls like that. Though my eyes were grey.

Their blue eyes stared, afraid. No wonder, after seeing me ambushed and pinned to the deck by a foot.

I thought I'd escaped my troubles by stowing away across the Pacific, but they'd only begun.

"Sparky, Sparky, Sparky. Aren't you exactly what I'm looking for? Get up. Now!" The foot moved off my chest.

I closed my eyes. This can't be happening.

Out here on the ocean, the city's September heat was long gone. The cool breezes smelled of fish and smoke from the ship's stacks. I shivered in my white sailor dress I put on only that morning for school. I had no idea then that I'd end up here.

I still didn't want to believe that of all nightmares, I had to run into Petunia, the owner of the foot.

"Last call, Sparky, before I start dragging you."

My eyes popped open. She didn't look as wild and twitchy as she had this summer when she kicked me from a moving boxcar. Otherwise, she was the same Petunia.

She grabbed a hunk of my curly hair and twisted. "Yes, perfect. This will do nicely." She tugged, hard.

"I'm getting up! Please!"

Look at me, tough Sparky, begging and pleading. Petunia was older than me, maybe twelve. She was bigger and stronger. I had a reputation as a crack fighter from my street kid days, but I was no match for Petunia. No one was.

I clamored to my scabbed knees and stood. I clutched my stolen library book tight. That book was all I took with me for my journey across the Pacific.

"March," she ordered.

I saw the other stowaways quickly duck back into their lifeboat and pull the cover shut.

I was Petunia's prisoner, and she hated me.

As she marched me down metal steps, the party sounds grew louder. I heard the pop of champagne corks. Prohibition was no problem on this swanky ship. Bookie and his boss Chum-Chum might have stocked this boat with the necessary booze in ordinary times, but Chicago had run them out of town. They were off to new criminal adventures without me.

They weren't the only ones who'd left me behind. Tootsie LaFemme, the once silent screen star, and her mysterious assistant Gilbert Grossman, with his strange accent and scar over one eye that made me think of him as the goblin, were also off to parts unknown. After a long dry spell, she landed a movie role, but it was shooting somewhere outside Los Angeles.

I'd been living in Tootsie's Bunker Hill mansion in downtown Los Angeles since this summer. It was my first real home. And now? I was supposed to stay with my best friend Bobby in his book-stuffed house while they were gone. The problem? Bobby was mad at me.

On top of everything, school was a disaster, despite Bobby trying to help me catch up for all the time I missed from school while I was living on the streets and running for Bookie.

It was Cornelius, the kid who worked in his granddad's weird pet shop, who came up with the idea of stowing away across the Pacific. Only hours ago I decided this was a solid plan. Everyone was taking off. My life was over. Why not stow away? So I left everything I knew on Bunker Hill. Forever. It was for an unknown future across the ocean.

The bulls who were combing the docks for stowaways captured Cornelius before he got onboard. So I was going it alone. Only I wasn't. I was with Petunia.

I changed my mind! I wanted my old life back. But it was gone.

Petunia prodded me forward along hallways, down more metal stairs that felt cold on my bare feet, deeper into the bowels of the ship. We reached a metal door. Petunia pulled it open and pushed me through.

I landed inside a large room. A dozen girls, all about my age, eleven, stood tightly clustered together. They turned to stare when Petunia barged in after me. The girls wore sparkly costumes and glitter-pasted dance shoes. Around the room, more costumes hung on racks that bent under their weight. Colorful hats, fabric, ribbons, and shoes overflowed from boxes. The mess reminded me of Tootsie's maze of closets stuffed with her old silent movie costumes from when she was a big star.

"Found her!" Petunia shouted toward a small man in a suit standing at the back of the room. He was berating a sobbing girl in a glitter tutu. "You're doing everything wrong!" he snapped at the girl.

Goosebumps traveled up my arms. That voice was familiar. No, no.

Petunia hauled me toward the man and threw me at his feet. I looked up, up as the man turned his face away from the tearful girl and fixed his spectacles on me.

Mr. Beele. He was Tootsie's voice coach and was useless as far as I could hear, because Tootsie's singing sounded like a hollering duck. What I did know was that Beele disapproved of me from the moment he spotted me at Tootsie's mansion. He enjoyed talking about punishment for bad kids like me.

I froze. What would he do to me? Throw me overboard?

"I told you she couldn't escape from me," Petunia said with a satisfied chuckle.

Mr. Beele said nothing and kept staring at me. Finally, he frowned and said, "I never did like how this girl looks. She reminds me of a child who is most disobedient and needs direction, harsh direction."

The puzzle pieces snapped together. The hair. My curly dishwater-blonde hair looked the same as the stowaway girl's hiding in the lifeboat. Petunia was supposed to capture her and bring her back to Beele. Instead, she found me. With the hair, I could kind of pass for the runaway girl. Petunia probably decided I'd be more fun to torment.

"Oh, yeah," Petunia agreed. "I think some harsh direction will bring her in line."

"Excellent!" Mr. Beele's face lit up like it always did when he spotted me at Tootsie's house and tried selling her on his punishment ideas. Lucky for me, punishment wasn't something Tootsie or Gilbert were into.

Not so, Petunia.

Beele looked up, thinking. "Harsh direction," he murmured. He rubbed the thin hairs on his nearly bald head, plastering them flat. "Yes! Get her back in costume and get her ready," he decided. "Rehearsal begins in five."

He strode out the door. As he passed the girls, they huddled together, trembling, trying to keep as far away from him as possible. After he was gone, they relaxed but only a little.

Petunia threw a costume at me. It had tights, tap shoes, a red-white-and-blue top hat, and a red-white-and-blue sparkling, dress-like outfit that looked too small for me. "Hurry up. Get in it before the director gets back." When I didn't move, she barked, "I'm the production assistant, so you better do what I say or else!"

This was so unbelievable. "How did you get this job?" I asked.

Petunia chuckled. "Wouldn't you like to know." Then she fixed her crazy eyes on me, "Hup two! There's no changing rooms here, so don't get all shy. Pull that thing on or I'll pull it on for you!"

Cripes and cripes some more. It was a good thing the ship bulls nabbed Cronelius. If he were here, Petunia would have forced him into a glitter costume.

I ducked behind a rack of tights hanging from a clothes rack before I pulled off my sailor dress and struggled to pull on this crazy outfit. I rolled my stolen library book into my sailor dress to hide it. I worried if Petunia thought about my book too much, she might fling it overboard.

Through the legs of the hanging tights, I saw the tutu girl step up to Petunia. "That's a different girl," she said.

"So?" Petunia snorted, half laughing. "As long as she passes enough for the director, who cares?"

"I guess," the girl mumbled. I saw her fade back into the huddle of glitter girls. They traded whispers with one another.

"You done?" Petunia snapped as she pulled me out from behind the clothes rack. She tugged the tights up and pulled the glitter outfit down. "This isn't a strip show, you idiot. Where's your hat?" She found it and shoved it on my head, too hard. Where's your shoes?"

"They don't fit!" This was true. Those shoes were for a nine-year-old or a girl with little feet. My feet were too big anyhow from all my years of running around Bunker Hill barefoot.

"Make 'em fit." She jammed them on my feet. My toes had to crunch up to fit. Ow, ow, ow. "Good enough," she mumbled. "Where's your twirling stick?" I shrugged. I had no idea what she was talking about. Her face became dark, glowering. That was the Petunia I remembered.

Just in time, tutu girl came forward with a slim blue cane that had a red tip at one end and a white tip at the other. "It was over there," she told Petunia.

Petunia grabbed the cane, shoved it at me, and shoved me toward an open space at one end of the room.

"Places, everybody!" Petunia shouted. "He'll be back any second!" The girls joined me. I noticed I was in front, and they stood behind me.

"What am I supposed to do?" I asked Petunia. The girls looked nervously at each other but said nothing.

"Do anything," she said. "Doesn't matter. He'll get mad no matter what. So, who cares?"

I stared at her with my mouth hanging open.

Petunia grinned at me, showing all her teeth. "Smile, Sparky. You're the new star of the show."

PHOTO CREDIT: GUY VIAU

Rosalind Barden has long been fascinated by the history of Los Angeles's lost noir neighborhood, Bunker Hill. *The Cold Kid Case*, the first in her zany 1930s *Sparky of Bunker Hill Mystery* series is a #1 Amazon New Release and has been awarded multiple accolades, including the Firebird Book Award 1st Place for Cozy Mysteries. Over thirty of her short mystery and horror stories have been published, including her inspiration for the *Sparky of Bunker Hill Mystery* series, "The Monkey's Ghost," part of the FAPA President's Book Awards Silver Medalist anthology, *History and Mystery, Oh My!* She writes and continues to explore lost history in Los Angeles. Discover more at RosalindBarden.com.

Please Leave a Review

Thank you for reading this book. I'd be especially grateful if you could take a moment to leave a review, even a super short one. The number of reviews a book receives helps other readers discover it, and determines its visibility on Amazon and other platforms. Thank you!

Please Join My Reader's Club

Please join my Readers Club (free!) for bonus stories, updates, and subscriber-only giveaways:
https://rosalindbarden.com/join-readers-club/

Please Follow Me!

BookBub: @R_Barden
https://www.bookbub.com/authors/rosalind-barden

Instagram: @rosalindbarden
https://www.instagram.com/rosalindbarden/

AVAILABLE NOW!

AVAILABLE NOW!